CRIME IN THE CRYPT

A fiercely addictive mystery

CATHERINE MOLONEY

Detective Markham Mystery Book 14

JOFFE BOOKS

Joffe Books, London
www.joffebooks.com

First published in Great Britain in 2021

Cover art by Dee Dee Book Covers

ISBN: 978-1-78931-997-2

PROLOGUE

Marie Devlin was feeling distinctly hungover as she trudged up to the top floor of the Theresian Club on Monday morning, a bucket of cleaning materials in her hand.

Too much Chardonnay, she thought ruefully trying to ignore the headache building behind her eyes. But it had been a great party . . . just so long as her brother JJ didn't shoot his mouth off to the family. She didn't fancy her mother back in Dublin hearing about those drinking games.

At least Mum approved of the club. Though, according to JJ, it was because it was the next best thing to a convent.

Breathing hard and cursing the fact that the building didn't have a lift, she passed through the swing doors on the landing, heaved the hoover from a wall cupboard and made her way along to the far end of the corridor.

Thank heaven there were only three rooms to do up here. It was always quiet in the club coming up to Easter when bookings became a trickle and there were only a few residents still around.

She retrieved a crumpled piece of paper from her overall pocket.

Yes, just Rosemary Gough, Thelma Machin and Julia Porter to attend to up here and after that the senior staff bedrooms on the second floor . . . last stop the American professor on the first floor. Not too bad really.

She wondered what JJ would think if he saw Rosemary Gough's room. There was so much religious bric-a-brac it made the place a nightmare to dust, but she was used to it by now. The statues and holy pictures felt almost like old friends.

Mum would definitely like the little figurine of St Therese ('teh-rez') of Lisieux dressed in the flowing nun's habit, clasping her crucifix and roses firmly to her chest. Marie liked it too, though this morning she fancied the saint's expression held a look of sorrowful reproach . . . almost as though she knew *exactly* what the cleaner had got up to last night.

The bedrooms could do with a makeover, she reflected as she set to. They were perfectly neat and comfortable but so drab with the cream walls, sage green carpet, dull heavy furniture and curtains from the 1950s.

Mind you, Rosemary Gough was the epitome of drab, so the room suited her personality down to a T.

Marie wasn't keen on the mousy little woman with badly cut hair who blinked at the world from behind thick-lensed NHS specs and never seemed to have a word to say for herself. But at least she wasn't around this morning on account of it being her shift with the Great Ormond Street Volunteers. Personally, she couldn't imagine anything more depressing than having the likes of Miss Gough dispensing good cheer, but she supposed there was no great harm in her. And at least she never gave Marie any hassle. Not like Mr Nosy Parker David Manners.

The Irish girl's pretty face darkened at the thought of the deputy warden. Always poking and prying. To say nothing of trying to catch them out over every petty breach of the rules. For such a small, grey man, he had boundless self-conceit and seemingly endless energy when it came to prowling round the building. And when he 'needed a word', this somehow invariably happened to be when she and the other student cleaners were half-dressed or getting changed.

Creep.

Rosemary Gough and David Manners had the same taste in books — big fat holy volumes about the lives of saints. And they were mighty particular about them too . . . always noticed if she moved anything or if they weren't lined up *just so*.

She wondered how Rosemary managed to afford living at the club. Even with a discount for membership, it couldn't be cheap. Getting by on her pension, presumably. Plus, she'd been a resident for years and years, so maybe they didn't give her a hike when they put prices up . . .

The woman was tidy and organised. Not like Julia Porter. God, she simply *dreaded* the thought of doing room eighteen at the other end of the corridor. What on earth could anyone want with all those newspapers and magazines, not to mention the stuff from charity shops?

It was a wonder old fusspot Manners hadn't had a go at her about it. But then, there was something vaguely scary about Julia's appearance with all the witchy hair and heavy eye makeup. Plus, she absolutely *stank* of cigarettes, so maybe he didn't care to get too close.

Thelma Machin was a bit of a hoarder too, though not on the same scale as Julia. But at least *she* had some excuse for all those books and papers, being a supply teacher, whereas Julia was just a part-time receptionist at the Little Flower Institute in Kensington. Out of the three women on the third floor, Thelma wasn't too bad. Had to be getting on, seeing the way she stooped and her whiteish hair, but she was kind to Marie at the beginning when she was homesick and lent her paperbacks from time to time.

Yes, there were worse places to end up, Marie thought as she cleaned the sink, dusted and hoovered. The residents' rooms didn't have en-suites, so that was one less thing to worry about. She couldn't imagine living for years with a bathroom down the corridor. Just like being at boarding school.

Or a convent.

Despite JJ's jibes, the club was very comfortable, for all that it was no frills. She felt quite proud of the red-carpeted entrance hall with the reading room on one side and the television lounge on the far side of the dining room. Everywhere was traditional and old-fashioned, but there was no institutional smell of cabbage or anything like that. With its shut-in, faintly perfumed air, pictures in gilt frames and the bookcases with leather-backed volumes of religious classics, it had the feel of a Victorian parlour . . . the kind of place where Dickens or some other famous person might have lived. It was quietly impressive from the outside too, situated at the end of the Georgian terrace with a pillared portico that was rather grand.

Marie and the other two cleaning girls lived in budget quarters in the somewhat dingy basement with a shared shower, but their rooms weren't bad and there was a pretty garden round the back. Mr Up Himself Manners didn't like them using the garden, but Father Digby Peake, the warden, was relaxed about it. 'Just remember, no topless bathing,' he told them with a wink. That was the thing about Father Digby, he was always up for a joke and a laugh. Not a bit like she'd thought a priest would be, though the grey-black beard gave him the air of an Old Testament prophet.

Finished with Rosemary's room, Marie locked it carefully with her master key and moved down the corridor to Thelma's. She had settled into the usual Monday morning rhythm and her headache had mercifully started to recede.

There was the same holy paraphernalia in Thelma's room as in Rosemary's, though it was rather more upmarket, with all kinds of mementoes of St Therese of Lisieux. A bit like a shrine. Mind you, the club *was* named for her and the place was meant to be a centre for religious research. What did they call it? Oh yeah — *Theresiana* — so it was only to be expected that residents would buy in to the whole thing.

Sister Pauline the club librarian, who lived on the second floor, was forever on at Marie about the saint's cult. And Sister Roisin the chaplain wasn't much better, though at least she didn't keep pressing prayer cards into her hand. Sister Pauline was always cornering her about Mass and Confession, but Sister Roisin (pronounced 'Rosheen', as she regularly had to remind people) seemed to understand that Marie had other stuff to do. She was more easy-going . . . more laid-back. Gloomily, she reflected that Mum would disapprove of them wearing skirts and blouses instead of the full religious habit. But you could *tell* they were nuns, she thought, even without the clue of the little silver cross and chain.

Thelma's room didn't take long. At this rate she'd be finished in time for a quick coffee with the housekeeper Paolo Serrano before she had to go on duty in the dining room, ready to help the cook and serve snacks for anyone who wanted a light lunch.

She brightened at the thought. Dark-eyed Paolo was outrageously camp and such *fun*. Not all prissy and down-turned mouth like the live-in theology student Ignatius Fermor who lived on the second floor. He'd made such a palaver about 'cleaning his own room', you'd think Marie was some kind of prostitute trying to tempt him from the straight and narrow.

It'd probably do him a power of good to live a little.

She had arrived outside Julia Porter's room.

For some reason that she couldn't quite analyse, Marie hesitated outside the door of number eighteen, a hand rubbing the small of her back.

There was nothing to suggest anything was amiss. Everything on the third-floor corridor was the same as usual.

And yet, something felt different.

She looked about the hushed landing apprehensively.

All the bedrooms up here looked out onto Upper Montagu Street, unlike the second floor which had rooms with windows both at the front and back of the building.

The third-floor corridor felt somehow cramped and claustrophobic.

Airless. Silent.

As though the club held its breath.

Waiting.

Marie gave herself a shake.

That's what came of living in a place like this, she thought. You started to imagine all sorts.

But *still.*

She hovered on the threshold of Julia's room, unaccountably reluctant to put her key in the lock.

Snap out of it, girl, she told herself. At this rate she'd never have time for that coffee with Paolo.

She turned the key.

Afterwards, when she thought back on the scene, she said it was as though Julia was waiting for her, glassy eyes turned sightlessly towards the door, watching her come in.

Even if she hadn't seen the livid weal around the woman's neck, she'd have known Julia was dead.

From a little shelf above the bed, a statuette of St Therese looked on, waxy and inscrutable as though oblivious to the sacrilege that had taken place within the sacred precincts of her club.

1. A CASE LIKE NO OTHER

Late afternoon, on Tuesday 16 March, found DI Gilbert ('Gil') Markham enjoying some mild spring sunshine in Montagu Square. The daffodils were out, and the pale blue sky was as clear as if it had been freshly shampooed. All around was the sense of nature stirring and preparing to put forth her best.

Delightful.

Or it would have been, were it not for what had happened the previous day just a short distance from where he sat.

It was halfway through the Police Federation fortnight, an event which was living down to expectations as usual. He and DS George Noakes were the attendees from Bromgrove CID amid much wrathful muttering from Noakes about it being 'some other sucker's turn to go'. DCI Sidney ('Slimy Sid' to the troops) was also down at the conference, though moving in more rarefied circles than his disgruntled subordinates. 'Cos he's the big cheese an' we're jus' fricking *plankton*,' as Noakes put it, mixing metaphors with his usual crude brio.

With his lived-in pugilist's face, squat physiognomy, unruly salt and pepper hair (bristly as a lavatory brush) and dire dress sense, George Noakes was no one's idea of a lean, mean fighting machine. He was the despair of DCI Sidney, not least for his obstinate refusal to pay due deference to the shibboleths of political correctness.

But that was precisely what Markham *loved* about Noakes. That and the fierce loyalty which meant the grizzled sergeant would always have his back no matter what. There was also a refreshing authenticity about the uncouth manners that made Noakes, like some old gumshoe, stand out like a sore thumb amidst the careerists and diplomats of CID. He had compassion too, though not for 'scrotes', and a strangely poetic, almost romantic, side to his nature that he took care to keep well hidden from the rank and file.

Perhaps this was one reason why Markham's English-teacher girlfriend Olivia had taken to Noakes from the first. She too had a markedly subversive streak that made her impatient of smooth-tongued apparatchiks (of which there were all too many in her profession) and delighted in Noakes's outspoken honesty. At some level they were kindred spirits, and the gruff DS was devoted to her, to the considerable irritation of his wife.

Mrs Muriel Noakes was overbearing and snobbish, though with a marked *tendresse* for her husband's fastidious, elegant boss. No great fan of Olivia's boho chic and sparkiness, she persisted in her belief that 'poor dear Gilbert' had been ensnared by a designing hussy. Sex was at the bottom of it all, in her opinion, and she lived for the day when the handsome inspector's eyes would be opened. In the meantime, there existed an uneasy truce of sorts between her and Olivia who — in a strange way — had become almost fond of her protagonist.

'It's a love hate thing, Gil,' Olivia told Markham. 'But after the Bluebell affair, I saw how vulnerable she was.'

The 'Bluebell affair' was an investigation during which Noakes made the shattering discovery that Natalie Noakes, the apple of his eye, was not in fact his biological daughter but the fruit of his wife's youthful dalliance with a 'no-mark'. The discovery had consequences that had almost ended Noakes's police career, along with his partnership with Markham. But they weathered the crisis, although the DI was unsure to this day what had passed between Noakes and his 'missus'.

He and Noakes never talked about it. Nor did they talk about Markham's sad past as the victim of childhood sexual abuse. That was the thing. Somehow there was no need for words. But he knew that Noakes — the man Sidney dismissed as 'Markham's useful idiot' — comprehended it all without any need for explanation.

As for Noakes and Olivia. Well, *there* was something of a conundrum. Clearly the DS had a secret chivalric yen for swan-necked, Titian-haired women who looked like the heroines of his childhood picture books about King Arthur. Muriel Noakes, on the other hand, was as buxom and well-upholstered as the 'Miss Joan Hunter Dunn' celebrated by John Betjeman and others as goddesses of the English shires.

'A man can be in love with two women at the same time, Gil,' Olivia assured him.

He would have to take her word for it. But still, it was unfathomable. When he watched Noakes and his wife dance — another well-hidden secret being that the Noakeses had met on the ballroom dancing circuit — he was struck by the mysterious affinity which meant they moved like a dream. It was difficult to reconcile their chemistry on the dance floor with Muriel's sergeant-major-like approach to marital relations. Truly, what went on behind closed doors was a great mystery.

Weirdly, Noakes hadn't been remotely fazed by events at the Theresian Club. After the St Cecilia investigation, Markham had braced himself for superstitious mutterings and maledictions of the direst kind. But when DCI Sidney made the call and brought them in ('you being *au fait* with the religious side, Markham' — a none too discreet reference to Markham's Catholic upbringing), the DS took everything in his stride right down to the religious statues and pictures.

It turned out that Mrs Noakes was something of a fan of St Therese of Lisieux, the 'Little Flower'. So none of the anticipated invective against nuns, convents and the Catholic Church in fact materialised.

Markham wasn't sure what to make of this born-again Noakes, but as things stood he'd take what he could get.

DCI Sidney had suggested he and Noakes link up with DI Kate Burton and DS Doyle at Southampton Row.

Just like old times.

DI Kate Burton was the earnest, achingly politically correct protégée Markham had been disappointed to lose to London.

'It was for the best, Gil,' Olivia had told him brutally. 'Otherwise, she was never going to get over you.'

Olivia and Noakes were adamant that Kate had a 'crush' on him. For himself, Markham couldn't see it. Nonetheless, he knew it was good for Burton to spread her wings and leave Bromgrove. But he felt the gap left by his astute colleague. And he knew Noakes did too. For all their differences, the warhorse DS and university-educated highflyer had eventually shaken down together like an old married couple, their periodic spats as predictable as the changing seasons.

The DS had discovered an avuncular protectiveness towards Burton that he would rather have been flayed alive than confess to, while for her part she had learned to appreciate the wily shrewdness that made him second to none when it came to flicking suspects on the raw. The psychology graduate and dyed-in-the-wool old school copper had also discovered a mutual passion for true crime documentaries, though it was unlikely Noakes would ever acquire any enthusiasm for Burton's bible, the *Diagnostic and Statistical Manual of Mental Disorders.* Markham suspected that each missed the other more than they cared to admit.

And now circumstances had reunited them.

The fourth member of their quartet, DS Doyle, had moved with Burton to Southampton Row. Noakes was the lanky ginger-haired young detective's mentor in matter of football and the heart alike, with no abatement in their friendship arising from the latter's transplantation to the capital since Doyle made frequent flying visits to his hometown, especially whenever there was a chance of seeing his beloved Bromgrove Rovers in action. With his newly minted degree in criminal law, Doyle, like Burton, was on the fast track to success.

Markham and Noakes were staying at the Russell Hotel in Bloomsbury and, fortuitously, Olivia was booked in there too, courtesy of a CPD (continuing professional development) course at the University of London.

Given the leaden dullness of the conference seminars on 'Diversity for A New Millennium', neither the DI nor his DS was devastated to be called away. But the Theresian Club case promised to be like nothing they had ever encountered.

They hadn't personally secured the crime scene. That was down to DCI Moriarty at Southampton Row. The previous day had only allowed a swift recce of the club once Julia Porter's body had been removed. Too brief a visit to allow them to form any distinct impressions. But he'd sensed that Noakes was thoroughly intrigued by what on the surface appeared an inexplicable murder and by the whole otherworldly atmosphere the place exuded.

That was the thing about Noakes. He constantly confounded expectations.

And now the residents and staff had been dispatched to a local B&B while forensic teams combed the premises. His own 'Gang of Four', mandated by the powers that be to take over the investigation, was due to meet at Southampton Row on the morrow. In the meantime, he awaited Olivia's emergence from her final seminar of the day at the Senate House.

For a moment, he felt nostalgic for the terraced graveyard of St Chad's Parish Church in Bromgrove where he invariably gathered his thoughts at the start of each new case. Then he reproached himself for being an old stick-in-the-mud. A change was as good as a rest, and this investigation promised something unique.

A check of his watch told him it was time to head for Malet Street to meet Olivia. With a final glance at the daffodils, he said a silent prayer for the soul of Julia Porter. Whatever had brought her to that lonely end in the Theresian Club, he would not rest until they had ferreted it out.

* * *

Later, Markham filled Olivia in on the events of the day as they unwound over a banquet at China City just off Russell Square. From an Anglican background, she had a keen interest in religion, though professed to be lukewarm about holy luminaries.

'St Therese . . . Oh yes, I know the one you mean,' Olivia said with an expressive eye roll. 'She was that French nun in an enclosed order at the end of the nineteenth century . . . the Carmelites, wasn't it? Therese Martin . . . died at twenty-four from TB. Actually,' she pulled a face, 'I remember seeing some creepy footage on YouTube from when they exhumed her body before lugging it back to the convent, all part of the rigmarole before she could be beatified . . . called 'Blessed' or whatever happens before they make someone a saint.'

She chewed her dim sum meditatively then added, 'Didn't she have these really pushy sisters in the same convent who sent out some notebooks of hers instead of the standard obituary? I read somewhere they chopped up her bed and clothes so they could send them out as relics . . . just like some creepy cottage industry?'

Markham chuckled. 'That's right. The notebooks ended up being published as her autobiography, *Story of a Soul.* But even before she died, they were beavering away collecting hairs and tears . . . There must have been something in it. Apparently in Fiji her image stopped a tidal wave and on other occasion it sent a horde of Chinese bandits packing.'

'Her *image* . . . Ah, I remember that too, Gil. It's all coming back to me now . . . She had a thing about flowers and said that after she died she would send down a shower of roses so the statues always show her with an armful of them . . . Honestly, all that *kitsch*.'

'That's her.' Markham's eyes held a mischievous gleam. 'And as for the "cottage industry", Noakes tells me they've got a piece of Therese's blanket in the Anglican church at Walsingham.'

She paused with a pork ball halfway to her mouth.

'How come *George* is up on all of this?' she asked.

'I believe Muriel enjoys the occasional flirtation with Catholicism,' came the wry answer. 'Apparently she went to see Therese's relics when they were on tour in this country.'

Olivia shuddered.

'On *tour*,' she repeated scornfully. 'God, isn't that a little necrophiliac-like . . . bits of her thigh and leg being toted round the UK like a rock star doing gigs. She even "played" Wormwood Scrubs . . .'

Markham smiled. 'I found it rather touching, actually . . . I suppose relics make ordinary people feel close to her,' he added simply. 'There's a shrine with her right arm, which wrote *Story of a Soul*, in the basilica at Lisieux. The convent has her ribcage inside an effigy of Therese on her deathbed, while there's some more bones in a vault directly underneath and other parts of the skeleton that travel the world.'

'Isn't it meant to be a sign of holiness if a saint's body doesn't decay?' Olivia demanded beadily. 'Aren't they supposed to be *intact*?'

'When Therese was dying, her sisters were obsessed with the idea of her body remaining incorrupt, but *she* was totally realistic . . . said there'd be nothing left of her apart from a pile of bones. Apparently she appeared in a vision to some theologian or other and told him, "It was the dress of my day's work that I threw off. I await the robe of the eternal Sunday; I do not care what happens to the other."'

'Hmm,' Olivia murmured appreciatively, 'that's rather beautiful.' Then she added slyly, 'Sounds to me like you've done some research, Gil.'

'Well, no doubt the academics at the club will fill me in on the theological side, but she's quite an intriguing character. There's much more to her than florets and fuzzy lambs and all the sentimental bad taste . . . They made her a doctor of the Church in the end.'

'I don't like saints made of multicoloured plaster in sky-blue and pink,' Olivia retorted stubbornly. 'All flowers, and roses and twee goodness . . .'

'Oh there were plenty of thorns and brambles too, Liv.' Markham scooped up some chow mein while she watched him expectantly. 'Therese was a product of her limited bourgeois environment, but gutsy for all that . . . She might have been raised in a middle-class hothouse and wrapped in cotton wool to start with, but there was real heroism later on.' Markham was surprised by his sudden inexplicable ardour for this long-dead twenty-four-year-old. 'Not just her illness and the fight to become holy . . . She went into religious life all starry-eyed, but that convent of hers was anything but a collection of saints.'

Olivia frowned. 'Wasn't there a crackpot prioress who wouldn't let her have morphine when she was dying?'

'That's right . . . Mother Marie de Gonzague.'

She raised her eyebrows.

Markham grimaced. 'Yep, aristocratic dame, so probably looked down on Therese because she hailed from "trade" . . . lacemaking and watches.'

'She was a psycho about the morphine.'

'The family got round it . . . Therese's cousin was married to a doctor and he administered it surreptitiously once the disease started attacking her intestines.'

Olivia flinched. 'What a *soap opera*.'

'She rose above it, Liv. That's what I like about her . . . Her sisters and a cousin were all lurking round her bed — pens at the ready to take down any edifying last words — and she more or less told them to stuff it . . . When they asked her, "What will you die of?" she told them, "I shall die of *death*".'

Olivia burst out laughing.

'I'm beginning to warm to Therese,' she said.

'Oh, everyone's fighting over her. Feminists take the sociological line . . . lots of Freudian speculation about the relationship with her father and sexual repression.'

'Don't tell me, they decided she had a crush on the prioress.'

'As a matter of fact, yes.'

Olivia rolled her eyes. 'Shades of the St Cecilia investigation and dodgy convents . . . George is going to *love* this.'

'Well, he takes his lead from She Who Must Be Obeyed, so hopefully these days he won't be shrieking "No Popery" at every turn.' Markham took a long draught of his Châteauneuf-du-Pape. 'Actually, Noakesy seemed to know quite a lot about Therese.'

Liv's eyebrows shot up again.

'Muriel dragged him along to some talks at the Women's Institute and a surprising amount appears to have stuck.'

'I can't imagine him going a bundle on all the tinselly stuff . . . chucking rose petals at crucifixes and all the rest of it.'

Markham chuckled. 'No, but I reckon he admires her sheer bloody-mindedness . . . the way she waged a sort of guerrilla warfare against the other nuns who weren't prepared to work at religious life and give it their best.'

Olivia was thoughtful. 'How many of her family were in that convent?'

'Three sisters and a cousin . . . Plus, there was another sister who joined a different order.'

'No wonder the poor old prioress was paranoid, she probably expected them to mount a coup or something.'

Markham smiled. 'It wasn't just the prioress,' he said. 'There's this story about a nun who liked to come and stand at the foot of Therese's bed when she was dying to gloat over her sufferings. They were all pretty intense and neurotic, no doubt about it . . . very much the product of their times . . . "Fortress Catholicism", if you like.'

'Didn't her parents want to join religious orders before they married?' Olivia asked. 'I remember hearing they've been canonised too.'

'That's right, and one of the sisters is on the same track.'

'Blimey, just like a family business.' Olivia turned her attention to the prawn crackers. 'I still think there's something eminently *slappable* about this Little Flower of yours, Gil.'

'Oh, no question.' Markham's eyes were merry. 'Looking through the worthy tomes about her life, some of it's hilarious.'

'Go on. After a day of Postmodernist Feminism with earnest nerds, I could do with a laugh.'

'Well, when Therese was in the convent, she was praying for her sister Celine to join her but it looked like big sis might have fancied the bright lights . . . Anyway, when Celine went to a party, Therese started praying that the evening would be a disaster and got the whole community to join in . . . It ended with some young fellow asking Celine to dance, but they both found they couldn't take a single step, so Therese took it as a sign she was right.'

'God, you'd think it was an orgy,' Olivia said crossly. 'See what I mean . . . *Slappable*.'

'There was a relative who was quite normal, actually: Uncle Isidore. He was a pharmacist who was very comfortably off because of money from his wife,' Markham replied, amused by her fierceness. 'He didn't want Therese going into the convent at fifteen and he wasn't happy about the canonisation either, though the Church played all of that down.'

'I like the sound of old Isidore.'

'Well, he wanted his nieces to see something of the world before they renounced it.' Markham chuckled grimly. 'But he was on a losing wicket with Therese. When the family did a pilgrimage to Rome, she spent all her time praying to St Joseph to shield her eyes from seeing anything unsuitable. Even on her deathbed, she was asking herself if it was sinful to have enjoyed using perfume.'

Olivia whooped.

'*Priceless*!' She looked ruefully at the spread in front of her. 'There's nothing very ascetic about the way I've hoovered up this lot,' she lamented. 'Come on, Gil,' she pleaded, 'save me from myself.'

Markham duly helped himself to a spring roll. Suddenly serious, he added, 'But like I said, Liv, Therese was a product of her time. On the other hand, she was a giant in religious terms . . . her theory of "the Little Way" had a huge impact.'

'*Uh-huh.*' Olivia looked unconvinced. 'Wasn't that all about her offering stuff up . . . gritting her teeth when some nun splashed her with dirty water in the laundry or trying to ignore the one who kept sucking her teeth during silent prayer?' She pulled a comical face. 'I remember thinking it made her sound like some kind of weird Eastern fakir . . . totting up pains and ordeals like she aimed to break a world record.'

'Oh, there was much more to it than that,' Gil replied. 'But I think what endeared her to ordinary folk — the reason she's such a big hit — is the way she fought so hard to do everything as well as she possibly could, and did it with her very best smile.'

'*Ugh.*'

'I know, I know. But once you look past all the gilt they daub on her, it's actually quite remarkable . . . how she rose above all the crudeness and spite of convent life and tried to meet it all with love.' He shot Olivia a penetrating look. '*Love is blind*,' he quoted softly. '*It is a wild torrent that leaves nothing behind in the path where it has raged.*'

'Therese said that?'

'She did indeed.'

'Well, I guess I need to mug up some more on your Little Flower . . . Sounds like she was treated pretty shamefully at the end.'

'Oh yes, the way she died was a scandal alright. There was a French priest who wrote about it in the 1950s. His book made the Church really angry, but it was all true . . . TB just wasn't properly understood back then, and Victorian prudery played a part. The priest's sister died in a convent too, and she wasn't even allowed to have fresh air because the Mother Superior decided it wasn't proper for nuns to keep their windows open at night.'

Olivia made a disgusted sound.

'What about the sensible uncle?' she asked. 'Wouldn't he have kicked up a stink?'

'Uncle Isidore did his best, but Therese covered things up — even after she began coughing up blood. Her mother was just the same. Had a tumour in her breast for sixteen years before she said anything about it, and by then it was way too late.'

She shuddered.

'Poor little girl. And no peace at the end with those pesky sisters whipping out their jotters like demented stenographers.'

Markham smiled sadly. 'She had a great admiration for martyrs like Joan of Arc, but what she went through was infinitely worse than anything *they* endured.'

'She sounds like a sort of eternal schoolgirl,' Olivia murmured. 'Didn't she doorstep the pope in Rome and beg him to let her become a nun at fifteen? What were they all thinking of? How could her father have allowed it?'

'He saw it as a great honour for all of his girls to enter convents,' Markham said simply. 'That's the kind of family they were. He was thrilled when she became a nun and sent so many presents to the convent that they called him "Christ's postman".'

'Downright unbalanced if you ask me.' Olivia was reluctant to be won over. 'A *schoolgirl*,' she repeated.

'With a huge following,' Markham said. 'In the First World War, soldiers and airmen went into battle carrying pictures and medals of her. And that tradition has lasted right up until today . . . It's a real *cult*, believe me. Even Muslims revere her.'

'Presumably her sisters' PR campaign had something to do with it,' Olivia observed caustically.

'To start with, yes. They were determined to have her declared a saint . . . Celine was the artistic one who took her camera into the convent, so while the others got down to editing the notebooks, she was airbrushing her photos of

Therese . . . making her features more oval and heavenly . . . All quite touching really.'

'Makes me feel queasy,' was Liv's tart retort. 'So there was a family bandwagon.'

'In the beginning maybe . . . But it took off astonishingly. She was made a saint by popular acclaim less than thirty years after her death, when usually the process lumbers on for much longer. There were so many stories and miracles . . . The Church has a huge investment in her.'

Olivia's gaze was penetrating.

'Do you think the *Church* has got anything to do with this murder, Gil?' she asked. 'I mean, d'you reckon this Julia Porter was some sort of heretic, working against the Little Flower cult or movement or whatever it is, so they set out to punish her?'

Markham frowned.

'That's the strange thing. Julia Porter was just this middle-aged woman who'd lived at the club for many years . . . ever since she came to London. Devout Catholic with a job as a receptionist at the Little Flower Institute. Quiet and inoffensive by all accounts — a bit eccentric perhaps, but nothing worse than that.'

'Eccentric?'

'Something of a hoarder apparently. Obsessive about collecting newspapers and stuff most people would throw out. It was more or less under control, though . . . They could still get in to clean her room.'

'So she was a Therese groupie then?'

'Definitely . . . but there was nothing subversive about her piety, she was just hugely enthusiastic about the whole shebang.'

Olivia was puzzled. 'There must be a connection with religion *somewhere*, Gil,' she said wonderingly. 'I mean, look at where she died. The whole set-up's so, well, *unique*.'

'True.' Markham felt as though a weight had lifted just from sharing his impressions of the case. 'That club's a weird, closed world,' he continued. 'But at least there are only a few residents and staff there at the moment, because the place always winds down before Easter when visiting academics go home for the holidays.'

She flashed him a grin.

'Not too many fanatics to wade through, then?'

'Correct.' He sighed. 'Of course, what happened to Ms Porter may be nothing to do with St Therese and the Little Flower movement . . . but something tells me there's a link.'

'Well, while you're hot on the trail, I'll take a look at those books you mentioned . . . From what you say, it sounds like Therese wasn't just a pink bon-bon but quite a toughie underneath it all.'

'Be my guest, Liv.' He was pleased by her interest. 'Don't be put off by the sugar roses and lard clouds and all the rest of it,' he added dryly. 'They're just analgesics to take away the pain of the real story.'

'I'm up for a challenge, at any rate.' She chuckled softly. 'Me and George both.'

'Oh, I'd say Noakesy is shaping up to be quite a fan.'

'Muriel's indoctrinated him, then?'

'Well, he doesn't have much time for all the voodoo bollocks.'

Olivia laughed, recognising a direct quote.

'But he likes how Therese bucked the trend . . . didn't do anything grand or heroic but just kept at it in that dreary convent and made the best of a bad job.'

'A saint for the tryers, then,' Olivia concluded.

'Yes . . . the little people, if you like.'

She screwed up her face.

Markham's lips twitched at her expression.

'I know, it sounds dreadfully patronising,' he said. 'But Therese may surprise you. When you get past the infantilism, there's something irrepressible about her.' He set down his chopsticks with a satisfied air. '*Wow*, that was good.' Again, he smiled the rare charming smile that transfigured his darkly handsome features. 'When Therese was near the end and refused a cup of broth, the nun who brought it was offended and told her she wasn't a saint as her sisters pretended but not even a good nun. Apparently, she replied what a blessing it was to hear on one's deathbed that one hadn't even been a proper nun.'

'Feisty gal,' Olivia observed. 'I begin to see why she might appeal to George.'

'Well, he likes physical courage—'

'Bloody-mindedness.'

'That too. He seemed pretty fascinated by the clammy details of how she died . . . tubercular toxins, gangrenous intestines and all the rest of it. Sorry,' he caught himself up at the look on her face. 'That's not what you want to hear over a meal.'

'No, I can see how this saint draws people in,' she said slowly. 'Such a strange *subterranean* kind of life . . . locked up in that convent when she was just in her teens, being measured for her shroud from day one.'

'She *chose* it, Liv . . . to save souls. And as for the rest, God was the only doctor she ever trusted.'

'*Humph.*' But Olivia's gaze was tender. She could see St Therese had somehow got under the skin of her lapsed Catholic partner.

'Actually, she badly wanted to be a missionary and get sent to Indo-China, but in those days and with what happened to her health . . .'

'Awful. Walled up within four walls and no physical escape . . . brought up against your own shortcomings all the time with no let up.'

'I think that's part of why Noakesy admires her. Battling away day after day no matter what. She didn't even believe in heaven towards the end—'

'Can't say I'm surprised.'

'But she kept trusting right up until the last.' Markham reached across the table and took her hand. 'It may sound odd, but I somehow feel I owe it to Therese as well as that poor woman to find out what's going on in the club.'

‘A divine mission,’ she exclaimed. ‘Well, if the Almighty is on your side . . .’

‘There’s a tale about the woman who reformed the Carmelite order, St Teresa of Avila. The story goes that after some setback or other she was praying about it and heard Jesus say, “This is how I treat my friends”. To which she replied, “If this is how you treat your friends, it’s no wonder You have so few”.’

The meal ended in laughter.

2. A FOREIGN COUNTRY

'You should go on *Mastermind*, sarge,' Doyle was saying as Markham joined them in Kate Burton's office at Southampton Row the following morning. 'Seriously, this St Therese woman could be your specialist subject . . . I reckon you'd clean up.'

Burton, too, looked reluctantly intrigued, eyes darting to her beloved *Diagnostic and Statistical Manual of Mental Disorders* which held pride of place in the bookcase. Markham was willing to bet the psychology graduate was itching to look up *Religious Exaltation and Psychosomatic Disorders* in the index.

'Sounds a terribly hard sort of life,' she said.

'*You're telling me.*' Noakes was gratified by their attention. 'Getting up at five in the morning with jus' two helpings of soup an' some bits of veg a day.' He shook his head sorrowfully. Decent grub was one of his non-negotiables. 'An' kissing people's feet when you did anything wrong, an' if you broke something then you had to wear it round your neck . . .'

Markham was amused by the way his wingman had latched on to the more gothic aspects of nineteenth-century religious life.

'Five hours work a day an' prayer on top of that,' he broke in with a smile. 'With just a straw mattress to sleep on an' no heating. They bred them tough back then.'

'S'pose it weren't *all* bad,' Noakes scratched his chin dubiously. 'The boss nun felt quite sorry for her an' gave her a box with some hot coal so she could warm her feet up. Therese joked about it . . . said other nuns would turn up in heaven with holy things while *she'd* be carrying this hot water bottle.'

Markham chuckled. 'Doyle's right, Sergeant. We'll be hearing you on *Thought for The Day* at this rate.'

The DS tried to look suitably modest and failed.

'Well, our Nat went through a stage when she wondered about becoming a nun.'

A choking sound came from Doyle, hastily suppressed.

The DI remained impenetrably grave despite the mind-boggling notion of the pneumatic Natalie Noakes, doyenne of Bromgrove's nightclubs, wanting to take the veil. Of course the trauma of the Bluebell case, when she'd been in serious danger, might have effected a personality change but even so . . .

Burton carefully didn't look at him.

'Me an' the missus didn't want that for her,' Noakes continued. 'She'd too much *character* for that kind of life.'

Markham suspected the vows of obedience and chastity might also have presented problems for the Stroppy One.

'An' when you look at what happened to Therese . . . the TB an' her insides turning to cheese,' Noakes added sagely.

Doyle shifted restlessly. 'How come you know so much about it, sarge?'

It was an echo of Olivia's question the night before.

'The WI back home did these lectures on her. Thought I'd go along, see what all the fuss were about.'

Which, translated, meant 'the missus' had issued a three-line whip.

'Turned out to be quite interesting ackshually,' Noakes said. A thought struck him. 'Hey, I almost forgot. Therese were into murder an' all.'

'*What?*' Burton was startled. Even *she* hadn't envisaged a saint with homicidal tendencies.

'Not herself,' Noakes explained patiently. 'But when she were little, she heard about this bloke called Pranzini . . . He'd knocked off a couple of women, so they guillotined him. But jus' before he died, he kissed a crucifix three times. Therese decided it were her prayers that made him repent . . . That's what got her started on praying for bad 'uns, see. *Murder*.'

The word fell into the silence of the room like a heavy weight.

Murder.

'Well let's hope Julia Porter's a one-off and there isn't some nutter out there targeting religious hostels,' Doyle said uneasily. Then, 'Look, why don't I get us some drinks in from Costa next door before we get started.'

'Champion.' Noakes beamed at the younger man. 'I could do with one of them muffins an' all.' He patted his paunch complacently. 'No need for any of *us* to go in for that fasting malarkey.'

Doyle grinned. It was really a miracle the older man got through his fitness appraisals what with all the junk he put away. Any virtuous intentions formed during their last investigation at the diet clinic had clearly gone up in smoke, and Noakes was looking distinctly chunky. The horrendous combo of blue chinos, mustard sweater and ancient Harris tweed jacket didn't exactly help matters, while his pug-like features and ungovernable hair gave him the air of a bookie's runner. A greater contrast to the pinstriped Markham and Burton in her softly tailored charcoal two piece could scarcely be imagined. Doyle was satisfied that his own ensemble from the Dior Men's range covered all the bases. Edgy but classic at the same time. Perfectly unobjectionable attire for scouting around this weird religious place.

Happily oblivious of his colleague's reaction, as Doyle disappeared into the corridor, Noakes grunted amiably at Burton, 'You're looking chipper, luv. So how's it going with you an' ole Shippers then?' By which cordial designation he meant Professor Nathan Finlayson, the psychologist Burton had become close with during previous investigations and who bore a disconcerting resemblance to the serial killer Dr Harold Shipman.

'Well, with it being long-distance we don't always hook up as much as we'd like, sarge.'

That figured, the DS thought, since the pair of them were bleeding workaholics.

Markham smiled warmly at her. 'You're certainly looking well, Kate. Clearly Southampton Row agrees with you.'

Burton's nut-brown pageboy swung forward to hide a tell-tale blush, but she quickly recovered herself, intelligent brown eyes and snub-nosed little face glowing with pleasure at the compliment.

She still ain't over the guvnor, Noakes told himself. *Poor old Shippers.*

'So, we're taking over this case are we, sir?' she asked anxiously after some desultory chit chat, as though fearful the opportunity would be snatched away before they'd got their teeth into it. 'DCI Sidney's squared it, right?'

'Yes, Kate. He and DCI Moriarty are only too happy for us to take over.' A slight tightening of the well-moulded lips. 'In view of the "cranky religious set-up".'

Burton registered the distaste. No doubt those were Sidney's exact words.

The DCI's resentment of Bromgrove CID's legendarily reserved wunderkind, with his Oxbridge background and air of fastidious refinement, was an open secret. Sidney never lost a chance to needle Markham about how 'his other half managed to crop up in so many investigations', leading Olivia to christen her partner's boss Judas Iscariot. Burton herself never experienced any problems with Sidney, but it was hard to watch his pettifogging persecution of the man who had been her lodestar ever since she joined CID. It was a relief to be out of his orbit.

Now she said, 'How cranky *is* it, sir? I mean, the Theresian Club's a sort of centre for research, right?'

'Well, the intellectual engine room, the Little Flower Institute, is on Brompton Road, located round the back of Brompton Oratory.'

'Knightsbridge . . . That's within spitting distance of Harrods,' she frowned. 'Prime real estate.'

'It's down to Peter's Pence,' Noakes rumbled. 'Collections at Mass an' all the rest of it . . . That's how they can afford such a posh location.'

Burton ignored the Greek Chorus.

'And Julia Porter worked there as a receptionist,' she mused.

'Correct.'

'Musta known summat about crooked priests . . . corruption an' dodgy deals.' Noakes was keen to demonstrate he hadn't read *The Da Vinci Code* for nothing.

'Like what?' Burton was clearly flummoxed. 'How would a receptionist have access to information like that?'

'Came across it by accident,' Noakes persisted. 'Or she were earwigging an' whatever she found out, it spelled danger.'

'Hmm.' Burton tapped a fountain pen against her teeth. 'That all sounds a bit high-flown . . . Maybe it had something to do with her personal life.'

'She didn't have one,' Noakes objected. 'Went to work an' came home. No boyfriends, no socialising, jus' work, sleep . . . an' hoarding,' he added with a theatrical eye roll. 'Newspapers an' religious brochures, that kind of thing.'

'What about an intruder?' Burton persisted.

'Highly unlikely,' Markham said. 'Security at the club's pretty tight . . . Visitors have to be buzzed in, and I'd say there's little chance of a stranger being able to wander around without getting challenged.'

Sensing her frustration, he smiled encouragingly. 'It's not too great a pool of suspects and the place is generally quiet over Easter. Hardly any paying guests and pretty much just the staff in residence.' Markham slipped a hand into his jacket pocket. 'DCI Moriarty's done a briefing note,' he said, handing out copies. 'There were just three other residents in the club when Ms Porter was killed. Rosemary Gough, a retired secretary who volunteers at Great Ormond Street, and Thelma Machin, a supply teacher. Both women live on the same corridor as Julia.

'The senior staff live below the residents on the second floor. Father Digby Peake, the warden. David Manners, deputy warden. Two nuns, Sister Roisin Boden and Sister Pauline O'Connor, chaplain and librarian respectively. And finally the housekeeper, Paolo Serrano.'

'You said *three* other residents, sir.' Burton was scanning the piece of paper intently. 'Who's the third?'

'Let me see . . . ah yes, that's Ignatius Fermor. He's a theology student at King's, has a room on the second floor . . . plans to train for the priesthood, so they probably lodged him on the same floor as the staff out of deference to that.'

'Yeah, wouldn't want ole Rosie or Thelma giving him the glad eye,' Noakes leered.

'They're devout Catholic ladies of a certain age, so I'm assuming there's precious little chance of that,' Markham said dryly. 'I'd say it was more a case of ensuring he had mentors available. Sister Roisin is also a student counsellor for the university.'

'The DCI's listed four "members" on here,' Burton said. 'Donald Trevelyan, Margaret Bertram, Kenneth Robson and Anne Leadbeater . . . Do they live in the club too?'

'I believe they're former residents and as such have various privileges — their own pass keys, reduced rates if they want to stay the night, that kind of thing. They've all been involved with Theresian studies.'

'And just one visitor that day,' Burton continued. 'Tom Nevin.'

'That's right. He's their only paying guest over Easter. An American professor from the University of Florida.' Markham folded the paper and restored it to his jacket.

'I don't know all that much about this St Therese,' Burton said apologetically.

Noakes bit back the sarcastic rejoinder that sprang to his lips. If Burton ran true to form, she'd be better briefed about Therese than the pope before the day was much older. She probably already had a reading list burning a hole in her pocket.

'Oh, Noakes can bring you up to speed,' Markham told her, not without a certain sly malice as he took in her expression. 'He's a walking encyclopaedia on the subject.'

The DI cleared her throat. 'I had the impression her becoming a saint was some sort of vast propaganda exercise,' she said apprehensively.

'Yeah, but she were *holy* too,' Noakes said firmly as though he was determined to brook no misunderstanding on that essential point.

'Right, sarge,' she replied faintly. 'Er, what's with the "Little Flower" terminology then?'

'That's cos she were really modest an' didn't like boasting . . . said heaven's like a garden an' the really important saints — you know, St Peter an' his mob — are the big flashy plants, then there's folk like her filling out the bits in between . . . little flowers, see.'

'Sounds more like moss,' Doyle quipped as he arrived with their refreshments. 'Or weeds.'

Noakes frowned portentously.

'Only kidding, sarge,' the other said swiftly. 'This bird I'm seeing at the moment—' of whom further particulars would doubtless be vouchsafed to his mentor over a pint or four — 'she's a Catholic. Her mum's well into St Therese. Always doing prayers and novenas and things.'

The DS nodded approvingly. 'Yeah, she's a big deal. There's even the king of some tribe in Africa made her regent of his country. *Thass* how much they rate her.'

Burton absorbed this startling information as Doyle smoothly distributed the drinks and snacks. 'There you go, guv. Oatmeal latte and granola bar for you. Cappuccinos for me an' sarge, espresso for you, sir . . . and chocolate muffins to finish off.'

Noakes wasn't distracted for long.

'St Therese is probably the Left Footers' number one saint,' he observed wistfully through a mouthful of muffin.

Markham's lips twitched at the way Noakes made it sound like the ecclesiastical equivalent of Eurovision. For someone with a soundly Methodist upbringing, he was an unexpected adherent of this most ethereal of saints. Burton meanwhile was trying not to boggle.

The coffee was excellent. After a few appreciative sips, Markham turned to Burton.

'Even those without faith couldn't help but admire Therese,' he said quietly. 'She wasn't all about meek sentimentality. She had iron self-discipline for her whole life.'

Now *that* was a language Burton understood. She began to lose the startled look.

'She died of TB, is that right sir?'

'Yeah,' Noakes cut in. 'They threw everything at it . . . mustard plasters, blisters, the works . . . the local doc didn't know his arse from his elbow an' the boss nun were a jealous bitch.' Not unlike Sidney, he thought to himself. 'So the poor lass died in agony . . . didn't even believe in life after death by the end of it.'

'But she kept on loving and trusting,' Markham continued as his wingman paused for breath. 'Which is a large part of her appeal. She promulgated a doctrine called "the Little Way". I suppose you'd call it getting on with life as it actually *is* . . . very different from the inflated Christian fantasies of martyrdom and being boiled in oil. Coping with difficult fellow human beings and family instead.'

'She might've preferred the boiling oil to her family.' Noakes had rallied once more. 'Her sisters were in the convent, an' they were a right pain in the proverbial . . . I mean, even when she had jus' weeks to live, they kept pestering her with daft stuff about angels coming an' taking her to heaven an' asking her if she wanted to die on a feast day—'

'What did she say to that?' Doyle asked curiously.

'Told 'em her death would be feast day enough for her.'

Like Olivia the previous evening, Doyle's response was admiring.

'She had a sense of humour then,' he said with a grin.

'She fricking needed it,' Noakes said dourly. 'One of 'em even told her it wouldn't look good if she took too long about dying cos people might think her being sick were all a fraud. The bloody *cheek* of it.'

Burton looked as though her prejudices about the Catholic Church were being confirmed on the spot.

'All sounds very *medieval*,' was her measured response, though Markham detected the undertone of distaste. Then, 'Will there be clergy butting in, sir? Bishops . . . people like that?'

'I understand from DCI Sidney that Bishop Buckley requires an update in due course, and I anticipate the diocesan clergy will be taking an interest.'

Cue glum faces all around, as their thoughts travelled unbidden to clerical interference in the St Cecilia case.

'Is this murder something to do with the Church then?' Doyle burst out impatiently in another echo of Olivia. 'Was Julia Porter up to something they didn't approve of . . . badmouthing St Therese or doing something to make this cult or whatever it is look bad, so they went and bumped her off?' Even to his own ears it sounded far-fetched. 'It's like something out of a trashy thriller.'

'*The Da Vinci Code*,' Noakes put in sententiously.

'Yeah, sarge, but we're talking a hostel in the middle of London, not Vatican City . . . no wicked cardinals or anything like that in the picture.' The young detective's freckled open face was a study in bafflement. 'The whole set-up sounds pretty creepy . . . Sorry, sir, no offence,' he added, reddening at the remembrance of Markham's Catholic antecedents. Rumour had it that his former boss liked visiting old churches in his spare time and had a thing for religious history. Weird, but all part of the DI's unique cachet.

'None taken,' Markham said lightly.

Burton's face was closed, introspective, as usual when she was thinking hard.

Noakes's words came back to her.

Therese's sister told her it wouldn't look good if she took too long about dying because people might think it was all a fraud . . . Fraud.

'The Catholic Church has had lots of scandals involving dirty money,' she mused, revolving new possibilities. 'There was this book *In God's Name* which claimed Pope John Paul I was murdered because he tried to clamp down on corruption.'

Noakes was staring at her as though he feared she was about to launch into a lecture on church history.

'Maybe Julia Porter found out about some financial wrongdoing,' she said hastily. 'Something connected with the institute. She might only have lived in a hostel, but if the Little Flower Institute's big league and this Bishop Buckley wants updates, then maybe he's worried about something embarrassing coming out.'

'Money an' sex,' Noakes said oracularly. 'Though it don' look like Porter whooped it up. The only crush she had were on God.'

'God and St Therese,' Doyle amended.

'Right,' Markham said briskly. 'Time to get started. Today we're taking all the staff and residents. They're staying in Eton Lodge, that's the B&B two doors down from the club. I've lined up a visit to the Little Flower Institute for tomorrow, then interviews with those members who don't live at the club.' He ticked them off on his fingers. 'That's Donald Trevelyan, Margaret Bertram, Kenneth Robson and Anne Leadbeater.' He raked the slightly overlong dark hair which was another item in DCI Sidney's list of grievances against his handsome subordinate. 'If there's time today, we'll take another look at the club while it's clear of everyone.'

Markham noticed that Kate Burton continued to address him as if he was her superior, despite having now attained the same rank. It made him feel slightly uncomfortable about giving her orders, but she behaved like it was entirely natural. The way she and Doyle slipped easily into their former roles made his heart lift in anticipation of a harmonious working relationship.

The team got to their feet, nothing loath to crack on with surely the strangest case they had ever encountered.

It felt like a foreign country.

* * *

There was nothing supernatural about Eton Lodge, however. It was just an unpretentious but comfortable little hotel whose balding bespectacled manager, Mr Evans, was quietly accommodating and not at all fazed by having the police descend on them.

'You can have the lounge for interviews, Inspector,' he told them. 'I'll see that nobody disturbs you. There's complimentary tea and coffee on the sideboard.'

There was nothing especially heavenly or elevated about the Theresian Club's staff and residents either. As Noakes grumbled afterwards, 'They looked jus' like anybody else.' Markham wondered what exactly he had been expecting. A whiff of incense or swishing habits, no doubt.

In fact, the two nuns, Roisin and Pauline — dressed in 'civvies' without veils or habits — were decidedly downbeat in their sensible skirts, blouses and lace-up shoes. Like social workers or district nurses, Doyle thought disparagingly.

Both were Irish, Sister Roisin being the more attractive of the two, with broad open features, a buxom figure and brown hair cut in a feathery mushroom hairstyle which, though decidedly nineteen-eighties, gave her a youthful air. Sister Pauline was what Noakes thought of as 'stringy', with dark hair pulled back in a severe bun and a straight up and down figure. Thick black NHS glasses swamped plain features and made her look far older than her religious colleague. Neither of them had an alibi to speak of for Sunday night. According to Sister Roisin, she was working on the club's newsletter while Sister Pauline was 'doing her spiritual exercises'.

The two women spoke of Julia Porter in respectful tones — a 'committed Catholic, dedicated to her job' — which gave no indication what they actually thought of her. Reference to the dead woman's hoarding elicited only a murmured, 'To be sure she had a great devotion to St Therese.' And no, they hadn't noticed anything out of the ordinary in the club on the day she died, nor had they seen any strangers around the building.

'Well, *they* were bugger all use,' Noakes muttered after they had left the room.

'Early days, Sergeant,' Markham told him. 'And don't forget, they'll all be in shock.'

'Looked to me like they were taking it pretty well,' his wingman retorted. 'Not 'xactly prostrated with grief,' he added sarcastically.

'They'll see her as having gone to a better place,' Doyle suggested helpfully. 'It's in their job description.'

Next up was Father Digby Peake.

Like summat out of the Bible, thought Noakes, clocking the beard and slightly overlong hair. *John the Baptist or one of them from the Old Testament.*

The warden was a gentle, softly spoken character who struck Markham as more suited to the contemplative life than manager of a hostel.

'Holy Obedience means I go where I'm sent,' he told them wryly.

He and the two nuns belonged to the same religious order, the Brothers and Sisters of St Therese. 'Our Rule aims for a balance of prayer and apostolic work,' he told them before adding ruefully, 'but these days there seems to be less and less time for quiet reflection.'

With an air of mild embarrassment, he confided that he had been watching a film in the television lounge on Sunday evening. 'No one else was around. It was a Western. I ended up falling asleep in front of it.'

Afterwards, Burton said, 'I liked how he didn't pretend to be doing something holy. Another priest might've said he was reading the Bible or something.' Suddenly she grinned. 'When Pope John Paul I died — the one they said was murdered — there was a story he'd been reading a Western in bed, but when the cardinals discovered the body, they switched it for some prayer book because they didn't want it to come out that the pope liked trashy books.'

'Nowt wrong with Westerns,' Noakes said stoutly. Like Burton, he'd found the lack of pomposity appealing.

Along with the nuns, Father Digby would not be drawn on Julia Porter. 'The poor woman had no family here and very few friends,' he said. 'She didn't really mix with people in the club all that much . . . perhaps Sister Pauline now and again, but obviously there was no question of their being confidantes.'

'Why not?' Doyle was puzzled.

'We're very aware of the danger of "particular friendships",' the priest said mildly.

'What's he mean by that?' the young DS wanted to know after the priest had departed.

'They don' want the nuns turning into lezzers,' Noakes informed him.

Kate Burton visibly cringed, but before she could say anything Markham took the bull by the horns.

'If by "lezzers" you mean a prohibition on lesbianism, Noakes, I would say the idea is to steer clear of intimacies which might compromise their vocation and distract them from serving God.'

'Yeah, that an' all,' his DS said, not at all abashed. 'But there were summat shifty about the way Diggers said it.'

Noakes was on the money there, Markham thought with reluctant admiration for the shrewd antennae that had picked up on the priest's discomfort. For some reason, Father Digby had been ill at ease around the subject of personal relationships. The question was *why* . . .

If Father Digby was understated, the theology student Ignatius Fermor came across as being the finished seminary product. Bespectacled and bookish in sweater and flannels, he was good-looking with closely shorn dark hair and clean-cut features. Markham couldn't say what it was about the man that unsettled him, but he sensed the man had intense feelings, which he was careful to bank down. Like the others, he had no alibi for the night of the murder. 'I was writing a paper on the spirituality of St John of the Cross and its influence on St Therese.'

Of course you were, thought Noakes sourly. Presumably that was what passed for a good time with blokes like Fermor. Prissy little sod. Casting those looks up to heaven every few minutes so you could see the whites of his eyes. And it wasn't nice the way he somehow managed to imply that Julia Porter was insignificant as a gnat. But the question was, was he really as indifferent as he appeared . . .

The Spanish housekeeper Paolo Serrano was a different proposition. Tall and dark, he had a little pointed beard and eyes that danced in a lean El Greco-ish face, there was something puckish and engaging about him. 'Julia's room was a challenge for the cleaners,' he said, 'but they understood. All our *madres* are a bit like that as they get older . . . hanging on to their treasures . . . keeping them close.' He had been working out staff rosters on Sunday night before watching television in his bedsit. Serrano seemed an unlikely candidate for a murderer, but Markham sensed a reserve beneath the bonhomie . . . something withheld.

David Manners the deputy warden was next. A fussy, self-important little man who no doubt got up everyone's nose and made the lives of junior staff a misery. He clearly hadn't liked the dead woman, his lips thinning to nothing as he spoke of her room being a 'fire hazard'. It turned out Manners wasn't a Catholic, which came as a surprise.

'It's not *compulsory*,' he sniffed. 'In fact, I'm a Quaker, but the club has a strongly ecumenical spirit and many of our visitors hail from other denominations.' For all the brotherhood-of-man guff, Markham sensed anti-Catholic vibes emanating from the deputy warden when he referred to the troika of Father Digby and the nuns — almost as if a superstitious dislike of priests and nuns (especially the latter) hid not far below the surface unctuousness. Sunday evening had seen him watching a documentary about the Eastern Orthodox tradition. *Big yawn to that,* Noakes thought crossly. So that was yet another of them without a bleeding alibi.

The cleaning staff followed, but it was the same story. Nobody had seen or heard anything untoward. On duty in shifts at reception, they didn't recall any visitors.

'Gotta be an inside job,' Noakes said as they helped themselves to coffee. 'One of that lot,' he jerked a stubby finger at the door, 'had it in for our bag lady.'

Burton frowned at 'bag lady' but held her peace. She knew none would be more zealous than the grizzled DS when it came to doubling down and tracking Julia Porter's killer.

'But what reason did they have for offing her?' Doyle was frustrated. 'Sounded to me like she was barely on their radar.'

'That's what we have to find out,' Markham said quietly.

'Hey up, here's another one,' Noakes said as there came a knock at the door.

It was the American professor, Tom Nevin, with the weathered looks of a strapping frontiersman and a lazy Southern drawl that put Burton in mind of Clark Gable in *Gone with the Wind.* Tall, bluff with improbably dark hair for his age (out of a bottle, Noakes surmised), he spoke of the dead woman with respectful and apparently sincere chivalry. 'I come over to London most years,' he said. 'Julia was always very helpful when I needed anything down at the institute, but she was an independent sort of lady . . . I guess the word I'm looking for is *self-sufficient,* so I wouldn't say we were friends.' Like the rest, he'd spent a quiet night reading and listening to music in his room.

Rosemary Gough and Thelma Machin came in together, 'for moral support' according to David Manners who hovered in attendance until Burton firmly closed the door on him.

They were a pallid pair, Markham thought. Rosemary Gough was a shrinking dormouse of a woman, with reddened eyes and nose, who shrank into her high-backed Queen Anne armchair and spoke in a whispery voice that the detectives had to strain to hear. Thelma Machin was plump and doughy with a somewhat bovine appearance. But she showed a kindly solicitude towards her fellow resident who appeared genuinely traumatised by Julia Porter's death even though there was no evidence that they had been particularly close.

'Fellow RCs,' Noakes said glumly afterwards. 'An' living on the same corridor . . . meals together . . . kind of like being back at school.'

Markham recalled Olivia calling St Therese an 'eternal schoolgirl'. No doubt she would regard the long-term residents as a bad case of arrested development.

The two women had been knitting and writing letters respectively. So once again, no alibi for the night of the murder.

'Let's take a turn round the club,' Markham told his team. 'Get a feel for the place before they let everyone back in. After that, I want to get the incident room up and running. Then tomorrow we'll scope out the Little Flower Institute and see what the other members have to say for themselves.' He intercepted an exchange of glances between Noakes and Doyle. 'Don't worry, there'll be time for a pint.'

'Reckon we'll need it after all this spiritual oojah,' Noakes said firmly.

They were like explorers in uncharted territory, thought Markham as they left Eton Lodge.

Explorers without a compass.

3. THE INSTITUTE

In the event, it was just Markham and Noakes who attended the Little Flower Institute the following day on the blustery overcast Thursday morning, Burton and Doyle being detained by sundry administrative matters at their station to be followed by a briefing on Julia Porter's post-mortem.

Markham could tell his subordinate was well pleased it was just the two of them, which meant he had the opportunity to indulge his curiosity uninhibited by the presence of two sceptical colleagues.

The institute from the outside was nothing remarkable. Just another unpretentious Georgian building in a quiet square. Attached to it was a gabled yellow brick chapel with a central rose window beneath which was a pointed arch entrance flanked by two traceried windows. The chapel was unlocked and, peering inside, they found it an unusually intimate space — just a single aisle with wooden chairs on either side. Yet there was grandeur, too, in the form of a carved mahogany choir, striking blue vaulted roof, triple arches behind the altar and a dramatic clerestory whose two rows of stained-glass arches, six on either side, flooded the space with light. A statue of St Therese in the porch clasping her trademark crucifix and roses was less simperingly anaemic than the usual representations. It had a strength of character in the painted lineaments and a resolute square chin as opposed to the insipidly romantic oval they had seen on the prayer cards in Julia Porter's room.

There was no time to stand and gaze, however, for a bespectacled wiry-haired bantam of a woman suddenly appeared from nowhere. Markham introduced himself and Noakes, to which she replied that she was Miss Parkin, the senior receptionist, and they were expected.

Leading them back round to the entrance hall of the main building, with its striking red and black tessellated floor and a sweeping staircase that smelled pleasantly of beeswax, she escorted them to a modern two-storey extension at the rear of the premises. This consisted of library and seminar rooms arranged in a quadrangle around a glassed-in courtyard holding several display cases and cabinets. Following Noakes's inquisitive gaze, the receptionist asked, 'Would you like to take a look? We have a small collection of exhibits here, though obviously the principal relics are kept at the shrine in France.'

There followed an interesting half hour.

Markham was amused to see that the DS was dressed in what appeared to be his Sunday best, presumably with a nod to the religious side of their expedition, and wore a respectful expression quite at odds with his customary mulishness. Truly St Therese had worked some kind of miracle!

Walking around the little exhibition on tiptoe, as though fearful of disturbing the monastic hush, Noakes drank everything in open-mouthed, right down to the sepia photographs of veiled kneeling women and Victorian prayer cards.

He nudged Markham. 'See that lass in a wedding dress,' he said, squinting at one of the yellowing photographs, 'that's cos she were a bride of Christ, so they laid on the works jus' like a proper marriage.'

'Indeed,' Miss Parkin nodded approvingly. 'You'll recall that St Therese was desperate for there to be snow when it was her turn, though the weather was warm and damp and showed no signs of that happening. But would you believe it, during the ceremony the weather suddenly changed and when she was brought out, everywhere was covered in white.'

Noakes was clearly pleased to be acknowledged as a fellow expert, though attempted to disguise the fact with elaborate nonchalance.

'Blimey, some of 'em weren't half ugly,' the DS blurted as he moved along the photo montages along the walls, scrutinising groups of nineteenth-century religious people. Then he blushed violently, suddenly realising the blunder.

But Miss Parkin seemed unconcerned.

'True. And certain brides of Christ were jealous, petty and unkind, if not downright unhinged. When Therese's prioress was a novice — still in training, when they wear a white veil instead of black — she once threatened to throw herself out of a window. Luckily, they were on the ground floor at the time.'

Noakes was anxious to make amends.

'Therese were okay, though,' he said, pointing to some blown-up photographs of the saint . . . A bit peaky looking, but living like that'd do anyone in, 'specially a teenager.'

'Oh, many of the nuns — like Therese's sisters — lived to a great age, Sergeant. Despite the cold and the fasts and the lack of sleep. Therese seemed resilient enough to begin with — she was almost the only one left on her feet during the flu epidemic which killed three of the community — but later her health was undermined.'

'An' the medical care were bobbins.'

'Well, there was a great deal of ignorance and fear around tuberculosis, even amongst the medical profession, in those days.'

Noakes looked mutinous. 'They could've let her have painkillers or morphine,' he rumbled.

'The prioress had weird notions about narcotics and people turning into drug addicts, Sergeant. They *all* did.' Miss Parkin turned back to the picture. 'But you're right, it was no regime for an adolescent girl.' Then, recollecting herself, 'On the other hand, it's really thanks to the disease that her message ended up being transmitted to the world. To paraphrase Samuel Johnson, knowing that death was imminent concentrated everyone's mind — including hers. She called TB her lucky lottery ticket because it supercharged her mission.'

'Yeah, "the Little Way",' Noakes replied proudly. 'I know all about *that* . . . making the best of things even if you've been dealt a rubbish hand and don' have much of a life.'

Miss Parkin beamed at him, the rather fierce features softening in a manner that took ten years off her.

'*Exactly*, Sergeant. "Before we die by the sword, we shall die of pinpricks," was how Therese put it.'

'Gutsy,' Noakes said gruffly.

'Well, she was a great admirer of Joan of Arc, but theirs were different battlegrounds.'

Markham looked closely at the saint's features. 'It's a strong face.'

'Authentic images were suppressed for a long time because her sisters felt her chin was too prominent . . . it suggested stubbornness, which didn't conform to idealised Catholic womanhood.'

Markham didn't care to imagine Olivia's reaction to this revelation.

They moved on to cases containing Carmelite habits, various items from profession ceremonies and pieces on loan from the convent in France including a writing case that had belonged to Therese's cousin.

Best of all, in Noakes's opinion, were the table displays which contained 3D models of the convent buildings alongside archive photographs from the turn of the century. The brisk little woman unbent considerably as she saw how the lumbering sergeant pored over them.

'That's the enclosure door, locked from the inside,' she told him. 'No one could ever pass through there except for clergy or the doctor.'

'Like being walled up alive,' the DS said with gloomy relish. 'An' look at that mesh thingy going right up to the roof in the church,' he marvelled.

'That's the *grille*,' came the reply. There were curtains and shutters too so that no one could see the nuns in their chapel, and a little grate for them to take communion.'

They passed along to the mock-up of Therese's living quarters. 'Not much in their bedrooms,' Noakes went on.

'No, the cells were small. As you see, just bare brown wood and only the essentials . . . cross, holy water stoup, bed — well, the beds were really wood planks laid across a trestle, with a straw mattress . . . And then she had a stool, table, lantern, shelf and an hour-glass to tell the time.'

'An' her only a teenager,' Noakes said admiringly, contemplating the walls and passages adorned with biblical texts and shaking his head in wonder at this mysterious landscape.

Next was a model and pictures of the basilica in Lisieux. Such a giant building for someone nicknamed 'the Little Flower'.

'*Hey up*, what's this?' Noakes demanded peering into a cabinet which contained a knotted rope and little iron cross with spikes. 'Instruments of penance,' Miss Parkin replied sweetly. The DS shuffled backwards, shoes squeaking as though in alarm.

'You'd think it were penance enough having no sleep an' no decent grub without any of *that* kind of caper,' he muttered squeamishly as though suddenly confronted by an outcrop of S&M where he least expected it.

A picture of the *Holy House of Loreto*, the building the Holy Family was supposed to have inhabited in Nazareth before it was transported by angels to Italy, met with the DS's approval. 'Came up in one of our cases, that did,' he told the receptionist, tapping the side of his nose confidentially and ignoring her bemused expression.

Markham's thoughts flew to the art gallery investigation and the sinister riddle at its heart. Even now, the memory had the power to set his heart pounding. But he forced a smile.

'One of our investigations had an archaeological dimension,' he murmured.

Miss Parkin's expression cleared. 'Of course, you must come across some fascinating scenarios,' she said politely.

None as strange as this one, thought Markham, reflecting that there was something almost surreal about a world where girls and women chose to lock themselves up for life.

'St Therese visited the *Holy House of Loreto* when she made a pilgrimage to Italy,' Miss Parkin told them before ushering them along to view various 'travelling relics' of St Therese and her parents.

It was apparent to Markham that Noakes had come a long way since the St Mary's choir school investigation when he had taken a decidedly dim view of 'nasty religious tat,' regarding it almost as a branch of taxidermy and downright morbid into the bargain. On the present occasion, far from flinching at the velvet-lined lockets, pouches and pendants allegedly containing locks of hair, nail clippings, fragments of clothing and even the saint's 'last tears', he contemplated the little museum's treasures with a reverential interest that charmed the receptionist.

Whatever it was about this little saint and the peculiarly rarefied world she had inhabited, she had certainly got past Noakes's defences in a most surprising fashion.

All good things come to an end, however, and they finally got down to business in a little office behind one of the seminar rooms.

'I understand this is an important centre for scholarship, Miss Parkin,' Markham said after firmly declining the offer of refreshment.

'Oh yes, very much so. The institute shares artefacts and research with the Lisieux convent and the national shrine in Illinois. There've been significant bequests over the years too, so we host conferences and seminars, with visitors coming from all over the world.'

'Are all shades of opinion represented?' Markham enquired, choosing his words with care.

'Well, this is a Catholic foundation, but there's a spirit of honest scientific enquiry,' she said. 'After all, as St Therese said, we live in an age of inventions, so the institute embraces all strands of thinking.' She smiled ruefully. 'The thing is, so many factions have claimed this saint for their own . . . sociologists, feminists, theologians . . .' She sounded somewhat exasperated. Aware that Markham was regarding her quizzically, she added, 'Everyone's so preoccupied with "isms" these days, Inspector, that it feels as though *personal* religious devotion barely gets a look in . . . I think that's why it's so refreshing to find a saint who did her best with the hand she'd been dealt, like your sergeant said. She tried to be loving and generous from inside her insignificant little convent right up until her last breath.'

Noakes glowed with pleasure.

'Thass why she said she'd send down a shower of roses, after she'd died, like.'

'Quite so, Sergeant. In fact, we've got some first editions of volumes from the *Pluie de Roses* — the collected records of miracles performed by Therese — in the archives here on loan from Lisieux.' The hatchet features softened once more. 'She introduced quite a revolution when it came to the idea of heaven as a place of rest. As far as she was concerned, it was going to be a place of the greatest possible action. Hence that famous declaration, "I am going to spend my heaven doing good on earth."'

'Yeah, solid work ethic.' Noakes thoroughly approved of such industry.

Markham felt his way carefully.

'Presumably, some of the items you have here in the institute are valuable, Miss Parkin.'

'Undoubtedly so, Inspector. In certain circles — serious collectors of religious memorabilia — they would be regarded as priceless. But even in purely cultural terms, they are prized antiquities . . . heritage items . . . part of the Church's history.'

Markham and Noakes exchanged glances.

Could Julia Porter have stumbled upon a theft or some illicit transaction?

It was time to talk about the murdered woman.

'What can you tell us about Julia, Miss Parkin?'

'I didn't know her well,' the woman admitted, her face falling. 'I'm sorry for it now. Maybe if I'd made more effort, she'd have told me if there was something troubling her. But she didn't really let anyone close . . . she was reserved and, well, almost *secretive*.'

If there was a secret, Julia had quite likely paid for it with her life.

'Did she get the hump with anyone?' Noakes asked. 'Quarrels . . . arguments?' he prompted hopefully.

'No, nothing like that . . . I'd have noticed. As I say, she kept herself to herself.'

'What about staff from the club?' Noakes persisted. 'Was she pals with any of 'em?'

'Not really, though she seemed to get on quite well with Sister Roisin and Sister Pauline . . .'

'How close were they?' Markham asked.

'Well, obviously those in religious life always have to keep a certain *distance*—'

'Cos of the "particular friendships" thing,' Noakes put in solemnly, mightily pleased with himself for remembering this piece of lore.

Miss Parkin blinked furiously. She really had no idea the police were so well up on everything these days. Sergeant Noakes didn't look the type to take such an interest . . . It just went to show you should never judge a book by its cover. And there was something so *delicate*, so very *considerate* about his phraseology . . .

Meanwhile Markham could only be thankful that his wingman hadn't launched into a swingeing denunciation of homoeroticism in the Church.

'The sisters are mainly based at the Theresian Club looking after students and visitors,' Miss Parkin continued. 'But they help out here as well with exhibitions and conferences.

Julia was very devout and deeply interested in St Therese, so there was a natural sympathy between them.'

'Did Father Digby have much to do with Julia?' Markham asked.

Was it his imagination, or was there a sudden tension in the air?

'Not that I noticed,' Miss Parkin said somewhat stiffly. 'But he had a lot to do as warden, so he didn't get over here as often as the sisters.'

'How about Iggy wossname?' Noakes said. 'The trainee priest guy.'

She visibly thawed. 'Oh, you mean *Ignatius* Fermor. *Such* an asset. Heart set on the priesthood once he's finished his theology degree. Always very courteous to Julia, but they didn't have much to do with one another.'

No, he'd have taken good care of that, Noakes thought sourly, recalling the student's supercilious attitude when they interviewed him. On the other hand, Iggy probably thought it was worth smarming to Miss Parkin who was a few rungs up the ladder and altogether more personable than the witchy haired eccentric with a passion for hoarding.

Markham enquired suavely, 'Which religious order does Mr Fermor hope to join?'

'I believe his heart is set on the Brothers and Sisters of St Therese,' she replied happily. 'Another dedicated labourer in the vineyard.'

Noakes shuffled his feet. 'Is that the order which owns the institute?'

The DS watched Miss Parkin somewhat apprehensively as he put the question. RCs were notoriously touchy when it came to people asking about money. Probably on account of all that stuff about it being easier for a camel to pass through the eye of a needle than for a rich man to get into heaven . . .

But the senior receptionist didn't seem particularly troubled by the enquiry.

'The order and diocese are joint directors,' she said. 'It's complicated . . . interlocking trusts and so forth . . . the

Archbishop of Westminster — the Cardinal — has ultimate oversight.'

Noakes pondered this. All sounded pretty kosher. But like his old dad always said, where there's muck there's brass.

Markham too was thinking hard. They'd need to follow up the financial side, see if there were any murky alleyways lurking behind corporate due diligence.

He smiled at Miss Parkin.

'Religious scholarship often generates factionalism and disputes,' he said easily. 'Were you aware of anything like that here . . . any controversy in which Julia might have got caught up?'

'Like I said, Inspector, everyone wants a piece of St Therese . . . including the atheists.'

'The *atheists*?' Noakes leaned in.

'On account of how she struggled with terrible doubts and temptations against belief.'

'Oh yeah,' the DS remembered. 'A kind of depression, right? But she said it were a good thing . . . being like everyone else an' having to work at it?'

'I couldn't have put it better, Sergeant.'

Noakes looked decidedly smug at this tribute. 'So, the atheists reckon she's really one of 'em?' he enquired.

'Well, there've been some highly contentious claims and studies,' the receptionist answered, a shadow crossing her face, 'including various Freudian interpretations. Extremely far-fetched if you want my opinion. But the whole point of the institute is to embrace research and opinions across a broad spectrum.'

Markham decided that he liked Miss Parkin and was pretty sure Noakes felt the same.

'No doubt some of this was offensive to the faithful,' he said gently.

'Actually, yes,' she admitted. 'When I went to a couple of lectures here, I didn't recognise Therese from what they were saying.' An angry flush mottled her cheeks. 'A lot of it was sensationalist and downright disrespectful . . . so *unfair*. There was nothing fake and phoney about her — she had a wicked sense of humour, so the nuns knew there'd be no laughs if she didn't come to recreation — and she was humble too. One of our visitors from abroad said her reserve and modesty put him in mind of the great Eastern cultures.' Markham recalled Olivia's comment about fakirs. 'So, to hear everything reduced to the lowest common denominator . . .'

The lowest common denominator. Sex, thought Markham.

It was a measure of the surprising sensitivity of which he was capable, that Noakes unleashed no salvoes about unsavoury church scandals but merely observed kindly, 'Reckon Therese don' have owt to worry about, luv . . . There's more'n enough of us in her corner.'

This clumsy sympathy elicited a smile.

'You're right, Sergeant. It's the curse of the age, isn't it . . . wanting to knock figures like St Therese off their pedestal.'

'Did Julia go to any lectures like that?' the DS asked.

'Just the one, I think. Like me, she had no time for rubbish.'

Markham made a mental note to find out more about the institute's programme of events.

'Did you notice if anything was troubling Julia lately?' he said.

'She seemed much the same as usual, Inspector . . . a bit quieter than normal, perhaps. But then, she was never a great one for chit chat.'

At that moment, the phone on the desk rang.

Picking up the receiver, Miss Parkin listened for a moment before saying, 'Right you are, I'll be along in a minute.'

Hanging up, the receptionist turned a bright professional countenance towards the two detectives.

'The non-resident club members are here, gentlemen,' she told them. 'I'll go and see that they're comfortable and then send them in to you one at a time if that suits.'

'Perfectly, Miss Parkin.' They stood courteously as she moved towards the door.

'When you're done, just pick up the phone and dial zero . . . Then, if you like, I can show you the crypt passageway that connects the institute to Brompton Oratory.'

At the threshold, she reached into the skirt pocket of her immaculate twinset.

'Before I forget, this is for you, Sergeant,' she told Noakes, handing over a picture card with a shy duck of the head. 'Seeing as you're clearly an admirer of St Therese.'

The DS looked hard at the picture of a statue.

'It's the *Virgin of the Smile*,' she explained. 'You'll remember that Therese had an episode of St Vitus' dance, or chorea, as a child—'

'Oh *yeah*.' The DS was animated now. 'Then the statue came to life an' cured her.'

'Correct.' A benign nod. 'There's a special prayer on the back.'

And with that, she whisked away into the corridor.

* * *

'You appear to have scored quite a hit there, Sergeant,' Markham observed.

'She's a nice woman.' Noakes, unusually for him, batted away the compliment. 'Seems like she'd have got proper upset if folk weren't respectful.'

'Julia Porter too by the sound of it.' Markham frowned. 'But somehow I don't see the murder being connected to any theological controversy . . . We'll need to get the institute's educational programme checked out, though . . . Perhaps Kate—'

'You can leave all that to *me*, guv,' the DS cut in with a comically proprietorial air, almost as though he held power of attorney over St Therese.

'Excellent.' Markham was amused. 'Judging by what Miss Parkin said, there were some lectures or debates where the facts appear to have been warped and Therese was presented as the victim of delusions . . . Passions can ride high in matters of religion, so maybe there was a difference of opinion that got out of hand.'

'She did get a bit antsy when you mentioned ole Diggers.'

'Make sure you don't call *Father Digby* that in front of anyone else, Noakes,' the DI admonished.

''*Course* not . . . But summat about him bothered her.'

'I agree—'

Markham broke off at a knock on the door.

If the detectives had been hoping for further enlightenment from the non-resident members, they were disappointed.

Anne Leadbeater was a well-preserved woman in her early seventies with a nimbus of white hair, cultured voice and pleasant manners. A former lecturer in women's studies at Birkbeck College, she spoke knowledgeably about St Therese and the history of the institute without being patronising or condescending, responding courteously to Noakes's apercus. Markham thought he could detect from her reserve about the dead woman that she had not liked Julia Porter, but this could equally have derived from the fact that they were poles apart in terms of personality and social background. Widowed some years previously, she had a flat in Crawford Street. 'Margaret Bertram and I live in the same block. It's very handy for the club,' she told them. It transpired that she had spent part of Sunday night in her neighbour's apartment playing cards before repairing to her own quarters.

'So, they're each other's alibi,' Noakes grunted after she had left the room. 'Don' mean to say they couldn't have been in it together . . . They've got keys to the club an' it's only round the corner.'

But it was difficult to discern a motive, thought Markham as they moved on to Margaret Bertram. Single and in her late fifties, the petite dark-haired dark-eyed woman was another cultured figure, recently retired from her job as librarian in the Humanities Faculty at Goldsmiths College. It turned out that she had started a PhD on St Therese but never managed to finish it. 'Perhaps I will now. My chance to make up for being a failed academic,' she said wryly, with a lack of chippiness that was rather endearing. When Markham enquired about the subject of her thesis, she told them, 'It was going to be about the manufacture of Therese's image . . . the extent to which she was *commodified* by the Catholic Church.'

'Starting with them sisters of hers,' Noakes put in.

She chuckled. 'Oh my, they were quite something weren't they. But once you get past the rose-watery production line — the lace frills and painted glass — there's this strange fire that glows through it all. If it weren't for the galloping consumption, who knows what else Therese might have written . . .'

'Is that what they called it in them days, then, TB?' Noakes was keen to add further nuggets to his store of knowledge, no doubt with a view to dazzling Muriel in due course.

'That's right, Sergeant.' Margaret nodded. '"Consumption" was the old-fashioned word for it . . . The illness carried a bit of a stigma if you were middle-class, because people thought it meant you came from bad stock or somehow brought sickness on yourself by your behaviour.'

Like Anne Leadbeater, Margaret was politely neutral on the subject of Julia but enthusiastic about the club. 'It's quaint and old-fashioned, but quite a unique place to live. David Manners is a pain, of course, but most of us just blow raspberries behind his back. Father Digby and the sisters are good fun, not at all strait-laced, and the staff are nice kids. Yes,' she sounded nostalgic, 'a great place to live.' Noticeably less starry-eyed about Ignatius Fermor, she nonetheless refrained from any snide comments about fanaticism or excessive piety.

'Respect for the cloth,' Noakes said sagely afterwards.

Donald Trevelyan, by contrast, was gleefully indiscreet. In his seventies and flamboyantly theatrical, this stocky silver-haired former resident didn't hold back.

'Oh, Fermor and his clique are simply *too much,*' he declared in a booming upper-class voice that proclaimed total indifference to anybody else's point of view. 'All that obsession with the rubric and sanctuary choreography . . . lays it on so thick, he manages to make the pope look a bit of a lefty. Julia was the same, of course, with her medals and novenas and holy pictures . . . *God*, sometimes it just made me want to *puke*, all that creepy bookkeeping of virtues and totting up good deeds. I'm quite keen on St Therese — not her poetry, obviously, because it's *awful* — but folk like Fermor and Julia were a real turn-off the way they carried on.'

Trevelyan's cheerful contempt for Julia Porter — along with his disparagement of the 'dreary twins', Rosemary and Thelma, and mockery of 'fussbudget Manners' — made him seem an unlikely murderer, but Markham knew better than to be taken in by what could have been a polished performance.

Like Margaret Bertram, Trevelyan evinced a real affection for the club and held Father Digby and Sister Roisin in clear esteem, though he pulled a sour face at mention of Sister Pauline who Markham suspected would have regarded his antics with a more jaundiced eye than her fellow religious.

Like most of the others, he had no alibi for Sunday evening, claiming to have fallen asleep at his mews house in Putney after over-indulging in a 'seriously good claret'.

It was the same with Kenneth Robson, a sandy-haired softly spoken young man with the sober mien of an accountant. 'Actually, I'm Don's accountant,' he told them. 'We overlapped at the club and have been friends ever since.'

It was an unlikely pairing, but as they talked with him it was obvious that Robson in his quiet way enjoyed being a foil to Trevelyan, savouring the outrageousness which spiced the older man's conversation. 'He's irrepressible, but good-hearted for all that,' he said with a wry smile on hearing how his friend had characterised Ignatius Fermoy.

Robson wouldn't be drawn on Julia Porter or the other residents beyond a bland expression of regret at her death.

Difficult to read, was Markham's verdict as the amiable former resident chatted easily about his time in residence at the club and move to Wandsworth the previous year. It appeared he had been working overtime for a client on the Sunday night. 'I was hard at it till quite late.' A self-deprecating shrug. 'Boring and predictable, but that's me I'm afraid.'

Boring and predictable. Markham wasn't so sure about that.

Miss Parkin reappeared so smartly on Kenneth Robson's departure, that it seemed she must have been hovering nearby.

'Now,' she said, 'how about I show you the crypt passageway and then I think you'll be ready for some refreshments.'

'*Crypt passageway* . . . That sounds very *Fall of the House of Usher*, Miss Parkin,' Markham said, endeavouring to shake off a feeling of discouragement after the unproductive interviews.

'Oh, it's worth seeing, gentlemen.'

'Lead on Macduff,' said Noakes, employing his boss's favourite catchphrase and earning himself further brownie points with their guide for being a 'literary policeman'.

He DS felt a certain flutter of anticipation.

A crypt.

That meant more history and old bones and relics.

And maybe a clue to murder . . .

4. DISTANT THUNDER

The crypt passage which connected the institute to Brompton Oratory did not disappoint. Accessed through the library's basement stacks, the chilly limewashed corridor, its vaulted ceiling supported on three pairs of pillars, was lined with cobwebbed wooden coffins stacked individually lengthwise on tiered shelving behind ornately decorated iron grates. Modern electric lighting in no way detracted from the eerie atmosphere of the subterranean chamber, which exuded a musty dampness leagues removed from the comfortable premises above.

Some of the lead-lined caskets appeared impregnable. Others, however, were in various states of decay, offering glimpses of rotting wood surrounds and discoloured velvet decorations.

The pillars were decorated with intricate engravings of foliage, birds and animals.

Noakes was puzzled. 'What's with them big leaves?'

'They're palms, Sergeant,' Miss Parkin explained. 'When St Therese was exhumed, a palm frond that had been placed in the coffin was found to be intact. It's a symbol of martyrdom and victory in heaven . . . they were used in ancient catacombs to show where Christians were buried.'

Noakes nodded sagely.

'The plants and creatures are meant to reflect Therese's love of nature,' their guide continued. 'When the nuns asked if she had visions, she said at night she dreamed of strange birds and creatures she had never seen before. Here, the sculptor stuck to the tried and tested, so you've got an eagle which represents the soul soaring to God . . . then there's the pelican standing for Christ's Passion, because of how the bird uses its own blood to feed its young when there isn't enough food . . . another image she liked is the lamb beside the lion—'

'Yeah, from the Bible,' Noakes cut in enthusiastically, memories of Sunday School coming to his aid. 'All about Jesus bringing peace at the end of time.'

'Quite so, Sergeant.'

Markham suddenly shivered. There was something quietly horrifying to him in this stony petrification of nature next to the rows of decaying corpses. It seemed to him too that the sinuous lines of the flora and fauna had something serpentine about them. As though paradise had been infiltrated by something demonic.

But Noakes was transfixed by it all, peering through the grates with delighted relish.

'What about skeletons . . . are there any ossuary thingies down here? Y'know, bone heaps?'

Endearingly, Markham thought, he sounded less like a hard-bitten CID veteran and more like one of the Famous Five.

Miss Parkin smiled indulgently and beckoned them down to the far end of the corridor where a narrow section of wall to the left of an arched oak door was covered by small plaques inscribed with messages and biblical texts.

'The Brothers of St Therese exhumed the remains of their founders in the mid-nineteenth century and translated them here before sealing off this part of the crypt.'

Noakes's face fell. It was clear to Markham that his wingman had been hoping to encounter some kind of ghoulish memento mori — grinning crania atop a heap of jumbled thigh bones and reeky shanks.

'Jus' boxes an' urns back there then?'

'I believe so, Sergeant . . . along with the odd brick vault.'

The DS gestured at a deeply recessed alcove to the right of the oak door which appeared to contain the twisted remnants of steel machinery.

'What about that?'

'Well, it's redundant now because the crypt's full and burials take place in Brompton Cemetery, but originally it operated as some sort of shaft with a hydraulic platform which brought coffins down from Oratory House — just above where we're standing — whenever there was a funeral for one of the brothers. The Oratory priests have got a private chapel which was used for Theresian funerals. They're a separate community,' she explained, 'but there's a strong tradition of devotion to St Therese and they have close ties to the institute.'

That was all they needed, thought Noakes glumly. Another mob of Holy Joes muscling in.

As though Miss Parkin intuited his sudden gloom, she added reassuringly, 'It's more a case of *spiritual* ties. The Oratorians don't do much socialising with the institute or the club . . . different ministries, you see.'

Given the rococo magnificence of Brompton Oratory, Markham had a hunch that the Oratorians' pastoral outreach focused principally on the capital's wealthier parishioners.

Contemplating the mangled remains of the catafalque, he observed, 'No doubt the elevator ensured a dignified ceremony.'

'Certainly, Inspector. We have some pictures in our archives room . . . eerily beautiful.'

Further to the right, just beyond the ruins of the lift shaft, was a spiral set of stone stairs.

'Where does that go?' Markham asked the receptionist.

'Nowhere,' came the prompt response. 'Like the lift shaft, it was blocked off years ago. The institute was built over the crypt as part of a Georgian conversion, but the reason for choosing this particular site was its proximity to the catacombs.'

'Presumably they aren't open to the public,' Markham observed.

'Sometimes we bring students and visitors down to the crypt . . . local interest, if you like. There are some distinguished clergymen interred here . . . that and the carvings you were looking at make it quite popular.'

Along with the frisson of the forbidden, thought Markham. Chapless skulls and mouldering shrouds hidden in this miniature necropolis in the heart of London . . .

Recollecting himself, he smiled at Miss Parkin.

'I believe my sergeant would happily remain here a while longer,' he said watching the DS who had bent down to examine a carving of what looked like a griffin on one of the pillars. 'But we need to brief the rest of the team.'

'Of course, Inspector. If you're agreeable, I'll take you out through the church. No doubt this isn't your first trip to Brompton Oratory, but it's always worth a visit . . . refreshment for the soul, as I see it.'

Spiritual refreshment wasn't exactly what Noakes took away from Brompton Oratory, his mind being absorbed by more worldly considerations.

'It's like a fricking palace,' he said to his boss once they had duly paid their tribute to the Oratory's neo-classical splendours and made their way back to the institute's front entrance. 'Must take a few bob to maintain.'

Contrary to his expectations, Markham had felt oddly unmoved by the magnificence of the famous Italianate interior whose soaring domes and lavish altars dwarfed the dim recesses where worshipers seemed almost swallowed up. There was an unreality about it all — a sense of detachment from the sordid present, almost as though the building was haughtily indifferent to the struggles of humanity.

'It *is* somewhat overwhelming,' he murmured. 'Though perhaps that had something to do with our coming to it straight from the crypt.'

'Yeah, *that* were creepy alright,' Noakes agreed. 'It felt as if all them dead priests were watching us . . . like they wanted to come out from behind the gates and do for us.'

'Well, I suppose we were intruders, Sergeant . . . It's hallowed ground after all, and yet their peace is constantly disturbed by gawking sightseers.'

'Ole Mother Parkin seemed to think it were okay,' the DS said dubiously, 'but I know what you mean. *Hey*,' his thoughts returned to their suspects, 'did you see Iggy Pop back there?'

'*Noakes*.'

'Oh okay,' as much as to say don't be a spoilsport, 'you know who I mean . . . the trainee priest bloke.'

'Mr Fermoy.'

'That's the fella. Well, I clocked him in that side chapel with the statue of St Joseph . . . the over-the-top bloke with the loud voice were in there too. It looked like they were having some kind of ding dong.'

'Mr Fermor and Donald Trevelyan . . . Are you sure?'

'Yeah. That's why I noticed 'em . . . cos they weren't being all quiet an' prayerful like other folk.'

'I must have been distracted by Miss Parkin telling me about the architecture.'

The DS grinned. 'You made her day, guv. I bet most of 'em couldn't give a stuff about flying buttresses an' the rest of it.'

'Well, to give credit where it's due, *you* were certainly an appreciative audience when she gave us that tour of the exhibits room, Noakesy.'

The DS tried to appear casual, but Markham was not deceived.

'There's summat about it draws you in,' Noakes said. 'Hard to imagine a teenager living like that . . . I kept thinking of our Nat.' While Markham wrestled with the notion of Natalie Noakes as a bride of Christ, his wingman appeared plunged in deep thought. Finally, he emerged from his brown study. 'Mebbe it were all cos Therese couldn't be a priest,' he observed. 'Miss Parkin said she wanted to be a missionary, but they didn't have equal opps in them days . . . guess she managed it in the end, though, after a fashion.'

'Indeed.'

Noakes roused himself. 'What now, guv?'

As he said this, Kate Burton and Doyle appeared, walking briskly towards them.

'Sorry we got held up, boss. The briefings went on forever and then we had to take the Tube because there's a demonstration in Marylebone and all the roads are blocked.'

'No worries, Kate. Look, why don't we find a coffee shop. Then we can compare notes in comfort.'

'Good idea.' Noakes was predictably enthusiastic. ''Sides,' he added virtuously, 'we were so hard at it this morning we didn't manage elevenses.'

* * *

The Brompton Café — stripped pine and very chi-chi, but snug and cosy for all that — was quiet and peaceful. Ironically, given where Markham and Noakes had just come from, the menu informed them that it was situated on the site of some former catacombs.

'There's no getting away from churches,' Noakes grumbled, but the refreshments certainly met with his approval. The coffee was excellent, and though Markham passed on the toasties, the fragrance of melted gruyere mingled pleasantly with that of his espresso.

It was obvious that Burton was deeply disappointed to have missed out on the museum tour and visit to the crypt, listening with rapt attention to Noakes's description of the Theresian exhibits and the subterranean chamber that connected the institute to Brompton Oratory.

'A vanished world,' she marvelled when he had concluded. 'I guess feminists would say Therese was quite radical in her own way . . . coming up with a mission even though social conditions meant a convent was her only real option.'

'Yeah,' Noakes agreed, pleased by this endorsement of his own hypothesis. 'She couldn't go an' be a priest or do heroic stuff like Joan of Arc or whatnot, but now there's this worldwide cult all on account of *her*.'

Doyle didn't want to be drawn too far down the byways of *Theresiana*.

'So the stuff in the institute's valuable, then,' he said with a touch of impatience. 'Maybe Julia witnessed a theft or something dodgy happening round these exhibits or whatever they are.'

'They never reported anything like that,' Noakes pointed out. 'Miss P would've told us if owt had gone missing.'

'Maybe it's something from their archives,' the young detective persisted.

'Or Porter could've had an Indiana Jones moment an' gone poking round in the crypt,' Noakes surmised. 'P'raps she came across summat down there . . .'

Now it was Burton's turn to sound impatient. 'Like what?'

The DS shrugged and turned his attention to the chunky fries that had accompanied his toastie. 'Dunno. But it's well spooky.' He shivered pleasurably. 'You shoulda felt the vibes.'

'Hmm.' Burton toyed with her own sandwich. 'From what Miss Parkin said, it sounds like there are times when the fur flies . . . lively debates and all that. Maybe Julia got drawn into some sort of faction fighting.'

'What . . . you mean with professors and scholars and intellectual types? But she was only a *receptionist*.' Doyle sounded incredulous.

'Religious fanaticism knows no distinctions of rank, Sergeant,' Markham reproved him. 'And Miss Parkin appeared remarkably well up on current academic debate about St Therese. Most impressive actually.'

Noakes grunted assent, feeling that he owed it to the old biddy.

'She's alright is that one. Really knew her stuff.' And appreciated his own insights into the bargain.

Doyle looked abashed. 'Point taken, sir,' he said. 'But do you really reckon Julia was up for all that? Everyone seems to think she was the type who minded her own business . . . stayed in her safe shell.'

Only it didn't prove to be so very safe after all, Markham reflected sadly.

He sighed. 'I agree, from all that we've heard of her it seems improbable. But it's a strange hothouse world with all kinds of undercurrents.'

'Like that convent Therese ended up in,' Noakes added lugubriously. 'Some of them nuns were weird as frick . . . power struggles an' bitching when they were supposed to be dead holy.' There was none so censorious as Noakes after his damascene conversion to the cause of St Therese, thought Markham with amusement. Much as he had done with Olivia, the battered veteran was now wearing the dead saint's colours like some knight from the annals of chivalry.

'Anything new from the post-mortem?' he asked Burton.

'Nada, boss. Julia died sometime between nine and half past ten Sunday night. Strangulation using a pair of her tights . . . no defensive wounds, so the likelihood is the killer was someone she knew. Forensics say she let them in . . . given the state of the room, there's no way of knowing if it was turned over. The world and his mother will have been in there at some time or other — cleaners, maintenance people, the odd visitor — so no use hoping for anything from prints. She was a hoarder . . . mainly religious stuff and *tons* of knick-knacks featuring Therese.' Burton shuddered fastidiously. 'She even collected St Therese *snow globes* . . . the woman might have had a . . . problem.'

Markham sensed that rational, sensible Kate Burton felt obliged to explain away Julia's intense commitment to the Theresian cult as a form of illness.

'She were lonely an' a bit bats,' Noakes said compassionately. 'Thass why she surrounded herself with all the tat. With her being religious, it prob'ly started off alright an' then got out of hand.'

'Forensics are going through everything from Julia's room,' Burton said heavily, 'but it'll be a nightmare job working out if the killer was looking for something.'

'And none of our potential suspects stand out,' Markham mused.

'Miss P were a bit huffy about Dig— Father Digby,' Noakes reminded him.

'You don't think the *priest* was at it?' The words were out before Doyle could help himself. At Markham's raised eyebrows, he hastily amended, 'I mean, having some kind of . . . *relationship* with Julia?'

'He certainly didn't strike me as the type,' Markham rejoined. 'Julia, on the other hand, sounds potentially the kind of woman who might have become somewhat *intense* around clergymen . . . Possibly that's what made Miss Parkin uncomfortable.' He turned to Burton. 'We'll need to run some discreet checks with the order.'

'Already on it, sir,' she replied promptly. 'I spoke to their Father Provincial over the phone this morning . . . He gave me a load of guff about how "religious formation" equips them to deal with unwanted attention.'

'But he didn't say whether anyone had tried it on with Father Digby?' Doyle asked in an exasperated tone.

'Or the other way round,' Noakes put in dourly.

'Looks like a visit may be called for,' Markham concluded with an inward groan.

'Why's the order called the Brothers and Sisters of St Therese?' Noakes asked irrelevantly. 'I though brothers an' priests were different . . . as in priests get to say Mass an' do the whizzy bits, while brothers are second division.'

Burton grimaced. 'I wondered about that, sarge. Apparently, it's all to do with humility. Their founder wanted to stress that everyone was equal.'

'One big happy family then?' Noakes grunted.

'Something like that . . . They've got separate monasteries with priests *and* brothers, and the nuns have their convents, but these days the order's very much involved with ordinary people — schools, universities, prisons . . .'

'A finger in every pie,' Noakes groused.

'Well, I get the point of the, what do they call them . . . *active* orders,' Burton said. 'It's the ones like Therese joined I struggle with . . . the Carmelites or whatever they're called. I mean, what do they actually *do* for anyone?'

'They pray,' Noakes said with impenetrable gravity. 'You know, get on the right side of God cos of the rest of us screwing up, try to make it up to him, like.'

Markham had always suspected that Noakes's private deity had much in common with Moloch, the wrathful divinity of the Old Testament.

Taking the stunned silence for agreement, the DS ploughed on, 'Plus they're meant to be married to God, right? There's all that brides of Christ stuff so, stands to reason they want to be alone with him cos that's what you do when you're in love.'

For some reason, Markham found this declaration rather touching.

'Yes, renouncing the world has its place in the scheme of things,' he said. 'I suppose we should see the contemplative orders as the powerhouse that supports the Church.'

Doyle looked as if he didn't care to suppose any such thing. 'Maybe Julia had some idea of becoming a nun,' he said faintly. 'Sounds like it might've been some kind of religious mania.'

Burton brightened at this suggestion, but before she had a chance to get started on *Religious Exaltation and Delusions*, Markham brought the discussion back down to earth.

'Look,' he said. 'As things stand, Julia Porter was just this colourless shadow but,' with some vehemence, '*somebody* wanted her dead so there must have been more to her than that.'

'Maybe it *was* just an intruder,' Doyle speculated. 'Religious hostels, halls of residence and places like that . . . they attract all kinds of nutters.'

'I don't think so,' Burton said slowly. 'Paolo Serrano and the staff had everything covered. They're positive there was no chance of anyone slipping in without being noticed.'

'Were they at the front desk the whole evening?' Markham asked.

'Until eleven o'clock,' Burton confirmed.

'In sight of the front door?' he pressed.

'Well, there's this little office behind the counter. They can make themselves a drink, listen to the radio, get on with their English language homework or whatever . . . But they're positive the buzzer didn't go and swear they didn't clock any of the members letting themselves in.'

'They're schoolkids,' Noakes muttered. 'Nothing to say they didn't bunk off or do their own thing cos it were Sunday night an' no one would catch 'em skiving.'

'Is there any other way into the building, Kate?' Markham enquired.

'There's the side door, but nobody uses it,' Burton told him.

Markham frowned. 'But technically they *could* slip in that way from Montagu Square.'

His fellow DI looked troubled. 'It's possible, sir,' she admitted.

Markham drained the last of his coffee. 'When we've finished our snacks,' with a pointed glance at Noakes who was eyeing the remains of Burton's toastie, 'let's head back to the club and see who we can round up.'

'Father Digby and the sisters are over at the institute this afternoon, sir, leading an inter-faith seminar for college chaplains. But David Manners and Paolo are on duty, and the residents are knocking about.'

'That Manners bloke is a right pain,' Doyle grumbled. 'Every time I turned around, there he was, watching me like he thought I might be going to nick the silver.'

'Snoops have their uses,' Markham said thoughtfully. 'Distasteful as it may sound, I'm hoping we can get Mr Manners to dish the dirt on his fellow inmates.'

Inmates. Almost as though the Theresian Club was some kind of prison.

Was that what it had become for Julia Porter? The poor woman barricading herself in room eighteen behind a mountain of sacred memorabilia . . .

'DCI Sidney's waiting at the club too,' Burton said. 'He wants a word before his speech on digital policing at four.'

'He bloody would,' Noakes muttered. 'Using us as the warm-up routine so's he can practise boring folk rigid.'

Markham grinned. 'Where's your spirit of charitable forbearance gone, Sergeant. Remember Therese's "Little Way".'

'She never met Slimy Sid, guv.'

* * *

In the event, however, Sidney was reasonably affable.

Because David Manners had buttered him up good and proper, Noakes thought sourly watching the deputy warden hovering unctuously over the DCI who basked in the deferential attention.

'Good man that,' Sidney honked when they were finally left alone, running a hand across his gleaming scalp.

Burton had taken an armchair as far away from the DCI's as possible, while Noakes and Doyle skulked apprehensively near the door.

God, she thought, watching Markham's lean sensitive features turned towards his boss. *Talk about Beauty and the Beast*. Of course, it wasn't Sidney's fault that, were it not for the uniform, his bald bullet head and horrible little goatee gave him the appearance of a sinister drug baron rather than the elder statesman aura which he was keen to cultivate. At least the eczema was in abeyance today . . . not a good look under the conference spotlights . . .

'I've scheduled a meeting with Bishop Buckley for tomorrow.'

Sidney's announcement snapped her back to reality.

Damn, damn and double damn. That was all they needed, the Catholic hierarchy barging in. No doubt His Grace would do his best to ringfence his clergy and steer the investigation away from the institute.

'Obviously, it's of paramount importance that God's work,' Sidney cast a pious glance heavenwards, 'isn't impeded nor any unwarranted aspersions cast on the diocesan religious.'

Burton noticed that Markham was looking distinctly strained.

She braced herself, anticipating Sidney's injunction to 'keep an open mind', i.e. pin the murder on some local lowlife as soon as possible. Sodding déjà vu.

Just at that moment, however, there was a knock at the door pre-empting the DCI's set-piece.

Paolo Serrano stood there, ashen faced.

Markham took one look at the housekeeper's face and rose. 'What's happened?'

'It's Father Digby . . . They've found him at the institute. He's dead.'

5. BODY IN THE STACKS

When they arrived back at the institute, Miss Parkin ushered them past little groups of frightened looking students to the library, a modern light-filled facility spread over two floors. Despite its age, it had something of Hogwarts about it, with its wood panelling, antique tomes and gallery reached by a winding wrought-iron staircase.

'He's in the stacks,' she whispered, leading them to a door behind the issue desk from where stairs led down to the basement.

The room housing the stacks was stark and cold compared to the upper levels, with long black-framed aluminium tables that ran between four aisles of steel bookshelves accessed by motorised drive wheels.

Father Digby sat slumped forward over one of the tables, with arms outstretched and his forehead bowed down. To the casual observer, it might have looked as though the priest had simply nodded off.

But moving closer, they saw clotted blood and brain tissue where the side of the priest's head had been staved in, with more blood congealed at the foot of his chair.

Some papers covered in spidery handwriting were scattered on the floor, as though they had been swept off the table by a furious hand, but otherwise there were no signs of a struggle.

A diminutive paper-suited man came forward to greet them. He had a gentle face and spoke softly, as though the murdered man could hear them.

'Sunil Dajani, pathologist,' he said shaking hands with each of the detectives in turn. 'Father Peake died late yesterday evening. There's no indication that he put up any resistance.'

Noakes turned to the senior receptionist. 'What was he doing down here, luv?' he asked gently. 'Is it open to anyone?'

'I've no idea.' She sounded genuinely bewildered. 'Of course, senior staff from the club are free to come and go as they wish . . . they have their own keys. People don't usually spend much time down here because it's more comfortable upstairs. But they might if they wanted something specific or needed to concentrate . . .'

'What about the issue desk?' Burton asked. 'Is there someone on duty there at night?'

'No, it isn't manned after hours. And reception closes at six p.m. After that, people use their pass keys. Alternatively, they can ring the intercom which connects to the janitor's flat.'

The receptionist swayed and Noakes put a steadying hand on her arm. 'Was it you who found him?'

'He didn't turn up to the inter-faith seminar which rang alarm bells, because he never misses any of the ecumenical events. The sisters couldn't remember seeing him since yesterday afternoon . . . We checked with Eton Lodge, and the manager said he thought Father Digby went out around half past nine that evening.'

Doyle was grateful they couldn't see the priest's face, screened as it was by his arms on both sides. Now he asked, 'Did Father Digby say where he was going?'

'He had to meet someone apparently.'

'Was there anything unusual about his manner?' Markham enquired. 'Did he seem agitated or upset?'

'No, apparently he was much the same as usual . . . didn't stop to talk, but then if he was making a sensitive pastoral *call,* he'd be focused on that . . . wouldn't want to chat.' The woman's homely face crumpled. 'We just took it for granted he'd be at the seminar when it was time to start.'

'C'mon, luv.' Heedless of contaminating the crime scene, Noakes steered her to a chair and squatted down on his haunches next to her. 'He wouldn't want you to beat yourself up. Like the doc says, he probably didn't know owt about it.'

The pathologist had not in fact said anything of the kind but, looking at the lumbering, gruff-voiced policeman with the piggy eyes, he chipped in readily enough, 'Father Peake didn't see this coming, Miss Parkin. It was all over in minutes.'

'Why don' we get you sorted with a cup of tea,' Noakes said to the receptionist, heaving himself upright, joints cracking like starting pistols. 'You're shivering an' it's like a fridge in here.'

'Temperature controlled,' she said faintly. 'We've got lots of rare books, you see.'

'You'd want your flipping thermals,' the DS grumbled taking her arm and easing her towards the exit, keeping up a flow of easy chat the while.

As they headed up the stairs, the words 'Little Flower' floated back down to the team below followed by some shaky laughter. Clearly Noakes's interest in Theresiana was having a soothing effect.

Markham reflected that his wingman had come a long way since the days when he would palm witnesses off on Kate Burton with an airy 'mine's three sugars, luv'. Not exactly in the running for New Man of the Year, but definitely an improvement on the unreconstructed male chauvinist of yore.

He got down to brass tacks.

'Could a woman have done this, doctor? Physically?'

'With the element of surprise, I would say yes.' Liquid brown eyes rested sorrowfully on the body. 'But it was a savage blow which required some strength . . . Of course, if the attacker was suffering from psychosis or if there was a brainstorm involved, who knows what physiological effects that might have produced physically.'

Kate Burton visibly perked up at the mention of psychosis.

'Do you think that's a possibility, Dr Dajani?' she asked eagerly.

'Well, your victim's a priest . . . an authority figure,' the pathologist said quietly, 'so I would say it's possible a delusional or obsessive fixation could be a possible factor in play . . . not necessarily full-blown mental illness, but something that might lead to an eruption of violence if the killer's buttons were pushed.' He looked at them gravely. 'There's also this.'

The medic opened his gloved hand to disclose a set of coral rosary beads in an evidence bag. 'The necklace was wrapped around his neck,' Dr Dajani said levelly as he handed it to Markham.

Doyle turned to Markham. 'They're for Hail Marys and things, right sir? So you don't end up saying more than you have to.'

It was an observation worthy of his mentor Noakes, but Markham suppressed a smile and replied gravely. 'That's right, a devotional prayer tool.'

'It's like the killer was showing contempt for Father Digby and everything he stood for,' Burton breathed. 'Making a mockery of him.'

The pathologist nodded. 'That's what I thought,' he said. 'It seems to imply a hatred of religious belief—'

'Or Catholicism,' Markham put in quietly. Where the hell did that leave them, given most of their suspects were devout believers?

'Maybe it's just Father Digby they hated,' Doyle volunteered.

'Or they could've left the rosary to confuse us,' Burton said. 'Get us looking for non-Catholics.'

'D'you think they wanted to confess to Father Digby about murdering Julia?' Doyle asked. 'Isn't there a rule priests can't repeat what someone's told them, even if they own up to a crime?'

'That's right,' Burton said slowly. 'Priests can't break the seal of the confessional . . . but maybe Father Digby wouldn't play ball and then things spiralled out of control.'

'It looks as if Father Digby could have met his killer by appointment,' Markham mused looking about him. 'Took them down here where it was nice and quiet and no risk of being disturbed.'

'But a woman's been murdered, boss,' Doyle exclaimed incredulously. 'What made him think he wouldn't be next?'

'Perhaps he didn't realise the person he came here to meet was the killer,' Markham replied. 'Perhaps he just thought they knew something and needed to get it off their chest . . . or wanted advice about what to do.'

Burton proffered another scenario. 'Or maybe he did know it was the killer and thought he'd be able to persuade them to turn themselves in.'

Doyle whistled. 'Hell of a gamble.'

'He might have felt invincible,' she said reflectively. 'What with having God on his side and all that.'

Hubris, Markham thought. It came in all manner of guises.

'He may have wanted to give them some form of absolution,' the pathologist said quietly. 'Pardon for their sins.'

Markham regarded the medic's calm features. He was as different as possible from bluff Doug 'Dimples' Davidson, their pathologist back in Bromgrove who was nicknamed 'Siegfried Farnon' on account of his resemblance to the irascible vet of the 1970s television series *All Creatures Great and Small*. But there was something reassuring and likeable about Dr Dajani.

'Any idea of the weapon, Doctor?' Markham asked.

'All I can say at this stage is a heavy implement . . . the dimensions of a poker or a candlestick, something of that sort.'

The pathologist then bowed courteously and gestured to the two hovering paramedics who waited with a folding stretcher.

'I need to move Father Peake,' he said quietly. 'There's a lift on the other side of the stacks which will take us back up to the ground floor.' He gave a puckish grin. 'From what I saw of your colleague, I imagine he'll have seen off any gawkers by now.'

Markham smiled too. 'Oh yes, he's very effective at routing the rubberneckers.'

The three detectives retreated to wait by the lift.

'In one sense, priests and nuns have it easy,' Burton observed unexpectedly. 'No worries about practical stuff — paying the mortgage, bills, putting food on the table, all of that . . . But on the other hand, they hear all kinds of things from people in confession . . . learn their deepest secrets.'

'Is that what you think this was, Kate?' Markham asked. 'Some kind of confession scenario . . . Father Digby offering the killer a chance to unburden themself?'

'It feels like that, guv.' Markham felt a fleeting twinge of discomfort at the way his fellow DI deferred to him, but it was clear she was entirely comfortable with the arrangement. 'Or maybe it's just the way the body was positioned . . . almost as though he was praying.'

'It looks as though he was going over some notes before the killer rocked up,' Doyle pointed out. 'And then they chucked his stuff on the floor.'

'Yes, we'll take a look once Dr Dajani's done, before the SOCOs get started,' Markham said.

'I've got my crime scene kit on me, sir,' Burton said eagerly, fishing out her plastic gloves and evidence bags, eager to learn if the priest's notes held a clue.

Doyle tried to visualise the sequence of events. 'So he came in here with some notes to go over while he waited. Then when the killer arrived, he went up to the front door to let them in—'

'Or they could've let themselves in if it was one of the senior people who had pass keys,' Burton interjected.

'If he had to let them in, then presumably they rang his mobile to say they were outside,' Doyle continued. 'Hey, what about his phone?'

'No sign of that, I'm afraid,' came the quiet voice of the pathologist from behind them. 'Looks like his assailant took it.'

They bowed their heads in respect as the sheeted stretcher was manoeuvred into the lift, doctor and medics squeezing in beside it.

'I'll be in touch, Inspector,' Dr Dajani said as the doors closed.

The detectives returned to the table where Father Digby had been sitting. With a quick word to the group of SOCOs who had begun processing the scene, Burton retrieved the sheets of paper and scanned them intently.

'It's just some notes about St Therese.' She sounded disappointed. 'Let's see. "Extraordinary family background . . . overstimulated awareness of herself . . . poetry and letters interesting but superficial, just the crest of foam on the deep wave" . . .'

Doyle's expression suggested his colleague might as well have been talking Swahili, but she ploughed on.

'"Thanks to her a form of life that always flourished, silently gained a face and a voice, she showed the true roots of Christian existence not the hollow pomposity that had corrupted the Church".'

Corruption. The word fell into the silence of the stacks like a stone into a deep well.

'"The Little Way", different from the grand style of sanctity . . . laypeople more important than the clergy—"'

'Bishop wossname won't like that,' grunted Noakes who had returned from attending to Miss Parkin and was padding across to join them.

'"A conflicted fighter . . . rose above a repressed nature and private torments . . . conquered herself."' Burton's voice trailed off, the initial flare of excitement swiftly extinguished.

She frowned at the sheaf of papers. 'Nothing revealing or radical in here by the looks of it,' she concluded. 'Of course, you know more about this kind of thing, sir,' she said politely to Markham, 'but none of it sounds controversial or provides a motive for murdering Father Digby.'

'There's the stuff about her being repressed and having torments,' Doyle said dubiously. 'Could be the Father was on to something sensational.'

Burton glanced down at the notes, speed reading their contents. 'Yes, but that's just by the by, almost an aside really . . . he doesn't say anything else about it.'

'Mebbe he planned to spill the beans,' Noakes suggested.

'About what?' Burton was exasperated. 'This is just a crib sheet for some sermon or other, nothing explosive, nothing for the Church to get worked up about.'

Noakes was thoughtful. 'Diggers might've been going to drop the H-bomb,' he persisted gamely. 'Whip out summat embarrassing . . . only he didn't have the whole picture yet—'

'Or didn't want to trust it to paper,' Doyle added.

Burton's shoulders drooped. 'Maybe it was just a random nutter,' she said wearily. 'Some weirdo who didn't like Father Digby's take on Therese.'

'It's gotta be connected to Julia's murder,' Noakes said. 'What with both of 'em living at the club and involved with this place.'

Markham nodded. 'Agreed. So maybe both of them were privy to a secret . . . something with the potential to discredit Therese's cult or compromise the Church.'

Burton's mobile sang out, making them jump. She moved away to a discreet distance as her colleagues glumly contemplated the crime scene and the SOCOs flitting about in their white suits like giant moths.

It was a short call.

'Bishop Buckley's with the DCI at Eton Lodge, sir,' she told Markham. 'They've brought the meeting forward . . . he wants an update asap.'

The group's gloom deepened.

'Trust the *chief* sky pilot to try nobbling us before Diggers even reaches the morgue,' Noakes groused. ''Course, you know what he's going to say, boss . . . wants us to keep our grubby mitts off his priests and nuns yada yada.'

'Sidney's probably got some local person lined up to take the rap,' Doyle concurred.

'Well, they're both doomed to disappointment if they think it's a case of our genuflecting to the hierarchy,' Markham rapped.

Noakes guffawed appreciatively. When the guvnor got sarky like that, it meant the gloves were off.

'What about next steps, sir?' As ever, Kate Burton was keen to fix an agenda.

'I want you and Doyle to check all the alibis for yesterday evening, but before that, arrange door-to-door checks for the area round the institute.'

'What sort of radius, boss?' she asked.

'Out as far as Exhibition Road and Queen's Gate to start with . . . Oh, and check South Kensington underground. I heard someone at the club say Father Digby didn't drive and took the Tube everywhere, so they may have him on CCTV. No cameras at the institute, worse luck.' He grimaced.

'You would think they'd want security, what with places like churches and synagogues being terrorist targets,' Doyle mused.

'The janitor does foot patrols,' Noakes told them. 'Nice old fella, been here for donkey's years.'

Doyle screwed up his face. 'Not past it then?'

'Nah. He's on the ball an' there's a son lives out Camden Way. His firm does their electricals.'

'See what they have to say,' Markham continued. 'Did they notice anyone behaving oddly, that kind of thing.' His tone suggested he didn't hold out much hope. 'After Noakes and I have seen off the bishop and Sidney, we'll see if anyone from the club can give us some more background on Father Digby. Now he's dead, there's a chance someone may open up.'

'I didn't have much luck with the Father Provincial, sir, but I'll try him again too,' Burton said. 'Murder puts a new slant on things.'

'Good. Father Digby's beyond being hurt now, but the full picture might help us catch his killer.' A thought occurred to Markham. 'What about his next of kin?'

'I would think the order will want to handle that side of things, guv,' Burton said crisply.

'Fine.' He sighed. 'It's unorthodox but fine. Let me know if there's anything I can do on that front.'

'Will do, guv. Also, they're allowing residents back into the club tomorrow and David Manners says we can set up an office there, so we don't always have to schlep back to the station.'

'Very considerate of him,' Markham said dryly. 'Presumably Mr Manners now steps up to become acting warden.'

Burton pulled a face. 'That's right, sir. There'll be an election by the institute committee to appoint a new warden, but in the meantime . . .'

'That bloke's a right little Napoleon,' Noakes rumbled. 'God help the staff.'

'Yeah, but snitchy types like him notice stuff,' Doyle observed shrewdly.

'Okay, we'll have a shot at pumping him later,' Markham replied. 'Miss Parkin was uncomfortable when Noakes and I asked her how Father Digby and Julia got on together, so it looks like there may be something to winkle out on that front.'

'Don' see it being like *The Thorn Birds*,' Noakes leered. 'Watched that with the missus. You know the one I mean . . . Richard Chamberlain's the priest who goes over the side.'

At least the DS didn't say anything about the clerical hero getting his leg over, which represented an advance of sorts.

'Diggers weren't 'xactly love's young dream,' the DS added in case they'd missed his point. 'Julia could've been the bunny boiler type, though,' he added meditatively.

'We won't share that theory with the bishop and DCI, obviously,' Markham said firmly.

Noakes pulled his shot-in-the-back face. ''Course not, boss. What do you take me for?' he said reproachfully.

'Come on,' Markham urged. 'The sooner we get that interview out of the way, the sooner we can get back to some real work.'

* * *

As it turned out, Bishop Buckley was far less oily and unctuous than Markham had anticipated. Tall and bespectacled with a fine head of silver hair (Grecian 2000, thought Noakes beadily) and a stoop, his manner and voice were precious and reedy, but Markham supposed that's how it was with some clergymen. As though they were pickled in aspic at an early stage of their personal development.

Mercifully, Sidney had already departed for what the DS termed the afternoon 'yawnathon' on digital policing, so at least they were spared watching him salaam to the diocesan representative whom Mr Evans had installed in the lounge with tea and biscuits. Judging from his weary expression, Markham suspected the bishop might have preferred something stronger, but it appeared Eton Lodge didn't run to a cocktail hour.

'The Church has been very much in the firing line over recent years, Inspector,' was Buckley's opening gambit after Markham had briefed him on their discovery at the institute. 'Had a bad press what with child abuse scandals and so forth.'

To say nothing of murky pockets of moral and ethical corruption, Markham thought.

But the DI said courteously, 'We're a church of saints and sinners, My Lord. And Pope Francis appears to be exercising the charism of discernment to good purpose. Cleaning the Augean stables.'

The bishop's eyes were sharp behind his spectacles.

'You're one of us aren't you, Inspector?'

Better not try that malarkey, thought Noakes. He wasn't sure what the guvnor meant by mucking out stables — sounded like one of his arty farty quotes — but he sure as heck didn't do *favours* when it came to murder.

His boss was courteous but steely.

'My allegiance is to the truth,' he said quietly. 'However, I have no wish to cause unnecessary embarrassment. You can be assured we will proceed with the utmost discretion.'

Bishop Buckley took the startlingly handsome DI's measure in one swift appraising glance. The intelligence he had received on Gilbert Markham suggested this was a man of integrity in whom there was a singular mixture of determination and hardihood, along with a notable absence of deference to authority. DCI Sidney might be manoeuvrable, but not this man. It would therefore be wise, the bishop thought, to proceed with caution.

'The cult of St Therese is open to misinterpretation,' the bishop said mildly, with a propitiating air. 'Indeed, many distrust it as a distasteful example of superstitious philistinism.'

'I reckon she's champion,' Noakes spoke up stoutly. 'We can't all float around on heavenly clouds an' she knew that.' He blew out his cheeks. 'Plus, she weren't too proud to tell God she couldn't be holy all on her own . . . needed a helping hand, like.'

Ah yes, Buckley thought. He'd heard about Markham's sidekick and the extraordinary symbiosis that made this partnership quite unlike anything else in Bromgrove CID.

'That's as good a summing up of the "Little Way" as I've heard,' he smiled at the DS. 'Personally, I regard her as the greatest saint of modern times . . . Pope Pius XI, no less, called her "the star of his pontificate"—'

'So, what's the problem then?' Noakes demanded, only partly mollified by the praise.

'In recent years, everything about Therese has been challenged,' the bishop replied. 'There's a sizeable contingent which sees the phenomenon of her cult as reactionary . . . counter-progressive and wedded to clericalism.'

'What's clericalism?' Despite himself, Noakes was interested.

'I suppose you would call it an overly obsequious attitude towards the clergy, Sergeant.'

In that case, the DS reckoned, Slimy Sid had a bad case of it.

Aloud, he ventured, 'So some folks think Therese an' her "Little Way" an' all the rest of it's a bad thing, right?'

'Correct.' The bishop paused. 'Feminists, in particular, have strong objections to what they see as the machinations of a church which oppresses women and turns them into victims.'

Noakes's mouth turned down at the corners.

Not that lot again. They cropped up all over the show. Made a right nuisance of themselves during the investigation at the 'fat' clinic.

'There's a demonstration scheduled to take place tomorrow afternoon outside the institute,' Buckley continued. 'One doesn't often see anti-Catholic protests in London, or indeed in the UK. Various . . . elements,' he hit upon Sidney's favourite word, 'feel that Theresian studies should have no place in an enlightened university curriculum . . . and there's the usual rent-a-mob looking to make trouble — claim priests and the Papacy are agents of capitalism.' He sighed heavily. 'Any suggestion that priests and nuns are somehow mixed up in a murder connected with the institute is the last thing the diocese needs. The impact on our work — on vocations — would be calamitous.'

'I'll issue a bulletin from Southampton Row with the minimum of information,' Markham said. 'Just a statement that we're investigating an unexplained death together with confirmation of the victim's identity. Staff at the institute have been instructed to stick to this line. There'll be no press conference until we've had a chance to follow up leads.'

Leads, what leads? said Noakes's truculent expression.

Markham looked Buckley in the eye. 'No salacious speculation,' he told him firmly. 'Not if I can help it.'

Noakes was incredulous. 'Are folk really going to pick a fight over this little lass who didn't even make it to thirty and spent most of her life stuck inside four walls in some mouldy little town?'

'Oh yes, Sergeant.' The bishop smiled grimly. 'People take sides.'

'Which side was Dig— er, Father Digby on then?'

'I believe he was on the revisionist side of the equation — wanted to assess St Therese as a product of her times.' A thin smile. 'He saw no conflict between such an approach and an appreciation of her theology.'

'Presumably this might have offended those with a more traditional view of the saint,' Markham suggested. 'A devout layperson, for example.'

'Or a fanatic,' Noakes retorted bluntly. 'Holy Joe with a screw loose.'

'I understand the first victim, Ms Porter, was highly religious and she had a great devotion to St Therese,' the bishop said thoughtfully. 'As did Father Digby, though his scholastic studies at Oxford caused him to subsequently adopt a sociological perspective . . . Ideologically, they were at opposite ends of the spectrum, so if they were murdered by the same killer, I struggle to identify a common factor — apart from their fascination with St Therese, but that of course is not an unusual trait here.'

'P'raps he had a foot in both graves.' Noakes was very pleased with himself for this witticism, though the bishop shot him a hard look.

Buckley abandoned finesse.

'Are you looking for one individual with a connection to both victims, Inspector?'

'The unique circumstances — their link to St Therese through the club and institute — and the fact that the murders happened one after the other strongly suggest they were murdered by the same person, My Lord.' Again, Markham held the clergyman's gaze. 'But we are keeping an open mind and will be liaising with Drugs and Vice in relation to local offenders.'

Good luck with that, guv, Noakes thought. A job for Kate Burton and her spreadsheets. If Sidney wanted them to go after fruit loops, Burton could come up with enough data to convince him and Buckley that they had the local psychos in their sights.

The DS heaved a portentous sigh of the 'time's a-wasting' variety.

Buckley took the hint.

'I must leave you to your work,' he said.

About bloody time.

'Jus' one more thing.' Noakes said in his best Columbo fashion as the bishop made for the door. He was buggered if he were going to 'My Lord' him. 'Did Father Digby ever have any problems with women? Y'know sex stuff.'

The temperature dropped several degrees.

'One assumes his sacred office precluded such an eventuality,' was the frosty response.

Markham wasn't assuming anything of the kind, but directed an almost imperceptible jerk of the head towards his wingman.

Leave it for now.

As the clergyman vanished into the hall, David Manners appeared.

Time for the black-washing to commence.

6. SHOWER OF ROSES

The deputy warden took the news of Father Digby's demise impassively, announcing that he would pray for his soul.

No other reaction, though it seemed to Markham that he looked even greyer and more faded than before.

'Was it murder, Inspector?' Manners asked.

'For the time being we're treating it as an unexplained death.'

Though no doubt the details would find their way out eventually. They always did. He could only pray the institute was less of a leaky sieve than other organisations they had investigated.

'In the meantime,' the DI went on, 'we're anxious to understand more about this cult of the Little Flower.'

The deputy warden pursed his lips. '"Little Flower" . . . Little Nettle might have been a better name for her.'

Markham and Noakes were taken aback by the wordplay, since David Manners hardly looked the type to engage in witty repartee.

Perhaps they had misjudged him. Noakes didn't approve of the disrespect.

'St Therese is a big deal to some folk,' he growled. 'There's no call to sneer.'

The deputy warden sniffed.

'In her lifetime, she was very keen on being ignored and reviled,' he retorted. 'She said she wanted to be a "grain of sand under the feet of all". Her doctrine was all about nothingness, in imitation of Christ you understand.' There was a distinct edge to his voice. 'So I doubt she would disapprove of honest criticism.'

Before Noakes could re-enter the fray, Manners continued in his schoolmasterish way, 'Obviously I'm not denying her impact. By 1915, nearly a million copies of her autobiography were in print and letters reporting miracles arrived at a rate of one thousand a day by 1925—'

'Yeah, the *Pluie de Roses*,' Noakes replied ponderously, with more than a suggestion of Franglais. 'Shower of Roses,' he translated helpfully.

'Indeed.' Now it was the deputy warden's turn to look taken aback. 'There was undoubtedly something extraordinary about the way the whole thing snowballed,' he told them. 'Between 1897 and 1925 more than seventeen million relics were sent out by Therese's convent.' A wintry smile. 'Either her cell was atomised, or the fragments multiplied miraculously—'

'Like the loaves and fishes,' Noakes cut in.

Markham suppressed an urge to laugh at the deputy warden's boot-faced expression.

'You have reservations, Mr Manners?' the DI interposed before his wingman got stuck into the Scriptures.

'One of the popes — I forget which — said her *Story of a Soul* seemed to him more like the story of a "steel bar". Many scholars are impatient of the romantic formulas.' A swift glance at Noakes. 'But arguably it isn't possible to have a moderate belief in God, and certainly with Therese it was all or nothing.'

'I take it you've contributed to the debate, sir,' Markham said courteously.

'A couple of monographs while I was doing my MA in Comparative Religion at Lancaster University.' A note of pride crept into the man's voice, and when the DI looked interested, Manners became expansive.

'There's considerable interest in the cult in Quaker circles, especially the socio-medical viewpoint.'

The anti-Catholic one, you mean, thought Noakes wrathfully, forgetting the St Cecilia investigation when he was inclined to shout 'no popery' from the rooftops.

Manners couldn't resist lecturing his captive audience. 'The family was remarkably interesting, especially the parents' Josephite marriage — the way they initially lived as celibates, in accordance with the tradition that Mary and St Joseph refrained from a normal sexual relationship . . . It seems likely the home environment resulted in neurotic difficulties and repugnance for Therese's body. I mean, she was given a doll dressed as a Carmelite nun when she was a child . . . Her uncle, quite a sensible man by all accounts, was absolutely appalled.'

Markham remembered Olivia's approval of 'Uncle Isidore'.

'Then there was the early loss of her mother, followed by her sisters' entrance into the convent . . . and,' Manners shot another wary glance at Noakes, 'the *strange* dynamic with her father. The whole set-up very likely induced a morbid mentality that made her seriously unbalanced. How many children of ten go round saying the neighbours "didn't think about death enough"?' He nodded sagely at their surprised expressions. 'Yes, from the psychoanalytical perspective she's a fascinating study. You could certainly see her as a child broken by loss. It's arguable that mysticism was her escape route from human abandonment and the experience of being forsaken.'

No stranger to familial abandonment, Markham felt a sharp stab of pain at these words. But before he could say anything, Noakes had taken up the cudgels once again.

'Okay, so the family's a bit weird. But *she* were down to earth . . . saw it through an' did her best,' he said stubbornly.

Noakes had a lot of time for people who 'did their best'.

Manners blinked apprehensively.

Markham judged it was time to bring their conversation round to the dead priest. 'I gather Father Digby shared this revisionist perspective.'

'Well, he belonged to the "New Historicist" cabal.' Something in the deputy warden's tone implied that faction was to be regarded as inferior. 'But of course, theologically speaking he was aligned with traditional Catholic teaching.'

'Presumably that puts him in the same camp — if I can use the word — as Julia Porter.'

'I would say so, yes.' The deputy warden was clearly torn between reluctance to speak ill of the dead and an impulse to self-aggrandisement.

A moment later, self-aggrandisement won the day.

'One might say there was something *backward* about their slavish adherence to the cult, as opposed to a more *cerebral* stance which probed its foundations.'

There was no doubt as to who was included in the latter cohort, Markham thought wryly.

'So you think it unlikely these murders would have been committed by a fanatic — someone who felt Julia and Father Digby had somehow disparaged St Therese or the cult?'

'I don't see how either of them could have offended any of the faithful given their personal *conservatism*. Julia was a devout soul.' *A not very bright one*, his tone seemed to say. 'While Father Digby's scholarship certainly didn't raise any doctrinal challenges.'

Noakes had had enough of the deputy warden's supercilious tone.

'Where were *you* yesterday evening?' he demanded.

An angry flush rose up the scraggy neck.

'I was here at Eton Lodge drawing up contingency plans for the interim period when I will be acting warden,' he said stiffly.

'Anyone able to vouch for you?' the DS persisted.

'No. As far as I am aware, everyone retired early. Julia's death has come as a terrible shock to our community.'

With one exception, Markham thought scrutinising the deputy warden closely.

Noakes was fed up with dancing around the bleeding maypole.

'Did Father Digby ever have problems with women?' he demanded. 'What about him an' Julia?'

'If you're imagining these murders are part of some love triangle,' the deputy warden's voice dripped with disdain, 'then I'm afraid you're barking up the wrong tree.'

'Were you aware of Father Digby having *any* sexual entanglements?' Markham asked.

'He was . . . *relaxed* with women,' Manners said. 'Especially young female students.' Clearly the deputy warden disapproved. 'It was possible he misread the signals on occasion . . . Julia made a bit of a nuisance of herself before getting the message.'

Markham wondered if it had been Manners who took it upon himself to deliver a warning.

'Prissy little sod, ain't he?' said Noakes afterwards as they sat over coffee provided by Mr Evans who discreetly left them in peace.

'It sounds as though there *was* some sort of issue with Father Digby and Julia, Sergeant.'

'An' Miss P knew about it,' Noakes agreed. 'Cos she were dead awkward when we asked about the two of 'em.'

The DS thought intently. 'But Diggers an' Julia were singing from the same hymn sheet . . . Sounds like they both bought into the cult big style, so it's not like they were — whatchamacallit — heretics . . . wouldn't have got up the nose of a nutter or some cult groupie with a fixation about Therese.'

'Yes, Mr Manners was a more likely candidate given that he's a sceptic.'

Noakes scratched his bristly chin. 'How come Manners ended up as deputy warden seeing as he's got such a down on the lass.'

Markham was amused by the easy familiarity with which his wingman referred to the saint. Evidently they were well on the way to being friends. Well, he thought, Therese had presumably attracted unlikelier disciples . . .

He considered Noakes's question. 'The club and institute plume themselves on having an ecumenical spirit as well as embracing all shades of Theresian scholarship.'

'Plus, Manners'd be good at sucking up to the right people.'

Markham's lips twitched.

'That too.'

The door to the lounge opened suddenly, and Tom Nevin appeared.

'Oh, I'm sorry,' he said in his deep Southern drawl. 'I didn't realise anyone was in here.' He hesitated on the threshold.

'That's alright, sir,' Markham waved the professor to an armchair. 'We're just trying to get a handle on the "Little Flower".'

'You could spend a lifetime doing that, gentlemen, and you still wouldn't have plumbed the depths.'

After bloodless David Manners, there was something soothing about the big American with the voice like molasses.

'My sergeant here is a big fan of Therese,' Markham told him.

'Is that so?' Nevin beamed at Noakes who squirmed self-consciously. 'Well, for a gal who aimed to become invisible, she certainly made up for it in the afterlife.'

'Did she *really* aim to become invisible?' Markham asked. ''Mr Manners rather makes her sound like a spoiled middle-class brat playing some sort of game . . . like an internal strategy for survival because she was psychologically damaged, a narcissist even.'

Nevin frowned.

'Oh, you don't want to let Dave put you off,' he said. 'All the folklore about totting up sacrifices — never leaning against the back of her chair and only getting reheated fish heads and leftovers for her supper — is just, well, window-dressing. She was far more heroic than that.'

Manky fish heads for supper constituted pure heroism in Noakes's book, but he held his peace, waiting for more and grinning inwardly at the thought of how the deputy warden reacted to being called *Dave.*

Nevin smiled at the untidy detective who looked like he had got dressed in the dark.

'I can give you a reading list, Sergeant,' he said. 'That way you can get to know the real woman behind the legend.'

Noakes was gratified to be treated on an equal footing and warmed to the laid-back academic.

'Well, she were definitely heroic, what with the TB an' all that,' the DS ventured.

'Yes,' the other agreed. 'Strange isn't it that people had this romantic idea of the disease — spirit shining through the flesh — when it was often a downright disgusting way to die. Haemorrhages, gangrene, suffocation, starvation, stomach hard as a rock . . . bedsores and oedema, tongue like a grater . . . coughing up pieces of tissue like bits of liver.'

Markham had a feeling that Tom Nevin's students probably relished the ghoulish inventory.

'Then there were her sisters and the other nuns badgering her about having a holy death,' the professor continued, 'worrying about who'd receive her last look — of course she said the prioress — and whether the angels would come for her. Meanwhile, Therese was suffering so badly, she told them if she'd been an atheist she wouldn't have hesitated to take her own life.'

'You're *kidding me.*' Noakes leaned in, fascinated. 'An' her a nun.'

Nevin was visibly delighted by his eager audience, so Markham relaxed in his armchair and enjoyed the American's conversation. Burton and Doyle would soon be back, but in the meantime perhaps something might emerge from this exchange which would yield a clue . . .

'Yes, she told it the way it was,' Nevin went on. 'Advised the nuns to keep all medications out of a terminal patient's reach. Gave practical advice about them needing to have better food and more warmth . . . They made the improvements after her death, but it was too late for her to enjoy them.'

'She weren't just some masochist then,' the DS observed.

'Oh no. Everything was related to her faith. But she had a very human side. Said she fancied an éclair a fortnight before she died.'

Cake. Now *that* was more like it, Noakes's expression seemed to say.

Somehow, the homely details were bringing the saint vividly to life, so that Markham almost felt she was in the room with them. Noakes was avidly lapping it all up in a manner that would have astonished his colleagues back in CID.

'Don't get hung up on the incidentals,' Nevin advised his new-found adherent. 'The key thing is the way she dismantled all the boundaries of her psyche — and yes, she *was* a cosseted middle-class girl — to give herself to God. There was a will of iron there.'

Markham remembered what David Manners had said about the steel bar.

'Darn impressive,' Nevin said. 'And then, when she was about to turn twenty-four, with no husband or home or child or even one real friend—'

'Cos of the particular friendships thing?' Noakes put in.

'Exactly, Sergeant.' Nevin's tone was warmly approving. 'Well, when everything had been stripped away, she had terrible temptations against belief . . . No more fancying she saw her initial *T* written in a starry sky . . . just this terrible void and terror that she was being tempted to blasphemy. So she ended up singing simply of what she *wanted* to believe . . . feeling that she was like the atheists but trusting in God. *That* was the heroism.'

Atheism.

'Is it possible that Julia *didn't* in fact subscribe to the common pious perception of St Therese?' Markham asked carefully. 'Could she have been working against the cult in some way?'

Even as he asked the question, he felt the improbability of such a scenario.

Nevin, however, wasn't thrown by it.

'You're thinking she might have been some sort of fifth columnist . . . the enemy within?'

'I know it sounds as though we're clutching at straws, Professor, given what we know of Julia. The notion of her being murdered over differences of belief is a stretch . . . it seems petty.'

Nevin considered this.

'Actually no, Inspector, it's not really. Therese said it herself, "Everything is so big in religion".' He took his time before continuing, 'And there are plenty of people who see her as infantile, sexually repressed and egotistical.'

Markham recalled Miss Parkin's distress at the reduction of Therese's story to the lowest common denominator.

The American said earnestly, 'Father Digby says you've got to see her as living in an age when invalidism was a respectable means of power for women and understand the Catholic piety of the time. If we see her in *context*, then the Freudian interpretations of hysteria and sexual repression fall away.'

Nevin referring to the murdered priest in the present tense was a shock.

But of course, he wouldn't know Father Digby was dead.

Unless . . .

Right on cue, Noakes brought the conversation round to the club.

'Reckon you must be looking forward to getting out of here,' he said gesturing round the lounge. 'It's nice an' cosy, but you've got everything to hand next door. Must be like a home from home.'

'True, but there was time to pack my computer and a couple of books, so I was able to get on with my article last night.'

There it was — his alibi for Father Digby.

Markham scrutinised the American for signs of self-consciousness but couldn't see any indication of discomfort. The man was perfectly at his ease, loose-limbed and relaxed, one leg crossed over the other at the ankle.

'What are you working on, sir?' the DI enquired courteously.

'It's a paper on Marie Guerin, Therese's cousin,' the other explained.

'Oh yeah, I forgot there was another of 'em in the convent with her.'

'That's right, Sergeant.' Nevin smiled. 'They used to play together at hermits when they were children.'

Hermits. Bleeding hell. What's wrong with a doll's house an' tea parties . . .

But Noakes, in his new character of Theresian aficionado, merely said, 'Was that Uncle Isidore's lass?'

'The very same. There were two girls. Jeanne married a local doctor while Marie followed her cousins into the convent. Jeanne's husband didn't exactly see eye to eye with the nuns' doctor when it came to treating TB.'

Noakes was willing to bet Isidore wasn't exactly chuffed with the whole set-up either.

'Ironically, Marie died of TB at thirty-five,' Nevin said.

'You'd think they'd have taken extra care to see another young 'un didn't go the same way as Therese. Downright *negligent* if you ask me. Prob'ly didn't get any morphine cos of Mother Looby Loo's hang-ups.'

The academic eyed Noakes consideringly.

'You really should take a trip to Lisieux, Sergeant,' he mused. 'I think you'd get a lot out of it . . . The chamber of relics at the convent is extraordinary. You can even see Therese's blond curls, which must have fallen past her waist before they cut her hair . . . they're all there preserved under glass, close enough to touch.'

'Reckon the missus might be interested in that,' the DS muttered gruffly. 'But sticking Therese's hair in a glass case . . . it's like she were *scalped*!'

'Oh, there's loads more besides . . . her habit and sandals, and of course the famous writing desk. And the basilica contains another museum in the crypt.' He chuckled. 'Even an atheist would have to agree that St Therese fulfilled her promise to come down from heaven to be among us.'

There it was again, thought Markham. *Atheists. The spectre of unbelief.*

With an effort, he brought his mind back to the conversation. 'Will you be unveiling new discoveries about St Therese, Professor?'

For the first time Nevin looked cagey. Hugging his knowledge close, Markham figured with amusement. No doubt he was hoping to make a splash in scholarly Theresian circles. Unworldly academics were always possessive of their 'finds'.

'There are descendants of the Martin and Guerin families who let information out from time to time, but only in a trickle,' Nevin said. With a shrug, he added, 'It's hard work getting them to turn on the tap.'

'Ah, knowledge is power,' the DI said.

'Something like that. I guess it's understandable they want to control Therese's image.' He looked frustrated for a moment.

Voices in the hallway brought the meeting to a close and Noakes and Markham were soon joined by their two colleagues. Tom Nevin bade Burton and Doyle a cordial good afternoon before disappearing back to his books.

'Any luck with Manners and the prof?' Doyle enquired once they were settled with cups of tea.

Markham duly briefed them, with many an interpolation from Noakes who was keen to display his freshly garnered knowledge.

'Blimey,' the young detective said at the close. 'Who'd have thought folk would get so worked up about whether some woman who died more than a century ago was the real deal or not.'

'"Everything is so big in religion",' Markham quoted.

'An' she's the Left Footers' top saint,' Noakes added.

'So if her reputation is tarnished, it reflects badly on the Church,' Burton said slowly. 'Potentially even enough to create a scandal.'

'That's right, Kate.' But Markham couldn't for the life of him see how to join up the dots between Julia Porter and the warden. 'Anything from the house to house?' he asked.

'Nothing, boss. And nothing from the janitor. But the CCTV at South Ken underground shows Father Digby leaving the station at five past ten last night. There was no one with him.'

'So he was on his way to the institute,' Markham mused.

And his lonely end in the stacks.

'Right,' he said. 'We've done Manners and Nevin. Let's see what we get from the rest of the residents. After that, we can check out the non-resident members. We'll take the line this was an "unexplained death".'

But to one of their interviewees, he thought, the news would come as no surprise. Not if his instincts were correct . . .

'There's that demo tomorrow, boss,' Burton reminded him. 'Do you want me to sort a police presence?'

'We can have a unit on standby,' Markham replied. 'But I think we should scope it out first. If it's small-scale, discretion's the best policy.'

As his subordinates scattered to their various duties, Markham reflected that the appellations of "Little Flower" and "Little Way" were seriously misleading. They suggested a miniature world with everything made to a bird-like measure. Sweet, fragile and delicate, just like the lace in which the saint's mother dealt.

But there was no filigree-coating to the reality of Father Digby's bludgeoned corpse.

Someone had killed twice because of this cult.

It spelled *danger*.

* * *

Friday morning was crisp and sunny, the institute slumbering peacefully in its little enclave as though the events of the previous forty-eight hours had never been.

The team had time to spare before the demonstration, so adjourned to the Brompton Café to take stock.

Once they were settled with drinks and toasties — Markham on this occasion succumbing to the lure of a croque monsieur — they reviewed their suspects' alibis.

'It's the same as with Porter,' Doyle said in a tone of profound irritation, 'all of 'em tucked up in their rooms like good little boys and girls. Mr Evans went up to his flat just after he saw Father Digby going out — said he wasn't aware of anyone else leaving the B&B. Guests have their own keys, and the girl at reception didn't see anyone—'

'How come?' Noakes mumbled through a mouthful of sandwich.

'Identical set-up to the club — kid sitting in a cubby-hole behind the counter. If anyone wants something, they ring the bell . . . No one clocks the comings and goings.'

'I checked with the non-resident members,' Burton said. 'Same story. All at home, either reading or watching the box.'

'Not exactly party animals, are they?' Doyle groused.

'Well, we're talking middle-aged and elderly folk,' she pointed out ruefully. 'A quiet evening in is what they're used to.'

'Not *all* of 'em,' Noakes said with heavy emphasis. 'Someone snuck out an' bashed the padre over the head.'

'Must be a cool customer,' Doyle observed. 'The way they managed to clean up and leave the building without anyone spotting them.'

Burton sighed. 'That's true. The killer was forensically aware, and secondary transfer means we can't narrow it down to anyone at this stage.'

'Makes you wonder about the SOCOs,' Noakes muttered tetchily. 'An' if there's any point to them at all.'

'When we find our killer and the murder weapon, their work will come into its own,' Markham observed.

Noakes scowled. 'Yeah, Professor Plum with a candlestick in the library . . . Worse than pigging Cluedo!'

Doyle shared his mentor's frustration. 'You'd think *someone* might have noticed a visitor wandering round with a bloody big pole or lump of brass.'

'This is a different world,' Markham said mildly. 'They shut up shop early in buildings like the club and the institute. You have to remember there's a value placed on hush.'

'Like the Great Silence,' Noakes said unexpectedly.

Doyle paused with a piece of sandwich halfway to his mouth. 'The *what*?'

Noakes was pleased with the effect of his revelation. 'In convents they stop talking in the evening an' keep silent till after prayers in the morning,' he confided. 'Have to use sign language, see.' The DS considered for a moment. 'Imagine a house full of women not being able to have a good yak.' Noticing Burton's frown, he amended hastily, ''S all about concentrating on the important stuff . . . not getting distracted.'

Markham smothered a smile at his wingman's placatory tone. Time was when Noakes would have ignored Burton's warning signals, but he had mellowed considerably since then. And, as with their shared passion for true crime, the ambitious university graduate and grizzled veteran were both intrigued by this mysterious new world of saints and relics.

Now Noakes said, 'None of 'em has a motive, guv. Julia were jus' some old maid with a thing for St Therese an' Father Digby were the same, only cleverer.'

'There *must've* been a connection,' Doyle mused. 'Maybe they were both on the same track . . .'

'What, you mean they uncovered some sort of *conspiracy*?' Noakes scoffed. 'Summat that'd blow the cult to smithereens?'

The young DS looked discomfited. 'When you put it like that, it sounds crackers,' he mumbled.

'No, it doesn't,' Markham said firmly. 'With *this* case, we have to think outside the box.'

'The cult's a money-making enterprise,' Burton said thoughtfully. 'Big business.' She wiped her lips daintily having, as usual, left half of her snack. 'I googled the stats last night and they're pretty incredible. When there was a tour of Therese's relics to the US in 1999, it covered a hundred and six cities and more than one million turned out. At the national shrine, fifty thousand filed past the casket in sixteen hours and they had to turn twenty-five thousand away . . . they'd waited all that time in freezing conditions. Apparently there'd never been anything like it. People were falling to their knees and smothering the plexiglass dome thing on top with kisses. And that's more than twenty years ago. If anything, she's even more popular today.'

Doyle was invariably impressed by facts and figures. 'So the Church goes into overdrive churning out postcards, prayer cards, coffee mugs and all the rest of it,' he said.

'Don' forget the snow globes,' Noakes joshed.

'Oh yes, it's a real production line,' Burton confirmed. 'And Lisieux is right up there with shrines like Lourdes. There's no getting away from Therese.'

'Wish she'd give us a nudge about where to look next then,' Noakes grumbled.

At that moment, Markham had the oddest sensation. As though a tall female figure in a brown nun's habit and black veil, with steady eyes and a resolute chin, was watching from the corner of the room.

He gave himself a little shake. This was not the time for hallucinations.

Noakes was shuffling his feet.

'My missus is coming down on the train tomorrow,' he said shyly. 'Knows the drill, so she won't be in the way or owt like that.'

Markham's old-world courtesy came to the fore.

'Always a pleasure to see Mrs Noakes,' he said. 'Perhaps she can make time for afternoon tea.'

Olivia would be less than entranced by the prospect of tea with Muriel. On the other hand, that business at the Bluebell had altered the dynamic of their relationship for the better. Liv had a kind heart, though increasingly she claimed her experiences at the chalkface gave her a jaundiced view of humanity. He suspected that she not only struggled with the all-consuming nature of his work but also secretly mourned her inability to give him a child of their own because of the abortion she had kept secret for so long, only revealing it in the aftermath of the Newman Hospital investigation and a fierce quarrel that had somehow cleared the air between them. Scars from the past — in particular a car-crash relationship dominated by coercive control — had carved a deep groove in her essentially sweet nature, and occasionally he almost fancied that she harboured some queer, indefinable resentment against him, as though the authoritarian overtones of his job recalled a bullying patriarchy that had kept her down. Such was her laughing wit, that it invariably charmed him into forgetfulness. But there were times when he felt thrown back on himself, felt there was something in Olivia's heart she tried to keep down but that sometimes surged up and took possession of her . . . something for which he did not have the remedy . . .

At some level, he knew that the guilt and anguish of terminating a pregnancy — albeit because of a dismal medical prognosis and the terror of enmeshing a child in the chaos of her personal life — had never left Liv and that, deep down, she believed her childlessness was divine retribution for the loneliest, hardest decision she had ever taken. Spiritually aware, with a lifelong commitment to Christianity, the sadness had endured, along with a residue of bitterness. Notwithstanding repeated assurances that he was equally happy whether they remained as they were or decided to adopt, he knew she was unable to rid herself of the belief that she was somehow deficient as a woman and had failed him in some crucial respect.

He became aware of Kate Burton's eyes on him and brought himself firmly back to the present.

'I seem to recall it was Muriel who got you interested in the cult of the Little Flower originally?' he said to Noakes.

'Thass right, guv,' the other said happily, always proud when any lustre accrued to his other half. 'Knows tons about her.'

Markham had difficulty imagining Muriel's reaction to Freudian theories of sexual repression, but the lady had a majestic ability to ignore anything unseemly, so it was more likely to be the romantic side of Therese's legend — her apotheosis as the exemplar of traditional self-denying and submissive femininity — that appealed.

'I look forward to tapping her brains, Noakesy,' he said, touched by the way his number two beamed with gratified pride.

Judging by the expressions on the faces of the other two, he suspected that Burton and Doyle would be 'otherwise engaged' on Saturday afternoon.

He looked at his watch. 'Come on, let's get over there and see what our rabble-rousers are up to.'

* * *

As it turned out, the small crowd that had gathered in front of the institute showed no signs of undue belligerence, despite the odd chant and placards with crudely drawn anti-Catholic slogans accusing the pope of being a bigot and homophobe.

An earnest Jeremy Corbyn lookalike was ranting about clerical sex abuse when they arrived, followed in short order by speakers accusing the Church of the repression of women and cover-ups.

Noakes yawned ostentatiously while Burton and Doyle tried to make themselves invisible. Markham reflected that the protests were seriously wide of the mark, since the current pontiff was by a long way the most liberal successor of St Peter ever to reign over the Vatican.

His number two looked round at the protestors and chortled. 'God, it's a right ole sneer-fest.'

The oratory washed over them.

'"Deluded . . . male domination . . . phallocentric hierarchy . . . ulcerations on the body of Christ . . . warped Christianity . . . need for truth before marvels . . . a woman's place . . . priest-worship . . . unnatural . . . treated like gods . . . false idols . . .'"

Markham almost felt he could write the script. Burton and Doyle merely looked embarrassed.

'Chuffing Nora, change the fricking record.'

Seeing as Noakes looked as though he was about to heckle, Markham decided to beat a tactical retreat.

'Nothing doing here,' he murmured. 'Let's head back to the club.'

Suddenly the front door of the institute opened, and a little procession came down the steps headed by four solemn-faced men bearing a litter at shoulder height. Behind them snaked a line of the faithful walking two by two, including residents and members of the Theresian Club along with Miss Parkin.

'That's well creepy,' Doyle breathed as he took in the two statues that faced each other on top of the flower-decked stretcher, one being St Therese in her austere brown habit clutching crucifix and roses while the other appeared to be a statue of the infant Jesus with the addition of a lacy alb over the top such as a priest might wear. Wearing a crown, the child held one hand upraised in blessing while the other clasped a golden globe.

Noakes was mesmerised.

'She took the name St Therese of the child Jesus,' he told them. 'Thass why they're carrying the little chap.'

Somehow the painted rosebud mouth and clustering plaster curls were disagreeable to Markham, the entire tableau making him think of Punch and Judy, so that he half expected a leering puppet to pop up between the celestial figurines.

He could tell Burton didn't like it either, though her features remained carefully blank.

Markham couldn't read the expressions of those in the procession, since they kept their eyes mostly downcast as prayers were recited. Only Sister Pauline looked up, her eyes glittering with an expression that was almost triumphant.

Ignatius Fermor appeared to be directing proceedings, intoning the first line of some sort of litany to St Therese while the rest chanted the responses. Tom Nevin brought up the rear with Donald Trevelyan and it seemed to Markham that the genial American, unlike the rest, appeared to be out of his comfort zone, his eyes fixed on those at the front with a troubled expression.

Most curious of all, the demonstrators fell silent as the extraordinary little troupe marched round the square before disappearing back into the institute. No jeers. No disparaging epithets. Just an uneasy silence.

As a gesture of defiant solidarity by the saint's supporters, it was remarkably effective.

'Talk about hocus pocus,' Doyle laughed shakily.

'It ain't hocus pocus to *them*,' Noakes reproved the youngster.

''Course not, sarge,' the other replied, wondering if his colleague's conversion to the RCs was on the cards. You'd have thought someone like Noakes, with his Methodist upbringing, would run a mile from all the fuss and flowers, he thought, but it seemed like he just couldn't get enough. The way they'd togged the child's statue out in that tunic thing, like he was some kind of bishop, was seriously weird . . .

Markham's voice interrupted his thoughts.

'Time to make our escape before this lot get their second wind,' he said.

A statuesque brunette appeared to have taken over the protest, leading the demonstrators in a chorus of ironic hand claps.

Noakes looked thunderous. 'Weren't so brave before, were they?'

'We've no call to interfere, Sergeant,' Markham said firmly. 'So long as they're decrying the shower of roses and not chucking missiles, we leave them to it.' Looking thoughtfully back at the institute, he added, 'Let's be thankful they haven't cottoned on to Father Digby's death.'

'Miss P won't like it one bit.'

'Can't say I'm enamoured myself, Noakesy, but we need answers, and we won't find them here.'

The sun had gone in now and he shivered, as though it was a portent.

For all the ostensible reverence of the Theresian procession, he had sensed an unmistakeable malevolence in the air. As though someone had thrown down the gauntlet and was there in the building behind them watching and waiting.

A killer on a mission.

As if this was only the beginning . . .

7. INVISIBLE PRESENCE

Markham and Olivia felt little inclination to go out on Friday night, instead choosing to dine in the impressively baroque surroundings of the Russell Hotel's principal restaurant.

'The décor's kind of turn-of-the-century bordello, but it grows on you,' Olivia commented, taking in all the gilding, marble and velour.

'Hmm, a bit oppressive perhaps. I vote we take Muriel to the Palm Court for afternoon tea tomorrow. It's brighter in there with the glass skylights and palms.'

'Ah, *tea with Muriel* . . . D'you reckon it's posh enough for Her Nibs? Wouldn't she prefer Harrods?' Olivia grinned. 'Nearer to Harvey Nicks.'

'She's not going back till Monday afternoon, so there's plenty of time for retail therapy. Noakes has promised to show her the institute, and I believe she wants to see Tyburn Convent in Hyde Park . . . there's a little museum with relics of martyrs who died during the Reformation.'

Olivia put down her knife and fork, temporarily distracted from her succulent Chateaubriand, and frowned at Gil.

'Has Muriel undergone a personality transplant or something?' she asked. 'I mean, what's the story with her and

Noakes going mad for saints and relics . . . are they planning to convert to Catholicism or what?'

Markham chuckled.

'More like they've discovered a shared passion for religious history,' he said wryly. 'Plus, the Catholic Church has the best human-interest stories because it gets to create saints. Anglicans have to make do with having the best hymns.'

'I wish they'd stick to the ballroom dancing . . . at least that's mainstream. The idea of Muriel swooning over dead nuns and medieval religious practices . . . well, it's a bit *weird*, Gil.'

'Muriel's nurturing her spiritual side more these days,' Markham observed. 'Thinking about the deep questions of life. It started when we were on the Beautiful Bodies case.'

Olivia gave a little shudder as she recalled the clinic investigation and its horrific conclusion.

'I thought that was just about unblocking her chakras or whatever they're called . . . This crush on St Therese sounds more like some kind of mid-life crisis.'

'Well, whatever it is, Noakesy's hooked too.' Markham smiled. 'He's talking about booking a surprise holiday to Lourdes and Lisieux.'

'Quite a change from the Costa del Sol,' she giggled before adding thoughtfully. 'So your little rosewater saint has really *got* to George, has she?'

'I believe it's not an uncommon phenomenon. She's the saint for ordinary people, after all. When you peel away all the gilt and gimmickry, there's something impressive about her . . . the way she died without belief in heaven or even any hope of getting there. She just pinned everything on God and tried to stay true to herself when everyone was yammering about angels coming for her and making a beautiful end . . .'

'What an awful death,' Olivia murmured. 'Decaying and rotting by inches.'

Markham felt sudden relief that he had finished his lamb.

Catching sight of his expression, she laughed sheepishly.

'I found time to check out the Theology section in the Senate House today. Made a nice break from *Gender and Sexuality in Postcolonial Literature*, I can tell you.'

Markham leaned back in his plush chair, savouring his Merlot. 'What did you discover, Liv?'

'Oh my dear, simply *horrors*!' she said in her best Joyce Grenfell voice. Suddenly serious, she added, 'I've never read anything quite so harrowing as the account of Therese's last months. And the way that prioress behaved was simply *diabolical*.'

Markham considered this. 'There's a tradition of religious superiors putting saints on the rack to keep them humble and detach them from human affections . . . a sort of discipline to make them holy.'

Olivia snorted.

'Therese thanked her for it in the end,' Markham insisted.

'She *would*.'

'There's a famous story of a Carmel prioress in Salamanca who ordered her nuns to carry a load of stones from one place to another and then back to the first site. When one of them complained about it being pointless, she said it was meant to teach them that in religious life obedience does not require justification.'

'She sounds like Slimy Sid in a habit.' Olivia retorted.

Markham grinned. 'Actually, George is with you when it comes to Mother Gonzague. Calls her "the old witch". Apparently, she used the nuns as maids whenever her aristocratic relatives came to visit . . . and fed her cat calf's liver and sugared milk when the nuns had bread and water.'

'Bet *that* wasn't part of the Carmelite diet.' Olivia sounded exasperated. 'Honestly Gil, I just don't buy all the supernatural guff about training Therese up to be a saint. The prioress was a real horror . . . seriously unbalanced.' Olivia took a deep draught of wine as she formulated her objections. 'It's only on account of her being a nun that people make excuses for what she did, when I think she was actually a nasty piece of work.'

'The way you tell it, she sounds like the wicked step-mother in a fairy tale,' Markham commented mildly.

'Well, I suppose the whole Therese legend *is* a kind of fairy story,' she replied. 'The obscure insignificant little nun locked away in a provincial convent who ends up conquering the world.'

'It does grip the imagination,' he agreed. 'And having four sisters and a cousin take the veil is something of a record too.'

'Plus having your parents canonised into the bargain. What a family!' She rolled her eyes. 'Next thing you know, the uncle and aunt will be up for sainthood.'

'Somehow I don't think so. Uncle Isidore kicked up quite a fuss about Therese becoming a nun so young and initially resisted the canonisation process.'

'Sounds like he was the only one with any common sense.'

Markham laughed, enjoying her caustic commentary. After the cloying ambience of the club and institute, Olivia's astringency came as something of a relief.

'Room for pudding?' he asked.

'I believe I can force myself.'

Once they were settled with deconstructed pear crumble and white chocolate panna cotta, Olivia returned to the subject of the investigation.

'So nothing useful came out of that demo outside the institute?' she asked.

'Alas no . . . though I'm getting a feel for the intensity surrounding the cult and its opponents.' He hesitated. 'There's something *unwholesome* festering back there amongst all the statues and prayer cards and relics . . . some secret. Maybe that's why Julia Porter had to die.'

'And you reckon Father Digby was on to it?'

'Yes, only I can't work out the connection.' Markham sighed. 'The Little Flower Guild is having a shindig at the club tomorrow morning — upmarket bring-and-buy sale, by the sound of it — so we'll swing by and observe the group dynamics.'

'Isn't that a bit insensitive of them, Gil, what with the deaths and everything?'

'It's a regular event apparently . . . one that Julia and Father Digby never missed, so it's "what they would want". And anyway, there's a special memorial service for them at the institute chapel on Sunday.'

'I'll come with you, sweetheart.'

He squeezed her hand gratefully. 'I'd like that.'

'So the bishop didn't try to rush through their funerals?' Olivia asked, remembering investigations where people in high places had pulled strings to speed up the obsequies.

Markham pulled a face. 'Doesn't suit Buckley's agenda. Not with him wanting this whole thing to stay under the radar.'

'*Can he*, I mean, keep it under the radar?'

'Possibly not. We're doing a press conference on Monday, and Kate says reporters are already sniffing around.'

'But you haven't got a lead on anyone?'

There was an interruption as the waiter cleared their plates. Once Markham had ordered coffee, he picked up the thread.

'The club's back open for business,' he told her. 'It's a strange atmosphere there at the moment — muted, *brooding* — but I suppose that's only natural . . .'

The excellent Italian coffee gave him a welcome jolt.

'I picked up on some kind of tension with Donald Trevelyan—'

'The loud Colonel Blimp character?'

'That's the one . . . There's something simmering between him and the buttoned-up theology student Ignatius Fermor. Whatever it is, I think the housekeeper Paolo Serrano's involved . . . I've got nothing definite to go on, just looks and this feeling of something under the surface. The rest of them seem pretty much as you'd expect. It's probably snobbish and elitist of me, but I tend to distinguish between them as the intellectuals and the, how shall I put it, less advanced souls.'

Olivia's eyes danced.

'Who are the intellectuals?' she asked.

'Margaret Bertram and Anne Leadbeater for starters . . . retired librarian and lecturer respectively. Cultured and level-headed. Good friends, though there's a fifteen-year age gap. You'd enjoy them. They managed not to antagonise Noakesy with too much highfalutin nonsense.'

She chuckled. 'Anyone else in the brainiac camp?'

'There's an easy-going American prof, Tom Nevin. Another one who wears his learning lightly. Then we've got Trevelyan's mate Kenneth Robson . . . accountant, quite colourless but intelligent and civilised. The chaplain, Sister Roisin, seems a sensible woman.' He paused. 'And of course there's David Manners, the deputy warden with his MA in Comparative Religion.'

'You don't like Manners,' she said swiftly.

'He thinks a lot of himself . . . a Captain Mainwaring character but without the laughs.'

'I take it George wasn't enamoured?'

'Well, Manners was sneery about St Therese, so that brought out Noakesy's Sancho Panza side . . . he pitched in to defend her.' He gave Liv a wry smile.

She made a comical face in response. 'I'd like to have seen that.'

'Noakes got on much better with Tom Nevin. In fact, it developed into a bit of a love-in . . . Nevin's the one who suggested checking out package holidays to the big religious shrines.'

'Okay,' she said. 'So who are the thickies?'

'I'm not sure that's the right word for them. After all, Thelma Machin's a teacher and Rosemary Gough worked as a secretary . . . Sister Pauline's a trained librarian.'

'Something about their mentality then?' she prompted.

'I guess so. They struck me as being less "evolved" in relation to their faith, if that makes sense.'

'Hmm. I think I know what you mean, Gil. Something unquestioning and bovine about them?'

'Yes, though Rosemary Gough's more dormouse than cow-like . . . seems perpetually on the verge of tears, though I gather she and Julia weren't especially close.'

'Neurotic?'

Markham thought about it. 'Quite possibly . . . Sister Pauline's certainly a bit intense, though there doesn't seem to be any harm in her. Just one of the Catholic old guard, whereas Sister Roisin's managed to move with the times.'

'What about the Thelma woman?'

'Placid and kindly. A very slow way of talking, but she teaches special needs kids so it probably comes from that.'

'How about the youngsters who work in the club?'

'Seem a decent bunch. Paolo's a people-person . . . emotionally intelligent, so probably pats things down when David Manners starts throwing his weight around.'

Olivia's lips twitched. 'Don't forget the woman from the institute . . . The one George calls "Miss P".'

Gil smiled. 'I was saving the best till last . . . She's a traditionalist and a fount of information about Therese and the cult. Looks a dry stick, but actually very good company and not a bit preachy.'

Olivia stirred her coffee meditatively.

'So what it boils down to is, you can't see *any* of them having done the murders?'

'Well, every time we try working up a hypothesis, it seems we end up in *Da Vinci Code* territory with far-fetched theories about a conspiracy that stretches all the way to the Vatican.'

She laughed, an uninhibited joyous sound that made the older neighbouring diners turn around and smile indulgently.

'*Priceless*. I can just see George googling cardinals to find his éminence grise.'

Markham could see the notion really tickled her fancy.

'No, it's got to be all about St Therese and her cult, Liv, rather than anything to do with embezzlement or shenanigans in Vatican City.'

'Something about this investigation reminds me of the Baranov case,' she said unexpectedly.

'How so?' Markham was intrigued, since his previous case of the ballet company murders hardly seemed to have much in common with ecclesiastical circles.

'Oh, just the way the ghost of someone off-stage seems more real than all the rest put together. St Therese is like George Baranov . . . this outsize personality you sense standing in the wings, so you almost fancy that if you turned round, you'd meet their eyes but then there's no one there.' Thoughtfully, she twirled her wine glass, looking into its ruby depths as though self-conscious about succumbing to the saint's supernatural aura. 'There was this strange picture in one of the books I was looking at . . . of the nuns in her convent around four years after she died. There they all were with this whopping great painting of Therese in the middle of the line-up . . . just as though she'd come back from the dead . . . Spooky. And apparently one of the nuns during the beatification proceedings testified that Therese had this strange kind of power over her . . . a kind of psychological sway like mesmerism . . .' Her voice trailed off, embarrassed.

But Markham was a receptive audience.

'Hmm, the saint and the ballet legend,' he mused. 'You know, I felt something of the kind with Therese when I was in the reading room at the club,' he admitted. 'It was eerie. I had a sixth sense she was watching me. It was the same with Baranov . . . the feeling of an invisible presence stalking me.'

'Better not share that with Judas Iscariot,' she riposted.

Markham grimaced, thinking of DCI Sidney's attitude towards flights of fancy.

'Sidney would call it "fey",' he sighed.

'A case of that famous flair getting the better of you, Inspector.' Olivia's imitation of his boss's honk was positively uncanny. She reached across the starched napery.

'You'll crack it,' she said softly. 'Having a saint on your side . . . well, that's got to be worth a few brownie points with the Man Upstairs.'

Markham lifted her slim hand to his lips, his eyes admiring as he contemplated her starry eyes and delicate features that were flushed with the fervour of her belief in him. Under the Empire-style chandelier, Liv's coils of red hair glowed like port wine.

It was clear the break from Hope Academy — or 'Hopeless', as the gritty comprehensive where she taught English was popularly known — had done her good, and her face was free of strain.

'I'm not sure how good my credit is with the Man Upstairs,' he murmured, his lips still pressed to her hand.

'I'll just have to start a novena to St Therese for you,' she countered mischievously. 'Clocking up the Hail Marys and Our Fathers has to count for something.' Then she gave him a saucy wink. 'Come on, I fancy an early night.'

* * *

Saturday 20 March was another fine bright day with clear skies and just the hint of a breeze. After a hearty full English, Markham and Olivia went their separate ways, arranging to rendezvous later that afternoon for tea with the Noakeses. 'I'll let the other two off,' he told her. 'Muriel in religious tourist mode won't be their idea of a good time.'

Meeting him outside the club, Burton and Doyle were ready with their polite excuses for the afternoon, the DI saying she planned to do some research into the origins of the Theresian cult at the British Library (on hearing which, Noakes silently mouthed 'School Swot') while Doyle was in training for his forthcoming Ironman Triathlon.

Markham felt momentarily nostalgic for Bromgrove Boxing Club and the ministrations of dodgy 'Doggie' Dickerson, the dreadful old villain whose run-down gym was a haven for local lowlifes and CID's finest, much to the disapproval of DCI Sidney and the higher echelons. It amused the DI to wonder what Doggie would make of St Therese and her followers. His New Age phase was well behind him, along with buxom Marlene who had initiated it, so it wasn't likely that Carmelite austerities would strike much of a chord.

On the other hand, just look at Noakes . . . he couldn't get enough of monastic lore . . .

Noakes looked almost dapper in what his boss recognised as his second-best Sunday suit, shiny spots and bilious blue shirt notwithstanding. The tufty salt and pepper hair was brilliantined within an inch of its life, and he smelt of cologne as opposed to fried food, no doubt in deference to afternoon tea with 'the missus'. His pigeon-toed walk suggested his best shoes were pinching, but one must suffer to be beautiful, thought Markham with a grin as he contemplated his subordinate.

The Little Flower Guild event looked about as exciting as haemorrhoids, the DS grumbled as they wandered through the downstairs rooms of the club which had been turned into a bazaar for Theresian books and memorabilia.

'Just keep smiling,' Markham murmured — aware that in Noakes's case that meant baring his teeth in a scary manner reminiscent of Jack Nicolson's sinister turn in *The Shining* — and endeavouring to cover any deficiencies with his usual practised charm. 'You can buy Mrs Noakes something,' he said with a happy burst of inspiration.

The suggestion worked, and soon the DS was happily engaged in discussing categories of relics with Tom Nevin who looked much more at ease now than he had during the institute's display at the protest the previous day.

'First-class is part of a saint's body,' he said. 'A piece of bone or flesh. Then there's second-class — that's something they owned or used, like a prayer book or rosary. Third-class is an item that's touched one of the other two.'

Doyle's expression suggested he found it a grisly racket.

'We don't worship the relics themselves,' Nevin explained kindly, registering the young detective's distaste. 'But they make us feel close to saints — it's a way of honouring what they did in their earthly body. A physical connection matters . . . think about the obsession with Princess Di memorabilia. And it's a fact that sometimes objects associated with holy people spark an interest where no amount of sermons succeed.' The gangling professor waxed eloquent. 'Therese's major relics have travelled all over the Middle East. Muslims call her "the little saint to whom Allah refuses nothing".'

Kate Burton's features were better schooled than her colleague's, but Markham could tell that she shared his squeamishness and found the entire set-up weirdly superstitious. However, she was quite taken with the various lockets, pendants and other antique reliquaries on display and listened with no small interest as Sister Roisin explained their provenance. The books too proved to be of interest, and she ended by purchasing a second-hand brochure about the basilica in Lisieux, Sister Pauline unbending noticeably as she popped it into a paper bag. Tom Nevin appeared uneasy around the two nuns as they chatted with simple piety to the club's visitors, no doubt feeling less comfortable amongst the hoi polloi than when mixing with his fellow academics.

Markham understood the sensation. Even sturdily sensible Sister Roisin seemed suddenly too full on. Too cloying somehow. Though her enthusiasm was going down well with the saint's admirers.

Markham suspected the little crowd had been swelled by reports of Julia Porter's death. *An actual murder on the premises*. But business was business, and the club's senior staff did a brisk trade in medals, prayer cards, DVDs and other sidelines.

It struck him that, like Nevin, Ignatius Fermor looked noticeably less sold on the proceedings than the nuns. No doubt the would-be seminarian had snobbish objections to the bric-a-brac side of things along with the rather unelevated clientele, but chairs were set out in rows in the dining room for a talk later by some visiting prelate which should satisfy his intellectual leanings.

Thelma Machin and Rosemary Gough browsed together, the latter looking somewhat less woebegone than the last time Markham had seen her and clutching a coffee mug with Therese's face on it. The mug was received with unconcealed horror by Margaret Bertram and Anne

Leadbeater who clearly didn't think much of the more downmarket souvenirs including tea towels, painted nuns and dolls at prayer. They were far more well-bred than Donald Trevelyan, however, who mimed being sick whenever he caught Paolo Serrano's eye. Seeing the DI from Bromgrove watching his friend's antics, Kenneth Robson gave him a discreet kick on the ankles.

'Blimey.' Noakes was flicking through a well-thumbed pamphlet. 'It says here that the nuns in Therese's convent weren't sure they'd be able to bury the elderly sister who founded the nunnery inside their chapel, so they went and got the local quack to remove her heart and preserved it in formaldehyde . . . an' it's still there in this cabinet thingy . . . jus' like a pickled onion.'

Kate Burton cringed, but Sister Roisin smiled indulgently at this most unlikely groupie.

'That's quite true, Sergeant,' she said. 'Mother Genevieve. She was so revered that they displayed her casket for eight days and her obituary appeared in the town newspaper. The nuns did eventually succeed in getting permission to bury her inside the chapel. For a good while after her death, they expected miracles to happen at the grave site, but none came.'

'Cos she weren't the special one,' Noakes nodded sagely, inadvertently making St Therese sound like the conventual equivalent of football's José Mourinho.

'No indeed, Mr Noakes. As you say, it was the Little Flower who became famous.'

Markham liked the woman for her unpretentiousness. As with Tom Nevin, she had the common touch.

'What's on the agenda for later?' he enquired, gesturing across the hallway to the dining room.

'Oh, Monsignor Barltrop's coming in this afternoon,' she said confidentially. 'He's going to give a talk on Therese's parents.' Seeing Noakes's confusion, she added, '"Monsignor" is a sort of honorary title for senior priests . . . They get to wear a purple sash.'

'I understand,' Markham said politely, 'that the parents have been raised to the altars too.'

'That's right,' the nun said happily. 'Such a wonderful exemplar for married couples.'

'Didn't Therese's dad go off his head cos of all his daughters leaving home to become nuns?' Despite the clumsiness of expression, there was a touching earnestness about the way Noakes said this, clearly thinking of the seismic upheaval in his life if Natalie ever upped and left.

Sister Roisin looked startled, but quickly recovered her poise. 'Well, we can't be entirely sure of all the psychogenic factors, Sergeant, but it was certainly a heavy cross for Therese.'

'Called her "his little queen", right?' Noakes said approvingly.

Markham had a feeling that when it came to winding a parent round their little finger, Natalie Noakes and the long-dead saint had something in common.

Sister Roisin could clearly have stayed chatting with this potential convert all morning, but another customer claimed her attention and the detectives moved on.

'We're not staying for the lecture are we, guv?' Doyle asked in tones of barely suppressed panic.

'Relax,' Markham reassured him. 'I don't think a police presence will exactly enhance the proceedings. We'll give it another five minutes or so and then leave them to it.'

He wandered from the reading room across the main vestibule and through the dining room towards the second smaller hallway outside the television room where the sound of raised voices made him turn sharply.

Tom Nevin and Sister Pauline stood halfway along the hall at the foot of a staircase that led to the club's upper floors.

Noticing the inspector, the American was the first to recover himself.

'Just as well the cavalry's arrived,' he said with an awkward laugh. 'Sister Pauline's running rings round me . . . I should've known better than to take on the Church.'

The two spots of angry colour on the nun's cheeks somehow didn't suggest to Markham that she had got the upper hand.

What were they arguing about? he wondered.

Whatever it was, they clearly weren't going to share anything with him. Nevin headed for the television room, while Sister Pauline disappeared through the hatch at the rear of the vestibule that led to the club's kitchen.

Then a movement above him distracted Markham's attention again.

He was pretty sure someone else had been eavesdropping on the conversation, but when he climbed the stairs to the first-floor landing and peered through the glass swing door that gave on to the corridor, no one was there.

Something about the encounter made him uneasy, but he told himself not to read too much into it. For all the bustling bonhomie of the Saturday bazaar, there was something almost febrile in the atmosphere. The unanswered questions about Father Digby's death hung in the air. His absence tangible. David Manners was everywhere, however, as though to ensure the club's secrets remained strictly in-house.

'We can keep tabs on the Yank an' Sister Misery Guts tomorrow, guv,' Noakes said when they finally disentangled themselves from the faithful a while later. 'Like as not he were jus' winding her up with some far-out stuff about St Therese.'

'Hmm. I'm not sure that nun-baiting is really Nevin's style.'

But the DI let the subject drop as they headed along Upper Montagu Street.

'Seeing as we've got plenty of time and it's a fine day, let's walk instead of taking the Tube,' he suggested. 'You can build up an appetite, Noakesy,' he added seeing that his subordinate was about to protest.

'Okay boss. Jus' so long as I don' turn up looking all hot an' sweaty. The missus won't like that,' the other replied cunningly.

'Oh, we'll take it at a nice sedate pace, don't you worry.'
And with that, they set off.

* * *

Afternoon tea was a resounding success.

The laid-back elegance of the Palm Court was very much to Muriel's taste, especially the way it 'brought the outdoors indoors' she exclaimed delightedly, surveying the abundance of foliage and potted trees. Personally, Olivia found the overall effect too much like a greenhouse, while the mosaic floor with its nymphs and shepherds smacked bizarrely of a bathhouse in Ancient Rome. But as George's 'missus' was in transports of delight, she did her best to join in. Indeed, seeing how carefully Mrs Noakes had prepared for the occasion — the stiffly lacquered hair, teetering high heels plus floral shirtwaister and stole that were somehow too mother-of-the-bride to be entirely successful — she felt her heart contract with something perilously close to affection. Even Muriel's arch demeanour towards 'Gilbert' somehow didn't grate as much as usual.

I must be getting soft in my old age, she thought to herself with an inner eye roll. Either that or the Little Flower's worked another miracle . . .

The tea was excellent and gloriously old-fashioned with, to Noakes's glee, piping hot floury scones and crumpets as well as the usual sandwiches and melt-in-the-mouth cakes.

The conversation too bounced along at quite a rate, aided perhaps by the champagne that Markham ordered as a 'touch of self-indulgence'.

Muriel, like Miss Parkin at the institute, was a staunch Theresian and had no time for the revisionist naysayers.

'As dear Prince Charles once said, people put you on a pedestal just to knock you off,' she said. 'And of course, holiness is always threatening to those without belief.'

'Didn't Therese line up with the doubters and unbelievers?' Olivia asked mischievously. 'I mean, isn't it part of her appeal that she was plunged into spiritual darkness at the end of her life?'

'Oh, but she *never* became an atheist,' Muriel said with an air of squelching further debate on the subject. 'And such a heavenly death. Altogether too good for this world.'

Mrs Noakes was clearly a fully paid-up member of the romantic lobby, Olivia concluded. A votary of Therese as the victim of divine love.

Happily, or rather unhappily for her husband, Noakes dropped the knife with which he was sawing at his scone, making a loud clatter that shattered the genteel hush of the Palm Court and distracting his other half from further controversial debate with Olivia.

Aware of his wife's frowning displeasure, he sought to retrieve the situation.

'I've jus' remembered. Doyle tole me a joke for you,' he said.

Muriel regally prepared to be amused.

'There's these schoolgirls at a convent school,' he began, before breaking into the most outrageously over-the-top Irish brogue that Olivia had ever heard. 'Sister Perpetua who's teaching 'em — their form mistress, like — asks what they want to do when they leave school. Bridget tells her, "I want to be a nurse" an' the nun says, "Healing the sick, that's wonderful". Then it's Mary's turn. She goes, "I want to be a teacher" an' the nun says, "Helping little children, excellent". But then Margaret comes up with "I want to be a prostitute" an' the nun faints. When they bring her round, Margaret says, "Sorry, Sister, it was the shock of hearing me say I wanted to be a prostitute". But Sister Perpetua jus' laughs, "Prostitute! Oh, I thought you said you wanted to be a Protestant!"'

The smile congealed on Muriel's lips at the punchline.

But seeing Markham chuckle — the DI deliberately exaggerating his amusement to cover the situation — she recovered her sangfroid, though her laughter sounded distinctly brittle.

Olivia too jumped into the breach. 'Amazing those tribal religious loyalties,' she said lightly as Noakes looked round uncertainly, fearful that he had somehow put his foot in it. 'The fault lines run deep . . .'

Markham smiled gratefully at his girlfriend as she deftly steered the conversation into calmer waters.

Afterwards when the Noakeses had left them, she chuckled. 'Poor old George. Muriel'll kill him for going all *Father Ted*.'

'He redeemed himself with that locket he bought her,' Markham said. 'But it was a close-run thing.'

'She liked the book with those anecdotes that Sister Rosin recommended,' Olivia added. 'That's really funny about the other saint — the one who founded the Carmelites — wanting to run away to Islamic Spain with her brother so the pair of them could get themselves martyred . . . like something out of El Cid.'

'Oh yes, St Teresa of Avila . . . much safer than Noakesy's awful jokes.'

They laughed companionably, but somehow Markham could not shake off the uneasiness he had felt earlier in the club.

As if a snake was hissing in his ear: *I'm not finished yet.*

8. ANGEL OF DEATH

Sunday 21 March dawned crisp and bright.

After a refreshing promenade around Kensington Gardens, Markham and Olivia made their way to the institute for the memorial service.

On their arrival, Miss Parkin, smart in a lightweight tweed suit and with freshly permed hair, beckoned them into the front hall with a confidential air.

'Very pleased to meet you, my dear,' she said kindly to Olivia before turning to Markham. 'We heard from Bishop Buckley yesterday that Father Digby's body is being released to his community on Tuesday . . . such a relief to know he'll be back with his family.' A telephone rang shrilly somewhere in the recesses of the building and she bustled off, gesturing apologetically. 'Duty calls, but I'll see you in the chapel, Inspector.'

Markham and Olivia wandered back outside and took a turn around the square arm in arm as they digested this piece of news.

'Looks like the bish swung it after all,' she said. 'He must've whispered in someone's ear.'

'I thought Buckley meant to hold back in case of attracting unwanted attention,' Markham mused. 'But I suppose letting Father Digby's order organise the funeral keeps everything low-key and under wraps.'

'Whereabouts are they based?'

'The main house is in Birmingham, but Digby's monastery is just outside Oxford . . . Woodstock, not far from Blenheim Palace.'

'I'm due back home on Tuesday,' she said. 'What if you and George take me and drop by the funeral en route.'

'Sounds like a plan . . . I can have a stopover in Bromgrove and then come back to London with Noakes on Wednesday.'

Olivia smiled up at him. 'You might even manage a workout at Doggie's,' she said slyly. 'Pretend you're pummelling Sidney.'

Markham groaned at mention of the DCI.

'Sidney's going to get antsy unless we narrow down the runners and riders for these murders,' he said. 'Unsurprisingly, he wants to keep well in with the clerical kingpins, and they want this fastened on some misfit — anyone'll do, just so long as there isn't any connection with the Theresians.'

'God, he's such a toady . . . royals, "slebs", telly people, bishops . . . is there anyone that man won't grease up to?' She scowled. 'What's he hoping for from the Church then?'

'Oh, there are plenty of juicy honorifics on offer . . . Order of St Gregory, Order of St Sylvester . . .'

She punched his arm. 'You're having me on . . . surely you have to be Catholic to get one of those?'

'No, some are for folk from other denominations . . . and don't forget, the likes of Buckley can always nudge the Church of England brigade — give Sidney a shot at the Birthday Honours.'

'God forbid . . . And I mean that as a prayer!'

'Oh, Sidney hasn't sold his soul for glory, Liv. It's just that he had quite a hard start in life — single parent family, dad bailed out early — and his wife's a few rungs up the social scale. I think it made him terminally insecure, with a thickening of the professional arteries into the bargain . . . He's one of those who became obsessed with authority and discipline to shore up his own self-image. Reminds me of that Victorian admiral who said, "It is better to go wrong according to orders than to go wrong in opposition to orders."'

'If you hadn't ignored Sidney's orders, the team would never have solved the last half dozen cases,' she protested. 'Isn't it about time he thought about getting it right?'

Markham chuckled. 'There's a decent man beneath it all.'

'You have to look bloody hard,' she grumbled. 'And Brunhilde's unbearable.'

He smiled at this reference to the DCI's Valkyrie-like spouse.

Markham's obsession with fairness could be exasperating, Olivia fumed to herself as they walked along. A major handicap that she just had to swallow. But it was also part of the reason why she loved him. The man simply didn't have a mean bone in his body, and he didn't care one jot about renown or baubles or class . . . or any of the things that loomed so large for others, herself included.

In fact, there was something positively unnerving about Markham's capacity for submerging his own identity and absorbing himself in the fragile, anxious interior lives of others. At times it made her feel uneasy — unworthy even — because she lacked the same empathy for human fallibility.

She dragged herself back to the subject under discussion.

'So Sidney won't go along with fitting up some local fruit loop?' she enquired with heavy sarcasm.

'Liv,' he said, half amused, half exasperated. 'You've been spending too much time with Noakes . . . "fruit loop"!'

'You know what I mean.'

He sighed. 'There's pressure to make this one go away.'

'But it's not Sidney's patch, so the buck doesn't stop with him,' she protested. 'No reason for Bromgrove CID to carry the can. Kate's team are technically the lead on this.'

'Yes, but we happened to be here and Sidney invoked my, er, unusual credentials.'

'Cos the rest of them are pagans and he figured you understood the God squadders' lingo?'

Markham was unruffled. 'Something like that,' he agreed equably. 'I'm due to meet up with DCI Moriarty tomorrow . . . he and Kate are doing a fixated threat assessment—'

'That makes the cult sound like royalty or the diplomatic corps,' she responded drily.

'Well, St Therese *is* Catholic royalty,' he laughed. 'But essentially it's a trawl of the religious fanatics and local mental health patients. Hopefully it will buy us some time and get His Grace off our backs.'

'You reckon it's an insider, don't you?'

'Has to be, Liv.' He paused in front of an impressive bank of red camellias. 'I felt it yesterday in the club at that funny little sale. The killer was there under our noses. Hiding in plain sight.'

She shivered and he tightened his arm around her.

'Come on,' he said, 'let's bag our seats in the chapel.'

Olivia knew that he would be making a silent promise to Julia and Father Digby.

Whoever hurled you into eternity, I will find them.

* * *

The statue of St Therese just inside the chapel porch met with Olivia's approval. 'No thorns on those roses, but at least she doesn't look like a total nitwit,' was her trenchant verdict, much to Markham's amusement.

Inside, the building smelled wonderfully of wax candles, pine and polish, with the perfume of lilies and gardenia in the air.

As they slipped into seats on the left of the main aisle towards the back, Olivia looked up wonderingly at the blue vaulted roof and the clerestory. It was as though she had been translated into another firmament where seraphim might appear at any minute to serenade her. Somehow, she felt at home. The soft grey encaustic flooring with its stippled raised dots, together with the rows of wooden chairs and limestone bas-relief Stations of the Cross, struck a modernist note that was echoed in the plain stone altar. This should have jarred with the copious statuary and two side altars whose frescoes, above carved wooden tabernacles and altars inlaid with gilt, featured the inevitable angels and cherubs. But oddly enough the overall effect was harmonious, suggesting a poignant attempt to bridge "old" and "new" pieties. There was no communion rail in front of the altar and behind it just the plain triple arches with a large wooden crucifix underneath.

Craning her neck to see the rows of stained-glass windows that bordered the vaulted ceiling, Olivia made out sunbursts, doves and other symbols, along with a jaunty little boat lined with haloed faces . . . *Christ calming the storm*, she thought, pleased with herself for having identified a gospel story.

To the left of their seats was a Byzantine icon that she recognised as being Our Lady of Perpetual Help, a cult propagated by the Redemptorist Fathers. Touchingly, instead of the usual pose with his right arm extended to give the world a blessing, the child Jesus had both his hands curled tightly around Mary's, looking scared as he contemplated angels hovering above carrying the instruments of crucifixion. She noticed that Gil's gaze was riveted on the icon. He knew all about childhood anguish, she thought, registering the sadness in his eyes and his faraway expression.

Recollecting himself with a start, Markham took stock of the congregation.

It looked like a decent turnout — everyone from the club present and correct, except for Tom Nevin and Paolo Serrano, together with a sizeable contingent of what were presumably university and institute staff. The Noakeses sat near the front next to Burton and Doyle, with Muriel resplendent in a long black mantilla that was more appropriate to an audience with the pope than a simple memorial service. Doyle was clearly fascinated by her rig-out, casting apprehensive sidelong glances at the DS's wife as though he expected her to break into a Tarantella.

The service, conducted by a stocky balding priest with haughty aquiline features and a strong resonant voice, was brief but dignified. Hymns were sung, accompanied by a small pipe organ to the side of the altar, and instead of a eulogy there were reflections from St Therese's own writings. One in particular caught Markham's attention.

'Let us pray for the souls who have no faith, who, by the abuse of grace, lose this precious treasure.'

Did the killer believe that Julia and Father Digby had committed an abuse of grace? Was that why they had been killed?

Markham felt this case was somehow slipping away from him, even though he had done everything possible to soak himself in the unique ambience of the Theresian Club and Institute.

Over the years, he had grown to depend on the solution to murder investigations coming almost instinctively, or subconsciously, after he immersed himself in the network of relationships and circumstances that connected suspects.

But this time there was no organic revelation of motive. No unfolding of human nature.

He let his thoughts drift, almost somnolent in the heavily scented air . . .

Liv gave him a sharp nudge. The celebrant was winding up.

'Pope John Paul the Second said that the saints virtually never go out of fashion.'

'Muriel'll like that,' Olivia murmured. 'Nothing worse than a saint past her sell-by date.'

Markham grinned, returning the nudge with interest.

'Therese reminds us,' the priest went on, 'that the most fundamental and universal truth of the gospel message is that God is our Father and we are his children. We should therefore keep an untroubled heart and rejoice in our nothingness . . . Only little children and those who are like them shall be admitted to the heavenly banquet.'

'He's clearly never met the juvenile delinquents I teach,' Olivia muttered.

'When invited to contemplate the value of Therese's Little Way, you may think: much ado about nothing. But

I urge you to follow the example of Julia Porter and Father Digby Peake who found in her *Story of a Soul* the means of obtaining great graces from God . . .'

'Not enough to stop them from getting murdered,' Olivia objected sotto voce.

'To the tepid and lazy Christian, in her headlong quest for a total and obliterating union with the divine, Therese Martin might appear as violent as the devil—'

Suddenly, at the word 'devil' there was a crash behind them as the heavy oak door burst open.

The priest halted in mid-sentence and the congregation turned to stare as a uniformed policeman looked swiftly around the congregation before spotting Markham and beckoning him urgently.

The DI moved swiftly to the porch, followed by his colleagues and two dozen pairs of eyes.

'What is it, Constable?' Markham asked once they were safely out of earshot.

'You're needed back at the Theresian Club, sir. There's been another murder.'

Markham felt suddenly, unnaturally calm, almost as though he had been expecting it.

'Keep everyone here for now please, Constable. No one goes anywhere until I give the word.'

And with that they were off, leaving a sea of watchful white faces in their wake.

* * *

The laundry room in the basement of the club was an old-fashioned affair cluttered with drying racks and pulleys as well as the usual appliances. Stuffy and airless, with somewhat grimy walls of a sickly yellow hue, it clearly hadn't been renovated in many a year. No doubt the trustees preferred to concentrate their spending on the club's public areas as opposed to its utilities and staff quarters.

Tom Nevin's body was slumped across the top of a washing machine whose spin cycle thrummed eerily in the silence. A kitchen knife protruded from the back of his neck.

'I didn't realise anyone was down here,' Paolo Serrano told them, looking more El-Greco-ish than ever in the gloom of the basement. 'Thought they were all at the institute for the memorial service. Decided to put some washing on while it was quiet . . . That's when I found him.'

Voices in the passageway announced the pathologist's arrival.

'He's all yours, Dr Dajani.' Markham steered the housekeeper out of the laundry room into an adjoining stockroom where there was a dilapidated armchair upholstered in faded cretonne.

'Sit down, Mr Serrano,' he said, pressing the other into the chair and pulling up a rickety stool while his colleagues squeezed in alongside him. 'When did you last see Professor Nevin?'

'Last night in the dining room with Mr Manners and the others. We offer supper at the weekends . . . nothing fancy . . . baked potatoes, salads, omelettes, toasted sandwiches. The residents quite often have a meal together on Saturday evenings if they've nothing else on. Mr Nevin went into the reading room afterwards . . . he had some work to finish.'

Serrano coughed, a dreadful hacking cough which sounded shockingly loud in the silence of the basement.

'Chuffing Nora.' Noakes eyed him beadily. 'I know the Little Flower had dodgy lungs, but you could give the lass a run for her money.'

Paolo Serrano might have looked pale and gaunt, Markham thought, but he was also young and wiry.

For all Tom Nevin's Davy Crockett physique, the housekeeper had a good thirty-year advantage. And it looked as though the American had been ambushed from behind, so his attacker had the element of surprise . . .

Serrano pressed the palms of his hands on his knees as though they were suddenly sticky.

'My chest rattles like . . . how do you say it, a cart-horse. It's the same with everyone in my family.'

'Well, we don't want you keeling over on us just yet,' Markham said lightly. 'Would you like some water?'

'I'm fine now, Inspector.' The man licked dry lips. 'It was just so horrific coming across Mr Nevin like that.' His hand moved up to the sallow forehead, then down past those hollow cheeks to the little pointed beard, finally coming to rest on his shirt front. 'And after what happened to the others . . . It's like the Angel of Death is picking us off one by one . . .'

Before Noakes had a chance to say what he thought of this interesting comparison, Dr Dajani's head appeared in the doorway.

'I'm ready to move the victim now, Inspector, if you'd care for a word.'

'Of course.' Markham turned to Doyle. 'I'd like you to take Mr Serrano back upstairs and see he gets some hot tea please, Sergeant. Then once you've got his statement, arrange for someone to drive him over to the institute.'

'Can I tell the others what's happened, Inspector?' Paolo asked.

The news would be everywhere soon enough, with no chance of avoiding a press conference.

'I have no objection,' Markham said, 'but it's in everyone's interests not to sensationalise these deaths, understood?'

Serrano nodded. 'Will the residents be able to come back here?'

'Not for the time being.' Markham calculated the SOCOs would need at least forty-eight hours. 'I'd be grateful if you could give Sergeant Doyle your master key and any security codes for the building.'

'Of course, Inspector,' the housekeeper replied calmly.

The DI addressed Burton. 'We need to liaise with the institute and with Oratory House . . . arrange temporary accommodation while forensics do their stuff. Easier to keep everyone there rather than take over Eton Lodge again.'

His colleague almost clicked her heels, keen as ever to sort the practicalities. 'I'll follow you up in a minute,' she told Doyle as he escorted Paolo Serrano away.

'Anything for us on time of death, doctor?' she asked the pathologist hopefully.

'I would say around midnight last night.'

'He came down here to wash his smalls?' Noakes asked incredulously. 'At fricking midnight!'

'Maybe he couldn't sleep?' Dr Dajani suggested. With a charming lop-sided smile he added, 'My wife suffers from insomnia. Doesn't try to fight it . . . just gets on with household chores till she's tired herself out.'

'Does it work?' Noakes grunted.

'Sometimes . . . Better than lying in the dark and fretting. She says it helps if she's got something on her mind.'

Something on her mind.

Did Tom Nevin have something on his mind? Was that why he came downstairs at midnight to the laundry?

And if so, what?

Markham's mind was racing, but he didn't give this away as he turned to the medic.

'No doubt as to cause of death, doctor?'

'None at all, Inspector. Massive blood loss and shock. I'll let you know more once I've had him on the table.'

As Burton hurried upstairs, Markham and Noakes followed the pathologist back into the laundry room and stood to the side as he directed two paramedics bearing a sheeted gurney towards the stairs which led up to reception on the ground floor. Poignantly, the American's left arm momentarily slipped free of its covering, dangling down to the floor, before the stretcher-bearer lifted it back into position. As the sombre procession passed the detectives, it seemed almost impossible to credit that the man who had regaled them with anecdotes about St Therese only a short time before was now on his way to meet her in that mysterious bourne to which she had been called when barely out of her teens.

As he stood there, some words from the memorial service came back to Markham: 'St Therese had no time for grisly representations of death as a grinning skeleton menacing poor sinners. "It is not 'death' that will come to fetch me," she said, "it is God. I tell you, death is not, as pictures tell us, a phantom, a horrid spectre. It is just the separation of soul and body — no more than that." '

Bowing his head, Markham found himself praying that Therese would make good on her promise and that, in crossing the mysterious threshold, Tom Nevin had been set free.

'I'd like to have a look at Mr Nevin's room,' he told Noakes once they were alone once more. Perhaps in the academic's bedroom they would find a clue to break the case.

'Leave it to me, boss.' The DS sensed his guvnor needed a moment. 'I'll fetch the pass key an' wait for you on the first floor,' he added heading for the stairs.

'Thanks, Noakesy. You can send the SOCOs in now.'

Mercifully, the subdued hum of the washing machine had now stopped, and there was quiet once more.

Markham looked around him.

He felt curiously light-headed in the stuffy room. But strangely enough, all his sensations were heightened as though this last victim's soul hung a little way above his head, waiting to see what he would do.

Justice, he breathed. I'll have justice for you.

* * *

Tom Nevin's quarters on the first floor comprised a comfortable double en-suite facing towards the street, with two armchairs and a large writing desk. Appropriately enough for a building dedicated to the cult of the Little Flower, the magnolia walls were adorned with various botanical prints. The carpet and curtains were an inoffensive pale green, and altogether the room wore a pleasant aspect which Markham imagined was conducive to scholarly research.

'Mostly ole pictures.'

Noakes was disappointed as he examined items on the desk.

Markham joined him, carefully scrutinising what appeared to be photographs from the turn of the century.

A game of croquet, Rue de la Chaussée. Left to right: Celine, Monsieur and Madame Guerin, Francis La Néele, Jeanne and Marie Guerin.

'Ah,' the DI said thoughtfully. 'I believe this is Uncle Isidore with his wife and daughters Jeanne and Marie . . . Francis La Néele married Jeanne, so he's the son-in-law—'

Noakes's head reared up. 'Ain't he the doctor who tried to smuggle morphine in when Therese got very bad with TB?'

'The very same.'

'An' Celine's her sister, right?'

'Correct.'

Noakes appraised the composition critically.

'Celine don' look like it's a bundle of laughs,' he concluded. 'But then, if you're thinking about going into a convent you prob'ly shouldn't be whooping it up.'

'Hmm . . . Isidore Guerin was a pharmacist who came into a fortune after inheriting from a relative of his wife. Bought a huge country estate called La Musse . . . I imagine he wanted Celine to have a taste of worldly pleasures before she gave them up forever.'

'Here's one of La Musse,' Noakes exclaimed. 'Blimey, they're all at it again . . . playing croquet an' looking dead chuffed with thesselves.'

'It was a kind of status symbol, Sergeant. Showed the world they'd arrived.'

The DS continued turning over pictures and squinting at captions.

'Hey up, Celine's holding hands with a bloke in this one,' he declared excitedly. 'Oh no,' in tones of disgust, 'he's wearing a long frock an' a dog collar . . . gotta be some trainee priest type.'

They continued examining the pictures. Clearly the Guerins had enjoyed a pastoral idyll available to only the very rich.

'Uncle Izzy's Marie weren't bad looking,' Noakes said finally in a tone which suggested he wasn't particularly taken with the other females. 'Sweet little thing . . . nice smile too. Hey,' he pounced on some more images, 'here she is in the convent wearing a weirdy bonnet an' cape jobbie. Scrubbing the floor . . . bit of a comedown after bleeding croquet!'

'That's what postulants wore in those days — the new entrants who hadn't taken *any* vows. And, as for the chores, they all had to do manual labour.'

'Yeah, but to go from being lady of the manor to Mrs Mop!'

'It was her choice, Noakesy.'

'Bet ole Izzy Wizzy didn't like it,' the other said stoutly.

'Maybe not,' Markham conceded. 'But in those days, devout Catholic parents like the Guerins wouldn't oppose a genuine call to the cloister.'

'Yeah, or God might smite 'em with a thunderbolt,' his wingman said with lugubrious satisfaction.

The DS was clearly fascinated by Marie Guerin's trajectory from spoiled chatelaine to convent slavey, but finally tore himself away to declare, 'Don' see anyone killing the prof cos of this lot. I mean, it's jus' research for that piece he were writing . . .'

Markham frowned, gazing round the room. 'No sign of his laptop.'

'Paolo thinks Nevin had it in the reading room but forgot to take it upstairs with him. He were absent-minded like that, always leaving stuff lying around . . . Any road, it ain't there now either.'

'He probably meant to collect it on his way back from the laundry room,' Markham said thoughtfully.

'Only someone had nicked it,' his wingman gloomed.

'Looks like it.'

Noakes rumpled his Brillo pad hair till it stood up in fierce little spikes.

'Paolo said Nevin used to go for a wander at night. Like the doc thought, it were a regular thing cos he didn't sleep well . . . pottered round doing jobs an' stuff till he got tired.'

'So people knew this was his routine?' Markham's voice was sharp.

'Yeah . . . He usually put a wash on or did some ironing or whatever to help him get off. It were a big joke. They called him the "Midnight Cowboy".'

'More like a sitting duck,' the DI said sombrely. Then, 'Did Paolo say if the other members — the ones who live out — were around last night?'

'Yeah, one big happy family . . . Everyone wanted to stick close an' have a meal cos they were getting over the shock of Julia and Father Digby, see.'

Markham's brow furrowed. 'Doesn't exactly narrow things down.'

'What's the plan, guv?'

As the DI outlined the itinerary he and Olivia had decided on, Noakes visibly brightened at the prospect of a there-and-back trip taking in Father Digby's funeral and an overnighter in Bromgrove.

'But tomorrow we have our meeting with DCI Moriarty and a campaign plan to draw up,' Markham continued.

Noakes nodded solemnly. 'Gotta divvy up the tasks,' he said. 'Checklists an' all that cobblers. Right up Burton's street.' *And thank chuff not mine.*

Markham took one last look around the peaceful room.

'I want everything in here bagged,' he said. 'Everything about the Guerins and Therese's wider family. Who knows,' he added softly, 'maybe the gardens of La Musse will guide us to the heart of the maze.'

Noakes peered at the books and papers on Nevin's desk.

'Most of it's in French,' he said in tones of dismay.

'I guess that figures,' Markham observed. 'Given he was researching Therese's relatives.'

'Your Olivia speaks Frog, right guv? Mebbe she could give 'em the once over . . . see if there's summat juicy in there.'

Markham frowned a reprimand at his colleague, before asking: 'Such as?'

'Some big secret that folk kept quiet about . . .'

'And then somehow our victims got tangled up in it?' Markham tried to keep the scepticism out of his voice.

Noakes looked mutinous. *Well, have you got a better idea?* his face seemed to say.

The DI gave himself a mental shake. It was better than nothing, and he was willing to bet Olivia would jump at the chance to root about in Tom Nevin's collection. For all her scoffing, he could tell something about the deceptively sentimental Theresian legend had her hooked.

'You're right, Noakesy,' he said generously, 'it's a good idea. Maybe there's something in the Guerin material that will bring things into focus.'

The DS was mollified. 'I'll get the stuff bagged up, guv.'

'We'll need to re-interview everyone from the club tomorrow once we've briefed DCI Moriarty. And there'll be a press conference to arrange.' Markham wasn't looking forward to that one bit.

'If they're anything like Scroteface Conors, the headlines will be real sicko stuff . . . y'know, pervy priests doing sex, drugs an' rock an' roll.'

Gavin Conors was the sleazy features editor of Bromgrove's *Gazette* and Noakes's particular bête noire.

'I think even Mr Conors would be hard pushed to concoct something like that from the bare facts, Sergeant.'

'Them lot never let truth get in the way of a good story.'

'Well, we'll just have to rein them in somehow.' At least there was one thing Bishop Buckley was good for. 'I'll ask the Diocesan Press Office to liaise with Southampton Row and prepare a briefing pack.'

Noakes grinned evilly. 'Yeah, lots of holy bollocks should spook 'em good an' proper.' It was clear his wingman had infinite faith in the Catholic Church's capacity for dissimulation.

The two men moved into the corridor and headed for the stairs.

Although the building was teeming with SOCOs, it felt eerily quiet.

What was it Paolo Serrano had said? The Angel of Death was picking them off one by one.

In that moment, it seemed to Markham he could almost hear the beating of its wings.

9. THORNS

The weather turned squally on Monday 22 March, rain lashing Russell Square as Markham and Olivia breakfasted together in their hotel's grandly named Conservatory Room.

'Just the one seminar this morning,' Olivia said happily as she slathered a croissant with butter. 'Which means I can get stuck into those French papers.'

'Because you speak fluent Frog.'

She giggled. 'It should be George attending the lectures on *Culture and Imperialism* . . . might cure his galloping xenophobia.'

'I very much doubt it,' Markham said drily. 'But he's certainly curious to know if Professor Nevin's research materials contain anything "juicy".'

Olivia sipped her coffee, suddenly serious as she thought of the academic's gruesome end.

'Maybe he *did* tap into something . . . St Therese's family background wasn't all hearts and flowers you know, Gil,' she said after a pause. 'There were aspects that were quite controversial.'

He raised his eyebrows. 'I gather your digging in the library's been productive then.'

'Well, the family was seriously peculiar, even by the standards of the time. The parents were so obsessed with sanctifying themselves, they didn't notice when Leonie — the middle sister — was being abused by the maidservant.'

'*Abused*?'

'Well, there was some kind of masochistic relationship going on . . . the maid was threatening and mistreating her . . . When the mother found out, she said she couldn't believe the things being done to the child "in cold blood".'

'Leonie's the latest member of the family being put forward for canonisation, isn't she?'

'That's right . . . She went ping ponging around different convents before ending up in the Visitation order. Sounds like she was the ugly duckling of the family — *literally* — kept breaking out in eczema from all the pressure to be holy. Apparently the poor kid said she belonged to a family of saints and didn't want to stain the record.'

'Hmm. *Noblesse Oblige* . . . Not overly incendiary though, sweetheart. Remember, you have to see the family in context. They were provincial nineteenth-century Catholics who took their faith very seriously.'

'You're telling *me*,' she snorted. 'Other kids ran and skipped at playtime. *Therese* did funerals for dead birds!' She paused before saying carefully, 'I got the feeling some of the commentators were skirting around stuff.'

Markham looked at her intently. 'What kind of stuff?'

'Oh, anything that would spoil the Church's narrative . . . "There was an unbalanced streak in the Martin family and Therese took it into the convent with her . . ." One of the nuns said it was uncanny the way Therese was literally *possessed* by God, in the same way the wicked are possessed by the devil.'

Markham started, recalling the words of the celebrant at the memorial service, when he said that to some people St Therese might appear 'as violent as the devil'.

'Maybe that's why she contracted a fatal illness . . . because at bottom of it, she *wanted* to die. Now don't get me wrong, Gil,' Olivia said hastily, 'I admire the way she battled on and made the best of a bad job.' This was an echo of Noakes. 'But I think she was far more *subversive* than the Church wants to admit. You can see it in that picture of her when she put her hair up . . . the one where she's trying to persuade everyone that fifteen's not too young to become a nun — stubby nose, stubborn chin, rectangular little face . . . not the drippy character on those godawful prayer cards.'

Markham recalled the image of the saint in a golden halo stamped on dishes and trays and bright plastic statues. He was inclined to agree with Liv that the real flesh and blood woman was infinitely preferable.

'Subversive maybe,' he mused. 'But not enough to threaten the cult surely?'

'There's the odd sociologist sniffing around Therese's backstory.'

'What did they uncover then?'

'She didn't have much formal education.' Olivia pulled a face. 'Too delicate and sensitive. But there was a stint at the local boarding school when she developed an intense crush on a schoolfriend — she was still obsessing about it thirteen years on — and later in the convent some kind of special relationship with a novice called Marie-Louise Castel who became Sister Marie of the Trinity.' Seeing that she had piqued Markham's interest, Olivia proceeded with relish. 'The prioress Mother Marie de Gonzague was jealous of Therese and her family, but everyone pandered to her, so when Therese's sister Pauline won a term as prioress, she appointed the old bat novice mistress and made Therese her assistant. That way, Mother M wouldn't feel threatened . . . Obviously Therese did all the legwork training new nuns, but she didn't have any *official* standing — God, the politics in that place were unreal — so Mother M was happy.'

'So Therese was responsible for training this Sister Marie of the Trinity?' Markham asked.

'That's right. She'd been a nun for six years by that point and Sister Marie was a year younger than her, which was a bit of a novelty since the rest of the community were much older. Looks like they became besties after a fashion, Sister Marie was an extrovert and quite attractive in the photos . . . tip-tilted features and laughing eyes. Therese wrote poems for her . . . all pretty hothouse . . .'

'Yes, but you're forgetting the fact that she was practically the convent's writer-in-residence,' he pointed out. 'And anyway, the embargo on "particular friendships" would have stopped things getting out of hand.'

'I'm not so sure, Gil . . . Therese tackled one of the novices about having an excessive affection for Mother Marie de Gonzague. She got so worked up, it makes you wonder . . . Maybe it was a problem for her too.' To Markham's amusement, she rummaged in her bag and whipped out a notebook. 'She wrote a letter to Marie—'

'*Woah.*' Markham grinned. 'Too many Maries . . . Which one do you mean?'

'Marie Guerin.'

'Oh right, I'm with you now. Her cousin . . . the one who followed her into the convent.'

The one Tom Nevin was researching.

'That's right.' Olivia assumed a mock schoolmarmish tone. '*Do* keep up at the back.'

'Giving it my best, sweetheart. So what was in this letter to her cousin?'

'Marie ended up in the convent eventually, but before that her father — Uncle Isidore — gave her a taste of city life. Turned out she had a bad case of scruples — got a bee in her bonnet about seeing nude statues in Paris, sinful thoughts, that kind of thing. Well, Therese told her, "I know these kinds of temptations so well."' Olivia's tone was triumphant as she air quoted, before riffling through her notebook for further allusions. 'And she told Celine that her heart "could easily be captured by affection" because she had no means to defend herself against mortal love. She even said she could have fallen as low as Mary Magdalen because of the temptation of earthly romance . . . And when she got obsessed with the case of that murderer who was going to be guillotined — Pranzini — she linked it to some sort of sexual awakening — said she was at the "most dangerous age for young girls". *How about that?*

'It's intriguing, Liv. I'm sure the psychologists would have a field day. But that kind of melodramatic language was par for the course back then. And any kind of sexual fallibility would have come out during the canonisation proceedings.'

'I guess so. Therese said she disliked her body . . . was never comfortable with it and found eating so shameful she said it was something you ought to go aside to do. Presumably that's why she didn't mind ending up sodding *liquified*,' Olivia said with a certain savagery in her tone. 'Very convenient all round.'

'So you see, there wasn't enough to threaten the authority of the Church.'

'Maybe Professor Nevin was onto something,' she insisted, not without a touch of defiance.

'Well, best of luck with it,' he said affectionately. 'Your perspective as a Therese-sceptic could be just what we need.'

'All things considered, I've come round to Therese's side,' Olivia told him earnestly. 'She's one hell of a strange saint, but I like her. Some of what she wrote is astonishingly profound for a twenty-four-year-old. And there's this *authenticity* which shines out once you chisel away all the sugar paste . . . But here's the thing — what if your killer's got some warped fixation with protecting the cult?' Impatiently, she tucked some wayward strands of red hair behind her ears. 'Though I don't see *how*.'

'You and me both, sweetheart.' But he was charmed by her enthusiasm. 'Therese must've cast some kind of spell to get you sleuthing like this.'

She laughed and blushed.

'It's quite exciting the way this case is connected to a real historical figure, Gil.'

'True . . . It's unique from that point of view. We've never had anything quite like it.'

Olivia reflected happily that for the first time in a long while she was integral to an investigation. Not just a spare wheel.

'The Catholic Church has been ruthless over the centuries,' she said. 'I could see them killing to keep Therese's show on the road.' She reached for another croissant, telling herself she'd have earned it by the time she ploughed through Tom Nevin's papers. 'But you know, their hang-up about protecting the "brand" is so damn *backward* . . . The minute any feminist scholars try to deconstruct Therese's writing — and there's lots of sexual language about being ravished and abandonment — the theologians scream blue murder, saying it's spiteful and vulgar.'

'Ah, pale, male, stale . . . and priests to boot,' Markham teased her.

'Well, obviously I'm exaggerating a bit,' she admitted. 'But there's nothing wrong with accepting that she was a *human being* with the usual hang-ups . . . even struggled to pray for most of the time. The way the convent edited those little exercise books to control her "image" was downright immoral . . . and God help us, the Church is still at it!'

'I hear what you're saying, Liv. And I'm sympathetic to the revisionist agenda because you're right, some of the aesthetics *are* uncomfortable. But I'm not sure any of it adds up to a motive for murder. Still,' he added, seeing her face fall, 'it will be interesting to know what Tom Nevin came up with . . . He wasn't a narrow-minded reactionary . . . quite the opposite . . . had a real thirst for information.'

'*A little knowledge is a dangerous thing*,' she quoted softly.

Those words echoed in Markham's ears after Olivia had left him.

Dangerous knowledge.

Had the American learned something that proved lethal? And were Julia Porter and Father Digby privy to the same secret?

Were the three victims bound together in some sort of conspiracy? Or did Father Digby and Tom Nevin have to die because they had inadvertently stumbled across something that led back to the murderer?

Markham glanced at his watch. Still too early for Noakes, which meant he had time for another coffee.

His thoughts drifted back to Sunday's memorial service in the institute's quaint chapel.

Strange how the prayers and readings had largely gone over his head at the time, as though he was holed up beneath some psychological plimsoll line. But now words and phrases came back to him.

Although the Lord slay me, yet will I trust in Him.

Did Father Digby go trustfully to his death, since his whole existence was arguably a novitiate for eternity? Or were the warden's last moments filled with unimaginable horror?

Markham was by no means confident that the priest's funeral would unlock the mystery, but he nonetheless wanted to follow him to the grave. It felt like the right thing to do. As though by such an expedient he could temporarily banish thoughts of the Grim Reaper and renew his faith in a God who saw all that was done in secret . . .

Lumbering into the restaurant, and seeing Markham's remote expression, Noakes thought to himself, *Hey up, the guvnor's off on one.* This being his shorthand for the DI's periods of mental abstraction.

Most probably his boss and Olivia had been chewing over the case, the DS concluded.

Noakes liked the idea of a joint enterprise. It was amazing how this little nun drew everyone in. The missus couldn't get enough of her, and his presents of a tray with Therese's face on it and locket (third-class relic *and* certificate) had been a great success. Muriel's approval even extended to Olivia. 'She seems less *flighty* these days . . . not so skittish and more of a helpmeet to *dear* Gilbert . . . Of course, a case like this is *bound* to raise her thoughts to higher things.'

In pursuit of that purer consciousness, Muriel had expressed her intention of visiting Tyburn Convent later in the day (via Harvey Nicks). In the meantime, she dispatched her husband to his 'working breakfast' with an admonition to 'go easy on the cholesterol', advice that he fully intended to ignore.

As he padded across to the hot plates where guests helped themselves, Noakes reflected that Olivia's fascination with the saint probably had something to do with Therese's convent being even bitchier than Hope Academy, both environments throwing up specimens of humanity who were arguably completely bonkers.

As he plonked bacon, sausages, black pudding, hash browns, baked beans and three rounds of toast onto his plate, Noakes felt quite chipper and ready to take on all comers. Okay so they hadn't got anyone in the frame yet, but with all those weirdos locked up together in the institute, it was just a matter of time . . .

Later that morning at Southampton Row, DCI Moriarty took Noakes's view of the situation.

'Cooped up together out of their comfort zone, someone's bound to crack,' he said comfortably. 'And don't worry, you can leave the press conference to me, folks. There's been a drugs raid in Brixton over the weekend, so—'

'A good day to bury bad news,' Noakes finished for him.

'Something like that,' the DCI agreed.

Moriarty was a handsome silver-haired officer with laughing eyes and a puckish, kindly face. Without anything explicit being said on the subject, it was clear he had grasped the position with Sidney and Bishop Buckley.

'Don't worry,' he said again. 'We'll give the vultures the bare minimum.' He grinned. 'I reckon I'm a match for DI Burton when it comes to throwing sand in their eyes.'

Burton wasn't sure how to take this backhanded compliment, but cleared her throat.

'Thank you, sir,' she said politely, smoothing the lapels of the smart houndstooth jacket she wore over a long matching skirt. 'That'll leave us free to focus on the suspects.'

'My pleasure.' With a gallant bow and a wink, he left her office.

'Ole Shippers might have competition there,' Noakes said to the DCI's departing back.

Burton pretended she hadn't heard this mischievous observation.

'The residents aren't very happy about being confined to the institute,' she said. 'Well, strictly speaking it's the Oratory House annexe, but the institute uses it for guests who stay the night. I let the members who don't live-in go home, sir. I hope that was okay . . . They're coming back this morning, so we've got everyone together.'

'That's fine, Kate.' Markham's eyes were thoughtful. 'Hopefully DCI Moriarty's correct and we'll catch them off-kilter . . . We need someone to talk.'

He briefed Burton and Doyle about Tom Nevin's research and Olivia's involvement.

'Sounds like a good idea, sir,' Burton said cautiously.

Doyle's open freckled face was the picture of bafflement. 'Are we saying St Therese was in a *relationship* with this other nun — the one she was helping train up or whatever it was — and the Church wanted to cover it up . . . but Porter, Digby and Nevin got wind somehow?'

Noakes looked as though he didn't like the idea of his 'special one' being tarnished by such salacious speculation, though he wasn't usually backward when it came to exploring theories of ecclesiastical deviation from the straight and narrow.

'Mebbe some rogue researcher dug up summat rubbishy about the lass an' then the higher ups panicked about scandal,' he suggested. 'Porter might've found out about it, seeing as she were a Therese freak, an' then the other two copped on to who killed her.'

'Sounds like the storyline for something off the TV,' Doyle replied dubiously. The whole religious angle was starting to creep him out. Seeing Noakes's missus in church the other day wearing that black lacy headdress number was seriously weird . . . like she was going to dance the flamenco or something. RCs were a dodgy crew, made him glad he was good old C of E. No danger of *them* going over the top.

He noticed Markham's eyes gleaming with amusement, as if the guvnor could read his thoughts.

Hastily, the young detective asked, 'Are we going to give it to them straight about how Digby and Nevin died?'

'Yes. There's nothing to be gained from holding back,' Markham said crisply. 'Not now that there's to be a press conference.'

He turned to Burton. 'What about Nevin's next of kin?' he asked.

'Just a sister, boss. She's a nun in Arizona. I've been in touch and set up a Zoom call for you with her later.'

At least the poor woman had her faith to sustain her. 'Thanks, Kate.'

It occurred to him that for those in religious life, death was akin to some sort of final exam that was easy to pass and eternal life like a summer vacation, while earthly existence was a school for understanding the workings of the Almighty . . . Though after seeing the mutilated bodies of Julia Porter, Father Digby and Tom Nevin, he found it hard to grasp the lesson.

'Come on,' he said, trying to sound positive, 'let's see if cracks are beginning to show with our suspects.'

* * *

Cracks were indeed beginning to show, but it wasn't clear that this brought Markham and his team any nearer to identifying their killer.

They interviewed the residents and members in a seminar room next to the little museum they had previously toured with Miss Parkin. The rain was still coming down heavily in horizontal gusts outside, buffeting the bedraggled looking garden, as though the forces of evil were coming closer.

Against this gloomy backdrop, they discovered more about the dynamics of the Theresian Club.

From Ignatius Fermor, they learned that both Sister Pauline and Rosemary Gough had histories of mental illness.

The theology student gave a fair impression of having this information dragged out of him but, as Noakes put it, 'You could see he were gagging to finger 'em as nutters.'

The gist seemed to be that Sister Pauline had been taken to task by her superiors for 'emotional attachment issues', while Rosemary Gough was a failed nun who had joined the Brothers and Sisters of St Therese in her early twenties but wasn't accepted for final vows due to periodic outbreaks of instability.

Sister Roisin subsequently confirmed the truth of these revelations but was anxious to downplay their significance. 'Those in religious life are human beings just like anyone else,' she said in an echo of Olivia's conversation over breakfast. 'It's wrong to see convents and monasteries as communities of higher beings who triumph easily over human frailty. We have to work at it. St Therese herself suffered considerable disillusionment on this score but,' the nun concluded happily, 'she turned it to her advantage.' Tactfully, she didn't ask the detectives who the source of their intelligence about Sister Pauline and Rosemary was. 'She'll guess it were Iggy Slimeball,' Noakes said trenchantly. 'But she's the type to make excuses on account of him training to be a priest.'

It was true, thought Markham. For all that she was clearly a sensible woman, Sister Roisin most likely had a blind spot when it came to the priesthood. He supposed the fact of the Catholic Church being increasingly under siege in the twenty-first century made it only natural that she should hold a vocation in some veneration though it struck him as being curiously backward for one who mentored university students.

Margaret Bertram and Anne Leadbeater were manifestly unhappy about the direction the Theresian Club was headed, seeing themselves as modernisers and the likes of Julia, Thelma and Rosemary as "dead wood". They didn't use those exact words, but it was clear there had been sharp differences. Like Fermor, they implied there was an element of mental instability involved, though they diplomatically refrained from providing specifics, merely referring to 'touchiness' and 'naivety'.

As Noakes pointed out, 'Them two got their stories straight before we arrived.' It was apparent the two women also had misgivings about Father Digby's 'fervour' and 'right-wing' approach but, just as with Sister Roisin, respect for the warden's priestly office put a guard on their tongues. There were no reservations when it came to Tom Nevin, however. The two women speaking enthusiastically about the American's engaging personality and scholarship. Intellectual snobs, thought Markham, but it was hard to see either woman as a killer.

David Manners made possibly the most startling disclosure, suggesting that the Theresian Club offered something of a safe haven for gay academics. 'Of course, the Quakers have a long tradition of inclusivity and respect for minorities,' he said primly. 'But we place a premium on decorum and civilised behaviour.'

'Who're we talking about then?' Noakes demanded bluntly, seeing that Manners was set to go round the bleeding houses.

'Our housekeeper and Donald Trevelyan make no secret of their preferences,' he sniffed. 'Professor Nevin was homosexual, and there are others of a similar persuasion.'

'Would that be Kenneth Robson and Ignatius Fermor?' Markham enquired.

'As to Ignatius, I couldn't say,' Manners replied.

Bet you could, thought Noakes with a spasm of dislike.

'Of course, *Kenneth* is a close friend of Donald's,' the deputy warden continued, as though to say, 'I rest my case'.

'Not giving it the full Danny La Rue though, were they?' Noakes grunted. 'An' it don' look like there was some vice ring operating out of the club . . . not 'xactly your standard pick-up joint, is it?'

Burton had cringed at the reference to the drag act, but she shared Noakes's distaste for the mealy-mouthed hypocrisy with which Manners threw his fellow members under the bus.

'What is his game?' the DS burst out after Manners left the room. 'Does he seriously think Porter an' the other two snuffed it cos the place had a touch of the Gay Gordons?'

Burton looked pained again, but over the years she had learned to overlook Noakes's chronic political incorrectness, placing it in the scales against his passion to win justice for the murdered dead.

'No, I don't think it was *that*,' Markham said slowly. 'He was just throwing us a bone by way of distraction.'

There was something about the deputy warden's demeanour that had puzzled him. An air of furtive excitement that he couldn't quite conceal . . . as though he was hugging something to himself.

Doyle recalled another snippet of information from Manners. 'Interesting how he said some of them thought Nevin was practically a heretic.'

'Not Margaret Bertram and Anne Leadbeater, though' Burton mused. '*They* thought he was a breath of fresh air . . . And Manners wanted to be in the intellectuals' camp . . . the trendy thinkers.'

'Not like the three old maids,' said Noakes dourly. 'Julia, Rosemary an' Thelma . . . along with Diggers an' the trainee priest. *Jesus, Mary and Joseph*, none of it gets us anywhere . . . I mean, who *cares* if Nevin went all Sigmund Freud an' had these whacko theories about Therese? Too fricking piddling for words,' he grumbled.

'Maybe not to someone who was obsessed,' Markham observed uneasily. 'Remember what Dr Dajani said about the possibility of a delusional fixation . . . that could be what we're up against.'

Miss Parkin, who brought up the rear of the interviews, agreed. 'Wars have been fought for much less,' she told them earnestly before adding, 'There's something very wicked going on here. I can *feel* it.'

No shit, Sherlock. But such was Noakes's liking for the institute's senior receptionist, that he swallowed the sarcastic rejoinder.

Back at Southampton Row, they congregated in Kate Burton's office. There was no abatement in the dreary weather and the room felt chill.

'I'll get us some hot drinks,' Doyle said, keen to escape the oppressive pall that hung over the group. Plus he fancied a treat from Costa.

Noakes turned round from kicking the radiator. 'Good idea,' he said. 'An' don' forget the muffins.'

The younger man executed a mock-salute and disappeared before Burton could veto the suggestion. 'I'll just pop along to DCI Moriarty and see how the press conference went,' she murmured. 'Back in ten, sir.'

While they waited, Markham reminded his wingman of the plan for them to attend Father Digby's funeral with Olivia before spending the night in Bromgrove and returning to the capital the following day. 'Maybe a trip out of London will help clarify things in our minds.'

'More weirdy priest stuff!' But the DI could tell his wingman was secretly pleased at the prospect of observing Father Digby's confreres in their natural habitat, almost as though he was an anthropologist studying the practices of some mysterious culture. It was something to tell Muriel about, given her newly awakened passion for all things Catholic, so he would score brownie points for that.

Once the others had returned from their respective errands and the room had warmed up, the team settled down to assess the state of play.

As Doyle said, it was slim pickings.

'Nevin died at midnight or in the small hours, when everyone says they were at home in bed . . . And we can't prove otherwise.' The young DS was exasperated.

'They're all pretty screwy,' Noakes said glumly. 'But it don' add up to anything.'

'What about the gay thing?' Doyle wondered before answering his own question. 'These days, it doesn't seem like anyone would — or should — care about *that*.'

Markham shared some of Olivia's research with them, amused to observe how Burton bristled at the notion of a 'civilian' (and Markham's partner) being co-opted. But gradually, interest in what she heard made the DI forget everything else.

'You reckon there's evidence for a sexual scandal connected with St Therese?' she asked eagerly. 'Something about this novice she was so friendly with?' Then, seeing Noakes's shaggy brows contract with disapproval, the DI added swiftly, 'I'm not saying any of it's true, but perhaps there's material out there that could be twisted to discredit the cult . . . and the Catholic Church.'

'Therese deserves better'n that,' Noakes objected. 'She were proper holy,' he insisted stubbornly, 'plus she never had time for owt dodgy, jus' wanted to get on with the job.'

Markham was strangely touched, *getting on with the job* being his wingman's highest accolade.

'Professor Nevin's research material may help to shed some light,' he said gently. 'In the meantime, we need to keep an open mind.'

'At least the press conference went without a hitch,' Burton said. 'DCI Moriarty was right about the journos being distracted by the drugs raid . . . He kind of patted things down with generalised stuff about a local crime wave.'

'Gets Slimy Sid an' the bish off our backs,' Noakes grunted.

The telephone on Burton's desk broke the silence that followed this remark.

'It's Rosemary Gough,' she said, looking worried. 'Apparently she's taken an overdose.'

Markham was on his feet.

'Noakes, with me,' he instructed. 'Kate, I want you and Doyle to hold the fort here. Brief DCI Moriarty and then follow up with the Brothers and Sisters of St Therese . . . find out which convent Rosemary entered and what went wrong. According to Ignatius Fermor, her career plans for being a nun stalled, so maybe the order can fill in the picture.'

It seemed scarcely possible that the diminutive, rather wretched looking woman peering out at the world from behind her badly cut fringe could hold the key to three murders.

But it was a break of sorts.

So far, the investigation's path had been strewn with thorns.

And the longer and sharper the thorns, the greater the satisfaction in unmasking this most elusive of killers.

10. GOD OF MEMORY

'Who found her?' Markham asked on arrival at the institute.

'I did,' Miss Parkin told them. 'Well, it was Sister Pauline who raised the alarm. I checked in St Stanislaus and there she was.'

Noakes scratched his head. '*St Stanislaus*?'

'Sorry, Sergeant, I should have explained . . . The guest rooms in Oratory House all have saints' names.'

'Why did Sister Pauline think something might have happened?' Markham asked.

'Well, Rosemary seemed a bit out of it before,' the receptionist told them. 'Glassy-eyed and unfocused, plus her speech was slurred. Sister Roisin and Mr Manners noticed it too.'

Markham thought back to their interviews earlier.

Now he came to think of it, Rosemary Gough *had* been on the verge of tears. But it seemed in keeping with her temperament, and Tom Nevin's murder had apparently hit her hard. For all his progressive tendencies, the American possessed an easy-going chivalry typical of those from the Deep South. And this kindness was not confined to Rosemary . . . Thelma Machin confirmed that he never saw them struggling with books or heavy shopping without offering to help. Both women regularly had meals with him when he visited

London, and it was clear Nevin exhibited none of the condescension the detectives had noticed in some of the other club members.

Markham could see Noakes wondering, was Rosemary Gough's breakdown the sign of a guilty conscience?

Miss Parkin's voice interrupted their thoughts.

'Rosemary took something for depression and,' a delicate hesitation, 'I think maybe she, er, self-medicated too.'

The two men looked at each other.

Booze.

'They've taken her to the St Dismas Clinic.' Even at such a juncture, Miss Parkin couldn't resist a pedagogic opportunity. 'Dismas was the Good Thief.'

'Oh yeah, the one who copped on to hisself an' said sorry to Jesus . . . An' Jesus said not to worry about it cos he'd square things at the other end . . . make sure the lad got into heaven.'

The woman smiled. 'I've always had rather a soft spot for him myself,' she said.

Noakes grinned back. *Miss P was on the level,* he thought. Not a bit preachy like your typical God squadder. Muriel said she calmed everyone down after they got called away at the memorial service. Got folks sorted with cups of tea and biscuits. Her and the missus had a nice chat about St Therese, and she gave her some fancy prayer cards with white lace round the edges . . .

Markham's voice broke into these agreeable recollections.

'Is that an NHS hospital, Miss Parkin?'

She looked faintly self-conscious.

'There are some private rooms reserved for diocesan clergy . . . and the institute has been fortunate enough to benefit on occasion.'

'Fair enough. Mates' rates,' said Noakes. Normally he'd be shrieking bribery and corruption, Markham thought wryly. It was a measure of the sea change affected by St Therese that the DS seemed untroubled by the idea of favours being called in.

'Do you have any update on Miss Gough's condition?' Markham asked.

'Apparently they had to sedate her . . . after pumping her stomach . . . she's in a very bad way — rambling and not making much sense. The clinic's not allowing anyone in to see her . . . Thelma wanted to go, but they said no.'

The DI fixed keen eyes on her.

'Would you say this is some sort of breakdown, Miss Parkin?'

The receptionist looked distressed.

'Yes . . . I suppose it's been brewing for a while now,' she said. 'Rosemary struggled with mental health issues in the past, and it looks as though things somehow came unstuck, unbalanced, at the club with the other residents.'

'Unstuck how?' Markham pressed her.

'I'm not sure . . . She and Julia were both quite intense — Thelma not so much — and there was a sense of them vying for Father Digby's attention . . .' Unlike Ignatius Fermor, she looked unhappy to be embroiled in a discussion of club personalities.

Blimey, thought Noakes. David Pain-in-the-Backside Manners had ridiculed any notion of a love triangle at the Theresian Club. But *this* was a development which put S-E-X front and centre.

After Miss Parkin, ever mindful of the obligations of hospitality, had left them to organise tea, the two men took stock.

'Looks like Rosy Posy fits the bill,' Noakes said brutally. 'Ole Julia were her love rival for Diggers so she lost it with both of 'em . . . an' then later on Nevin figured it all out, so she had to kill him too.' As far as the DS was concerned, the cards were stacking up nicely. 'The rosary beads left on the priest . . . that's jus' the kind of thing a religious nutter like her would do. She could've rocked up to confess what she'd done, thinking he'd cover up for her, but he said no an' then she wigged out . . . Or mebbe she came over all slushy an' romantic — said she loved him an' couldn't live without him blah blah — an' he were shocked cos he twigged she'd murdered the other one, so she had to kill him cos he *knew* . . .'

'Doesn't this strike you as all rather too convenient, Sergeant?' Markham asked, interrupting his colleague's increasingly detailed musings.

Noakes shrugged.

'Sidney'll lap it up,' he said. 'Not to mention the bish . . . Nowt scandalous about the cult or Therese for 'em to fret about — they can say it were jus' some poor cow who flipped when everything got on top of her.'

It was ironic, Markham reflected, that Noakes, erstwhile enemy of the 'Papists', clearly favoured a solution that avoided casting any aspersions on his much-admired Little Flower and her following.

And yet he knew from his wingman's body language that the DS also harboured reservations about the way in which Rosemary Gough had dropped into their laps. It seemed too . . . obvious.

'It's all too pat and you know it, Noakesy,' he said.

The DS sighed gustily. 'Well, we can shove it under Sidney's nose at any rate,' he said hopefully. 'Leastways until summat better comes along.'

Something better.

As things stood, Markham felt at a loss to know what that might be.

On Miss Parkin's return, he divulged their plan to attend Father Digby's funeral the following day. The receptionist clapped her hands softly like a child. The gesture put Noakes in mind of a little mole in one of Nat's picture books . . . *Wind in the Willows*. There was something endearing about it.

'I'm so glad of that,' she said. 'The institute needs me here right now, otherwise I'd have asked to go.'

As they sat over tea and slices of the receptionist's homemade fruit cake, Markham asked, 'Miss Parkin, what can you tell us about Marie-Louise Castel . . . the nun who was St Therese's favourite novice?'

The receptionist was startled.

‘Sister Marie of the Trinity?’ she asked.

‘Thass the one,’ Noakes confirmed through a mouthful of cake. ‘There were summat about her in a brochure at the bring an’ buy jobbie,’ he improvised.

Miss Parkin, reassured by his casual demeanour, visibly relaxed.

‘Oh, Sister Marie of the Trinity was a bit of a tomboy when she entered the convent . . . only twenty-three when Therese died . . . She was an important witness during the beatification process and lived another forty-six years after Therese’s death. Later, she developed tubercular lupus which disfigured her face . . . but she was brave through it all and said that in heaven she would follow Therese everywhere.’

Noakes shot the DI a meaningful look which went unnoticed by the receptionist, distracted as she was by the chance to impart further Theresian lore.

‘So theirs was something of a . . . privileged friendship then, Miss Parkin?’

‘That’s right, Inspector. Sister Marie was a true disciple of the Little Way. In the Lisieux archives there’s a letter she wrote saying how happy she was about the Church deciding to canonise a saint who never did anything extraordinary but just did all of the common things exceptionally well . . . It caused her great pain that the prioress wouldn’t allow her to nurse Therese at the end because of contagion, but she took comfort from the fact that Therese sent her a note saying she held an immense place in her heart.’

Noakes thought they might as well chance their arm while they had the chance to pump an undoubted expert.

‘What about the other Marie . . . Therese’s cousin?’ he asked.

‘Marie Guerin?’

‘Yeah . . . Uncle Isidore’s lass, right?’

Miss Parkin settled in comfortably for further explanation, cutting Noakes another slice of cake with an indulgent expression.

'Marie Guerin was another of the young nuns, a beautiful singer and talented pianist . . . just three years older than Therese.'

'Prof Nevin said she died of TB as well.'

'That's right, Sergeant. She was five months off her thirty-fifth birthday . . . didn't live to see Therese beatified.'

'Tough,' Noakes observed. 'She'd have likely wanted to be part of it all, what with her being family.'

'Well, she hung on long enough to know that Therese's *Story of a Soul* was making a huge stir, so that was some consolation. And she'd made great strides in her spiritual life because of Therese.'

'Did she find it hard going then?' the DS enquired sympathetically. 'Getting up at sparrow fart an' down on your knees half the day an' being kind all the time . . . plus half rations an' all the rest of it.' The heroism of half rations had made an indelible impression on Noakes.

'I think it was more a case of struggling with her own temperament, Sergeant. She was neurotic . . . given to introspection and self-preoccupation. Reading between the lines, she was possessive of Therese and suffered quite badly from jealousy.'

Jealousy.

'A complex character,' Markham said easily. 'I believe Professor Nevin was researching her story?'

'Yes, and he had generously offered to do some talks here on Carmelite traditions.' The receptionist suddenly looked very forlorn. 'I'm sure they would have been a great success.'

Markham gave her a moment to collect herself before asking, 'Was he on the brink of any new discoveries about Therese's family, Miss Parkin?'

'The Lisieux Carmel was very generous with its materials, Inspector . . . There's an abundance of correspondence between Marie and her parents, Isidore and Celine Guerin, about the progress of Therese's illness. But Professor Nevin hoped to track down Marie's letters to her sister Jeanne—'

'The other cousin . . . married to the doctor who wanted to give Therese morphine, only the prioress made him out to be a drug smuggler?' Noakes put in eagerly.

Miss Parkin smiled tremulously. 'That's putting it quite strongly, Sergeant. But certainly, the family was unhappy about Therese's medical treatment. Jeanne, Marie's sister, was married to Dr Francis La Néele, and there's a tradition in Catholic circles that after the beatification process began, Madame La Néele hid or disposed of the letters she received from Marie . . . Only one or two people knew about their existence and nobody was able to work out where they ended up.'

'Secret letters?' Noakes was like a truffle hound. 'Why did she want to hide 'em? I mean, here's her sister writing from the convent telling her all about Therese being ever so holy an' you'd think she'd want everyone to know.'

The receptionist seemed to choose her next words carefully.

'For a long time, Isidore Guerin resisted the introduction of the beatification process . . . in fact, the whole family was strongly opposed to it.'

Noakes frowned. 'What made 'em change their mind?'

'Increasing recognition of Therese's holiness . . . And then, her fame was spreading in a quite extraordinary manner.'

'And pressure from the Church authorities perhaps?' Markham ventured.

'Yes, that was no doubt a factor as well,' the receptionist replied calmly.

An unwelcome thought had occurred to Noakes.

'Mebbe the family knew stuff about Therese,' he said slowly. 'Personal stuff . . . an' they thought it might take the shine off her halo, like, if anything came out.'

Seeing that he was troubled, Miss Parkin smiled kindly at the burly sergeant.

'You could well be right,' she said. 'Intimate family jokes and stories wouldn't necessarily translate well . . . Some of the people Marie wrote about were still living. Also, certain material might have been an unhelpful distraction in terms of Therese's legacy.'

Markham respected the woman's honesty.

'You think some of these letters were potentially compromising because they could have tarnished Therese's reputation,' he suggested gently.

'The nineteenth century had a different mind-set,' she said earnestly, 'and women writing intimately to each other used flowery, extravagant language which these days might be open to misconstruction.'

'Enough to threaten Therese's cult?' Markham persisted.

'I don't think so, but of course I'm not qualified to judge.' The receptionist poured more tea as she marshalled her thoughts. 'St Therese was only twenty-four when she died. She was still evolving, still maturing . . . she was a very *human* saint. Along with her cousin and Sister Marie of the Trinity — her favourite novice — she had a mischievous sense of humour . . . Sister Marie nicknamed Mother Marie de Gonzague "the wolf", and the three of them composed a whole riff on the convent doctor . . . called him Clodion the Hairy after some Gallic chieftain.'

'Was there any question of Therese being in love with her favourite novice?' Markham asked, ignoring Noakes's thunderous glower.

But Miss Parkin did not look surprised. Evidently, she knew what he had been building up to.

'The friendship was very much a spiritual relationship, Inspector. It was Sister Marie to whom Therese confided her crisis of faith when she felt that heaven was closed to her.'

'You mean blasphemy?' Noakes definitely preferred the notion of heresy to the idea of any sexual shenanigans between the pair.

'Well, she never stopped trusting in God, mind, but there was a terrible period of darkness.' The receptionist spoke with deliberation. 'As for the letters from Marie Guerin . . . who knows what she said to her sister? But it seems likely the La Néeles — or maybe Isidore Guerin– decided the correspondence was somehow unhelpful . . . Actually,' Miss Parkin met their eyes defiantly, 'they were probably just being protective of the family, but I'm sure if anything the contents would only make Therese even more loveable.' She took a shaky breath, her features working. 'That's what was so wonderful about Professor Nevin's work . . . He was making her relevant to the modern age and accessible to everyone, not just Catholics.' The receptionist drew herself up. 'Pope Leo—'

'The one she begged to let her be a nun at fifteen when her dad took her to Rome?' Noakes cut in, 'She grabbed the poor bloke's knees an' wouldn't let go so they had to carry her away.'

'The very same,' Miss Parkin nodded approvingly. 'Well, when Pope Leo was opening the Vatican archives up to scholars, he said the Church has nothing to fear from the truth.' Collecting up their cups and saucers, she repeated firmly, 'Nothing to fear from the truth.'

Afterwards, as they sat in Markham's car, Noakes was sceptical. 'I can see where Miss P's coming from,' he said slowly, 'but somehow I don' buy it, guv . . . Sounds to me like priests an' bishops an' cardinals wouldn't like them letters coming out.'

'Not if the correspondence was indiscreet,' Markham agreed. 'And if Marie Guerin was seen to be neurotic and unbalanced, then there's a definite possibility that the Guerins decided to suppress the letters she sent to Jeanne La Néele.'

Noakes scratched his frowsy head.

'How come Cousin Marie managed to send letters like that in the first place?' he asked. 'I mean, wouldn't the mad prioress have put the mockers on it?'

'That's a good question, Noakesy.' One that had also occurred to Markham. 'In those days, a nun's superiors would have censored outgoing mail—'

'An' if there were owt dodgy, they'd tell the nun to change it,' the DS finished.

'Exactly.'

'Of course, Marie G could've smuggled 'em out somehow. Mebbe she were friendly with them nuns who did the errands . . . bought the shopping an' stuff—'

'The extern sisters,' Markham prompted thoughtfully. 'They didn't live inside the enclosure but had their own little house next to the convent. So it's true, they were free to come and go after a fashion . . .'

'Or mebbe she slipped it to the gardener or someone who was visiting.'

It would have been difficult to pass illicit correspondence to relatives in the parlour unless other nuns connived at it, thought Markham.

'Or the loony prioress might've taken her eye off the ball,' Noakes concluded. 'She were an aristo — had this sister, a countess, always dropping by with the rich relations, so she got the nuns waiting on 'em hand an' foot . . . doing their sewing an' laundry when they were meant to be praying.'

Markham reflected with amusement that his wingman's disapproval had a distinctly Torquemada-ish flavour.

'With everything that was going on, mebbe she stopped checking the letters . . . jus' waved 'em through.'

'All that I've learned about Mother Marie de Gonzague suggests she was a control freak,' Markham observed. 'But you could well be right about the system breaking down.'

'The thing is, boss,' Noakes eyed Markham beadily. 'It looks like Nevin could've been on the track of summat the Church didn't want coming out.' The DS blew out his cheeks in a characteristic gesture of exasperation. 'So as it stands, either there's some kind of sex triangle thingy going on with Porter, Gough an' Diggers . . . or it's all about a big fat secret the Church didn't want anyone to know about, only Porter cottoned on somehow an' it went downhill from there.' The DS scratched his paunch with a vigour that made Markham wince. 'Bagsy you explain to Slimy Sid about the letters . . . dunno if I could keep a straight face. I mean, can you imagine telling him about "special friendships" an' "spiritual conversations".' He scowled. 'Might as well jus' come right out an' say it were curtains for the cult if it came out Therese an' Sister Marie wossname were, like, involved.'

'That's definitely a conversation I'm keen to avoid, if at all possible,' Markham said. 'Somehow I don't think the sociology of Carmel in the late nineteenth century is really DCI Sidney's cup of tea.'

Noakes's face assumed a crafty expression. 'But I bet we can get Burton to push the line about Gough being in the frame cos she's screwy . . . Seeing as no one can get to see her, it means we can play for time. Should keep Sidney an' the bish quiet for a bit.'

Markham started the engine. 'Let's swing by Southampton Row and brief the others about this business of the letters. Then I want to catch up with Olivia.'

'An' I've gotta see the missus onto her train.' Noakes's doleful tone suggested he suspected the family finances might have taken a significant hit courtesy of Harrods and Harvey Nicks.

Markham knew Olivia would want to give the temples of Mammon a wide berth. Perhaps they could squeeze in a visit to Brompton Oratory. Should put him in the right frame of mind for Father Digby's funeral . . .

'Take some time for yourself once you've seen Muriel off, Noakesy.' He had a shrewd idea the other would appreciate the chance for a catch-up with Doyle, i.e. the sharing of scurrilous titbits about the Southampton Row crew, along with a dissection of the younger man's romantic prospects and assessment of Bromgrove Rovers' chances in the FA Cup.

'Ta, guv.' But even with this alluring vista before him, Noakes's mind was still running on the Theresian mystery. 'Happen Burton knows what happened to Gough when they kicked her out of that convent.'

* * *

In the event, Rosemary Gough's expulsion from the Brothers and Sisters of St Therese turned out to be less dramatic than Noakes had hoped.

'Whass it mean saying "her vocation lay in the world"?' he grumbled as Markham drove to Father Digby's funeral the following day, jabbing the air to indicate intense mistrust of namby-pamby lingo designed to mystify and confuse.

'Just that she wasn't suited to life as a religious, George,' Olivia smiled at him from the front passenger seat. '*Super tandem tuum*,' she grinned.

'Eh?'

'On Your Bike.'

'Oh right, I'm with you,' he guffawed, belatedly registering the joke. Then, shyly, 'What d'you reckon to all of this about Therese mebbe being an unbeliever . . . Or worse, given the spectre of an illicit entanglement with Sister Marie of the Trinity.'

'A lot of people think Therese was pretty amazing, George . . . Thomas Merton called her "a mighty child" — gave her top marks on his saint-score-o-meter.' Olivia locked eyes with Noakes in the wing mirror. 'Of course, you've got folk who carp about her being "lowbrow", but it's good to have a saint for ordinary people . . . You have to admire the way she settled for doing her best in that damp little convent when she really wanted to be a priest or a martyr . . . It rains a lot in Normandy,' she added inconsequentially.

Noakes had never heard of the Merton bloke — some religious boffin most like — but nodded vigorously.

'She had a rough old time of it,' Olivia went on, 'what with the funny upbringing and all the problems with scruples in her teens . . . losing her mother when she was just a toddler and then her father having a breakdown—'

'An' gangrene an' all that horrible stuff with the TB,' Noakes put in.

'*Exactly* . . . And yet she went on loving and trusting up to the very end.'

'She were a tough cookie, right enough.'

‘Tough’s the word, George. She said she spent most of her time surrounded by fog . . . the “night of nothingness”.’

‘But she hung on in there.’

‘Yes,’ Olivia said softly. ‘The bravest of the brave. She rose above all the crudeness, pettiness and spite of convent life and somehow transformed it by love. *I’d* say she was a believer alright.’

This time her smile was so radiant, that Noakes just basked in its glow.

‘Whatcha reckon to all this about Therese writing some iffy letters though?’

Olivia heard the plea in this question.

‘It’s a poser, George . . . Looks like Professor Nevin thought the Guerin papers — Marie Guerin’s confidential correspondence — might result in a radical reappraisal of St Therese.’

Noakes’s leg was jiggling. ‘In a *bad* way?’ he asked anxiously.

‘Well, possibly taking more account of the historical context and her upbringing. I mean, that kind of revisionism is inevitable . . . and *healthy* if it means we approach saints with greater honesty.’

‘By making out she weren’t so holy, then?’ Somehow the issue of Therese’s integrity was high stakes for Noakes.

‘I think it’s more a question of understanding the background,’ Olivia said gently, aware she was dodging a bullet.

‘But it don’ mean they’d cancel her being a saint?’

Olivia badly wanted to laugh but preserved an expression of impenetrable gravity. ‘Not at all, George,’ she said. ‘I don’t think “cancel culture” extends to canonisation.’ She looked to Markham for help.

‘Oh, I think the worst that can happen is they get *demoted,* Noakesy,’ his boss said easily.

‘So whass going on then?’ Noakes’s belligerence was an evident camouflage for his partiality towards Therese and the cult. ‘Are them letters the reason why Julia Porter got herself throttled?’

'I checked with the exhibits officer and there's a scribbled name on several of Julia's prayer cards,' Markham replied. 'Amélie *Lemarchand*.'

Noakes was unimpressed. 'What about it?'

'Kate's done some research and it transpires that Lemarchand was a distant branch of the Guerin clan,' Markham explained. 'Paolo Serrano mentioned that Julia spoke decent French . . . There was a postcard signed by this Amélie, so it looks like Julia *may* have had a link to Therese's family on Isidore's side. The Lemarchands live just outside Versailles . . . I've asked Kate to contact them as a matter of urgency. Hopefully she'll have something for us later tonight.'

'An' you reckon these Frenchies hold the key?'

'At least they may be able to shed some light as to why Julia could have presented a threat to the religious status quo.'

A portentous sniff was all that Markham received by way of response.

* * *

Father Digby Peake's funeral rites were the most transcendentally beautiful that Markham had ever witnessed.

The monastery in Woodstock consisted of a cluster of nineteenth-century buildings: a church of dressed stone; a shaded cloister; orchards and undergrowth on the side of a gothic monastery complex.

The walled cemetery resembled an old English garden, with scattered flowers around the tombs and tall grass in the paths. Markham, Noakes and Olivia lingered there amongst the geraniums and well-trimmed boxwood as a light drizzle fell before passing into the church which resembled an ancient longship, narrow and dark.

After a few minutes — barely long enough for their eyes to adjust to the gloom — a little bell sounded and members of the community entered, bearing aloft an open white, wooden casket which was placed on trestles in the centre of the choir stalls. Recalling the bludgeoning of Father Digby, Noakes studiously averted his gaze.

The requiem Mass proceeded with due solemnity. First the opening rites and then the clarion-call of the readings.

> *We shall not all sleep, but we shall all be changed . . .*
> *For this corruptible must put on incorruption, and this mortal must put on immortality.*
> *So when this corruptible shall have put on incorruption, and this mortal shall have put on immortality, then shall be brought to pass the saying that is written, Death is swallowed up in victory.*
> *O death where is thy sting? O grave where is thy victory?*

Bit of a tongue-twister, but Noakes liked the ringing vowels. It occurred to him that something like that must have been recited over little Therese's coffin all those years ago.

As his thoughts drifted, he remembered that Muriel had mentioned some weird stuff about the Little Flower's sister Celine when they first dug up Therese's body to rebury it in a stone vault . . . because obviously you couldn't leave a saint-to-be mouldering under a flower bed in some crummy little cemetery.

Apparently when Celine came into the marquee they'd put up at the entrance to the cemetery chapel — all shy and awkward in her big flapping nun's habit — all she could think about when she saw the bones laid out was getting hold of Therese's skull and giving it a kiss. She said Therese still looked lovely and then started stuffing little silk bags with bits of her clothes . . . Later on, they gave her the head and bones to wrap up so they could go back in the coffin in exactly the same position.

He'd felt a bit queasy hearing all this, but the missus said it was beautiful — just like when Thomas More's daughter took his head down from the spike on London Bridge after he was executed by Henry the Eighth so she could be buried with it one day. So that was alright then.

According to Muriel — who was thinking of giving a talk on it — Therese said she didn't have a problem with dying . . . something about being like a child waiting at a railway station for her parents to put her on the train. It didn't matter if she missed it, because there was sure to be another.

Noakes understood. He was like that about trains himself. Butterflies in the stomach and a sense that anything was possible . . .

Time for the sermon.

'Entering our order is the first step towards death,' the celebrant said as he began his homily. 'But we invoke the words of the Night Prayer that Father Digby recited every day of his life. "Let the dreams and phantoms of the night flee far away".'

That prayer was bleeding bobbins when it came to protecting the priest from a psycho killer, thought Noakes angrily.

Eyes sliding sideways, Noakes took in Olivia's pale, intent profile, ethereal and remote like a princess from Camelot. Somehow, she looked completely at home in the dim depths of the church, while *he* felt like a lumbering intruder. Markham too fitted right in, his hawkish chiselled features like the kind of face you saw on tombs . . .

The DS began to feel sleepy watching all the messing around with candles and incense. Then, just when he was feeling nice and settled, everyone promptly jumped to their feet and he was yanked out of a pleasant doze.

Bleeding hell, up down, up down.

At last, they got to sit again.

'Heaven will be a celebration like no other,' intoned the celebrant.

Noakes thought grimly that was the least Father Digby deserved after what he'd been through.

'Like St Therese of Lisieux, who said "I do not die, I enter into life", we commemorate the passing of our brother Digby with joyful gratitude that he has met the Lord.'

Hmm. Wish I had your confidence, mate, thought the DS.

Then he reproached himself for a lack of faith. Therese wouldn't be impressed with him being so lukewarm. On the other hand, happen she'd sympathise. After all, she had a bit of a panic about the Last Judgement — as if *she* needed to bother about stuff like that! — and told the whacko prioress she was worried she wouldn't know how to die properly . . .

A dig in the ribs from Olivia recalled Noakes to the present.

'Go forth, Christian soul, from this world, in the name of God the almighty Father, who created you, in the name of Jesus Christ, Son of the living God, who suffered for you. May you live in peace this day, may your home be with God in Zion.'

The pallbearers took up their positions next to the coffin, the skirts of their long black cassocks swishing about their legs.

Eerily, at that moment, Noakes had the impression Digby might have been looking one last time at the vaulted ceiling which formerly carried his prayers.

The little cortege wound its way out of the church and into the cemetery where a plot was waiting to receive Father Digby's mortal remains. It had stopped drizzling and a clear blue sky gave a sense of space and peace to this enclosure of the dead, as though the priest had at last found a fitting refuge from everyday storms and squalls.

The pallbearers set down their load and one of the brethren leaned over the coffin with a white linen cloth, reverently covering the corpse's face. Two more advanced with the lid which was carefully screwed into place. It seemed to Noakes as though they were moving underwater, so unhurried and graceful were their actions. As the coffin was lowered into its narrow home, a tall young priest began chanting:

'Praise be to you, Lord, for our Sister Death, from whom no living man can escape. Sorrowful are they who die in mortal sin; happy are they whom she finds living according to your will, for no second death can do them harm.'

'*Sister Death*?' Noakes muttered as the little crowd dispersed. 'Who wrote that cheery number then?'

'St Francis of Assisi,' Olivia told him.

'I thought he were all about birds an' animals an' loving nature,' Noakes said with the indignant air of one who had been sold a bill of goods. 'Y'know, like *All Things Bright and Beautiful*.'

'It's from his *Canticle of the Creatures*,' Markham explained. 'Death is portrayed as part of the life cycle . . . a passage to Christ.' He grinned. 'It's actually meant to be uplifting.'

'Gave me the willies.'

'You're a hard man to please, Noakesy,' his boss said.

'Yeah, well you don' want it sounding like Halloween. Whass wrong with summat about resting from their labours . . . "Where the wicked cease from troubling an' the weary are at rest". The missus' dad had *The Lord is My Shepherd* . . . same as on *The Vicar of Dibley*. Very nice too.'

Olivia linked his arm as they wandered past the little orchard.

'Oh George,' she said cosily. 'You're such a comfort.'

The tips of Noakes's ears turned pink at the compliment, though he was at a loss to know what he had said to cheer her up.

But Markham knew.

It wasn't what his wingman said so much as who he *was*. A card-carrying old school copper and unrepentant nonconformist whose very ordinariness somehow forced the genie of evil back into its bottle.

Maybe that's why Noakes was such a fan of St Therese — the saint of the common man, the obscure little nun with no pretensions to ecstasies and levitations who ended by outshining all the rest.

His eyes met Olivia's over Noakes's head, and a silent message passed between them.

Suddenly, his wingman pulled up short.

'Where'd *he* come from?'

'He' was Ignatius Fermor.

The theology student noticed them at the same moment but wasn't predisposed to chat. With a frigid bow in their direction, he disappeared towards the main house.

'They're not prisoners at the institute, Noakes,' Markham pointed out. 'Free to come and go, though they can't move back into the club for now.'

'Wasn't Father Digby his mentor?' Olivia asked.

'That's right . . . And Mr Fermor's training for the priesthood after all. Stands to reason he'd want to attend. I imagine he sees himself as representing the sisters.'

'There weren't any nuns in the church, Gil,' Olivia mused. 'Actually, come to think of it I was the only woman there.' She frowned. 'Isn't it meant to be a *joint* congregation — the Brothers and Sisters of St Therese?'

'They all belong to the same religious order, but looks like they decided to make it a men-only funeral.'

'Prob'ly had orders from the bish,' Noakes said dourly. 'No women in case the press got wind an' decided there were summat pervy going on with Diggers.' He looked hopefully across at the monastery's elegant facade. 'Are we going to the eats or what? We can keep an eye on Iggy Pop — see what he gets up to,' he added craftily.

'Sorry to disappoint you, Noakesy, but I understand they're not laying on any refreshments for visitors. Something to do with wanting to get straight back to their usual routine . . . After death, the essence of life continues. And of course, the community may be under instructions to keep everything low-key.'

'Stingy, that's what I call it,' the other huffed. 'After all that praying an' chanting, folk need a bun an' a cuppa.'

Olivia squeezed his beefy arm.

'Don't worry, George. Gil's going to stop off somewhere. *Aren't you, Gil?*'

But Gil had turned round to look back the way that they had come and was murmuring softly.

'"Where will they go if you forget them, God of memory"?'

Olivia's gaze rested lovingly on him. She had once laughingly compared her culture-loving policeman boyfriend to General Wolfe who famously declared that he would rather have written Gray's *Elegy* than take Quebec. But she knew it was his outlet for the sadness of his job.

Noakes waited respectfully while the guvnor communed with himself. He was used to these moments of fugue and decidedly proud of having a boss who quoted poetry. So what if some of them in CID said you needed a thesaurus to understand him. They were just jealous.

Finally, Markham was ready to leave.

At the monastery gates, they switched their mobiles back on (Markham not having wanted the Mexican hat dance to disrupt the funeral Mass).

Almost immediately his phone rang.

After listening intently, he said, 'See if the sisters know anything about it, Kate. We're stopping over in Bromgrove, but we'll be back at Southampton Row by lunch time tomorrow.'

'*Well?*' Noakes demanded, impatient to learn developments.

'Kate's tracked down the Lemarchands—'

Olivia was no less eager. 'The people who may know something about the letters Marie Guerin sent to her sister Jeanne La Néele?'

'That's right.'

'Were they in touch with Julia?' she pressed.

'It would appear so,' Markham said thoughtfully. 'Well, it was mainly this elderly cousin she became friendly with on a visit to Alencon, St Therese's birthplace. Amélie Lemarchand's very frail and suffering from arteriosclerosis, but from what Kate can make out it appears she might have given Julia certain letters from the Guerin family papers.'

Noakes was baffled. 'But the SOCOs didn't find anything like that in Porter's room, boss . . . It were all jus' religious tat.'

'The killer could have removed the correspondence, Noakes,' Markham said gravely. 'In which case, it wasn't a sexual intrigue or love triangle that led to Julia's death.'

They waited expectantly.

'It was the contents of those letters. Someone was prepared to kill so that they never saw the light of day.'

As he spoke, it seemed that the sky darkened, casting the monastery behind them into shadow. From somewhere deep within, a bell began to toll.

11. OPEN ALL THE DOORS!

'Why'd you reckon this Madame Lemarchand handed over a cache of letters to Julia?'

Olivia and Markham were ensconced in the living room of their apartment at the Sweepstakes, an upmarket complex off Bromgrove Avenue, having enjoyed a scratch supper of fish and chips followed by Ben & Jerry's chocolate chip cookie dough ice cream.

The weather had turned once again and it was stormy outside, but indoors all was warm and snug, their wood burner keeping them toasty and the heavy damask curtains in the living room drawn tight against the gloom. By tacit agreement, they had avoided talk of murder during the meal, but now over strong coffee their conversation turned to the investigation.

Olivia, sitting cross-legged on the carpet at Markham's feet, looked up at him expectantly.

'I've been wondering about that, Liv,' he said thoughtfully, 'but I'm blessed if I know the answer. It could be she just warmed to Julia . . . enjoyed reminiscing with her about St Therese's family history . . . wanted to give her something as a memento perhaps . . .'

'But wouldn't the family try to stop her handing over stuff that was private?' She frowned. 'I mean, if the contents were sensitive for some reason, surely they wouldn't allow the letters out of their sight.'

'It's not clear that they knew much about it. Miss Parkin from the institute talked about some "tradition" floating around and only a couple of people being in on the secret . . . It sounded like there was a fair amount of mythmaking surrounding the whole subject of the Guerin papers. Actually, Kate had the impression the family thought Madame Lemarchand might have been romancing when she talked about letters having come down to her from the La Néeles.'

'Hmm. I guess you could be right,' she said, thinking hard. Then, 'Maybe Julia took advantage of the old lady . . . if Madame Lemarchand had arteriosclerosis, she'd be vulnerable to someone wheedling the letters out of her.'

'True.' It wasn't an attractive scenario, Markham thought as he sipped his espresso. 'Of course, it might have come about innocently enough . . . Amélie Lemarchand showed Julia the letters and Julia offered to look after them . . . keep them out of the clutches of anti-Theresians bent on producing revisionist bombshells about romantic friendships or mental disturbance.'

'Maybe Julia had the idea of taking them to Father Digby,' Olivia mused. 'He was another right-winger, so she would have been sure of support. Plus, she had a bit of a thing for him, and a stash of Marie Guerin's letters was guaranteed to arouse his interest. *Hey*,' a thought struck her, 'what if she *did* pass them to Father Digby and that's why he had to die too . . .'

Markham smiled at her excitement. Twirling strands of red hair round her fingers, flushed and happy in the lamplight, she looked like a teenager rather than a thirty-something schoolmarm.

'Could be, Liv. One thing's for sure, those letters are key to the murders.'

'What d'you think is in them?' she asked, fascinated. 'It's got to be dynamite if someone was prepared to kill . . . A love affair between Therese and this novice, Sister Marie of the Trinity? Something about the three blood sisters who were nuns with her in the convent? A secret about the one who ended up in a different order . . . the sister they're thinking about canonising—'

'Leonie.'

'Or perhaps something murky about Therese's parents? Let's face it, Gil, the Church has invested heavily in the entire tribe . . . constructed a whole pilgrimage industry around them . . . not to mention a lucrative market in saintly kitsch.' She giggled suddenly. 'By the by, I wonder where Muriel's displayed her Therese tea tray?'

Markham chuckled.

'I gather she liked her locket too.'

'I'd forgotten about the relic! *Honestly*, Gil.' Her face was alight with mischief. 'Who'd ever have thought it . . . Muriel Noakes falling for the Little Flower!'

'St Therese has made unlikelier conquests,' Markham observed drily.

'But I mean, Muriel . . .'

'And Noakes too,' he pointed out.

'George bought Natalie a rosary . . . the biggest shiniest beads you ever saw. It'd qualify as an offensive weapon if you swung it round.'

'Well, they *do* call it the Church Militant,' he laughed.

'Seriously though, you don't think he's planning to convert to Rome?'

'No I don't. That Methodist upbringing and Sunday School go too deep for Noakesy to defect.' Markham considered some more. 'This may sound strange—'

'Try me,' she said softly.

'I think he feels *fatherly* towards Therese . . . and angry about the way everyone let her down at the end . . .'

'That awful prioress and the pestiferous sisters trying to force her into some preconceived mould of sanctity,' Olivia suggested. 'Not to mention the quacks who more or less killed her.'

'Yes, something like that,' he agreed. 'And more than all that, her courage and the way she kept trusting God—'

'Like a *father*,' Olivia finished. 'Yes, I can see how that would resonate with him.'

The couple fell silent, thinking about the hard-bitten copper whose world nearly fell apart with the discovery that Natalie was not his biological daughter. The possibility of his beloved 'Nat' ever discovering the truth precipitated the greatest crisis of Noakes's personal and professional life.

Seeing that this revived uncomfortable memories, Olivia steered the conversation into safer waters.

'George is quite spiritual in his way,' she mused. 'I noticed him at Father Digby's funeral drinking it all in . . . And I think he really likes hearing about saints and old churches, though he does his best to hide it.'

Markham laughed.

'I remember once when Sidney was being snide about my "religious leanings"—'

'Oh, don't tell me.' She imitated the DCI's nasal honk. '"You need to avoid affectation, Inspector . . . Remember, most people have zero interest in *churchy* stuff and don't care to be *lectured* or *patronised*. Too many *long words* and intellectualism is so *off-putting*."'

He pulled a wry face. 'Yes, words to that effect . . . Anyway, Noakesy was furious. Piped up about churches being part of our country's history, then reminded Sidney that the queen was head of the Church of England and a decent sort, so folk bleeding well ought to know about it.'

'Oh, that's brilliant, Gil. I'd love to have seen Judas Iscariot's face.'

'Well, it shut him up for once. Noakes topped it all off by saying he liked my "big words" and there was nothing wrong with people expanding their vocabulary.'

She was convulsed. 'George just doesn't give a monkey's, does he?'

'He can be pretty chippy when he puts his mind to it, but God help anyone who has a go at me. I honestly thought he was going to call Sidney an ignorant git or worse!'

'There's nothing petty or small-minded about George,' she smiled. 'People think he's just this vulgar oik, but he's secure enough in his own skin not to worry if someone else has more book learning.'

'True.' Markham smiled. 'He was always scoffing at Kate for her university "ed-u-ca-shon", but in reality he hoovered up every crumb of knowledge and secretly enjoyed it when she and "ole Shippers" got started on the workings of the criminal mind.'

'It's really naughty calling Nathan that . . . But I have to admit he does look like Harold Shipman.'

'Doesn't seem to have put Kate off,' Markham said drily.

'Are wedding bells in the offing, d'you think?'

Somehow, obscurely, Olivia knew she would feel more secure, and her jealous fears subside, once Kate Burton was spoken for.

'Who can say, sweetheart? But it's high time for Kate to have a bit of luck on the romantic front. She and the prof seem well-suited.'

Olivia decided to change the subject.

'How did your workout go?'

Markham stretched pleasurably. He had felt guilty about heading for the boxing club as soon as they arrived back in Bromgrove, but the bout with DI Chris Carstairs had done him a power of good.

'Doggie enjoyed hearing all about St Therese,' he said with a mischievous glint in his eye.

'*Come off it!*'

'I kid you not. Apparently his old mum was a "Cafflick", so he knew about the Little Flower and all the rest of it.'

'He didn't feel he was being patronised or lectured then?' she enquired sarcastically, thinking of DCI Sidney.

'Not a bit of it. Like Noakes, he said it's history and anyone with millions of followers and a cathedral built on top of her is well worth knowing about.' Markham grinned. 'In fact, I can see him and Noakesy settling down for a good old chinwag about Therese and the cult when all of this is over.'

'Do you think you *will* be able to get to the bottom of it, Gil?' she enquired with some anxiety. 'If these letters have disappeared into thin air, that's your best lead gone . . .'

Gently, he reached out and stroked the bright hair.

'I feel we're getting closer, Liv. Kate rang earlier. I've authorised her to drop a hint about the "French Connection" and make sure our suspects get wind of it—'

'You think that will rattle the killer?'

'Hopefully, yes. She's also going to imply that Tom Nevin may have given us something . . . whatever it takes to ratchet up the paranoia essentially.'

Even as he said this, Markham was aware it sounded thin.

'I'm not going to let the murderer slip through my fingers, Liv,' he said finally. 'I remember when I was just starting out in CID . . .'

Olivia listened attentively, aware that he hardly ever spoke of those early days which she guessed had been difficult.

'There was this case . . . It went to trial and we knew our man had done it, but he got off on a technicality because the CPS screwed up. I'll always remember the sound his shoes made when he went down the stairs behind the dock — the soles flapping as he literally ran to get away . . . Each step was like a slap in the face.'

The well-cut features of his face in that instant struck her as looking almost haggard.

'I've never forgotten the face of the woman he murdered . . . She was a slip of a girl with this cloud of dark hair.' Markham brought his clenched fist down on the arm of his wingback chair as though he wanted to smash something to pieces. 'We never got justice for her. Her father suffered a heart attack because of it and the mother never recovered.'

Olivia squeezed his hand in mute sympathy. She knew that was why he had chosen this flat in the Sweepstakes with its view of Bromgrove North Municipal Cemetery.

To keep his murdered dead close.

Markham let out a shuddering breath.

'I guess it got to everyone. My boss in those days was Superintendent David Hart . . . lovely man, a class act in every sense of the word. He kept this sliver of wood on a shelf in his office. It had a stain on it . . . like a blob of sealing wax, I used to think. Someone told me it was the murder weapon from that case, and it had blood on it. The higher ups weren't happy when they got to hear of it, but Hart dug his heels in and there it stayed. A reminder.'

He stared in silence at the floor for a while, obviously lost in memories. Olivia wanted to bring Gil back from the dark place where his thoughts had taken him.

'You've got Therese on your side, remember,' she said gently. 'Supernatural help has to count for something.'

With an effort, he roused himself.

'That's what Noakesy says. Apparently, when Therese was dying, the prioress — or Sister Loony Tunes, as he insists on calling her — suddenly stopped all the control freakery and called all the nuns to help pray her into heaven. *Open the doors*, she told them. *Open all the doors!*'

'Well, there you are, my love,' Olivia said firmly. 'You're pushing at the door right now and Therese is going to help you get through.' She spoke with more confidence than she felt. The "French Connection" might lead nowhere and then where would they be . . .

'Enough for tonight,' she told him. 'Let's treat ourselves to something thoroughly secular but not *Father Ted* this time!'

As she had intended, Markham burst out laughing.

'Didn't you say there's *Line of Duty* waiting for us on catch-up?'

'Talk about a busman's holiday,' she grumbled. But her voice was tender.

'I'll be up very early tomorrow, sweetheart . . . want to get a head start on the traffic, so we're back in London by mid-morning.'

'No worries.' She groaned and rolled her eyes, thinking of Hope Academy. 'And I'm due back at the snake pit

. . . ready to "cascade" the latest trendy thinking to my colleagues.'

'Is that what they call it these days . . . cascade?'

'Yep, that's the latest term of art for boring people rigid . . . Be sure to flash it at Sidney at your next briefing.'

And with that they settled down for their evening's viewing, banishing thoughts of what the next day might bring.

* * *

True to his word, Wednesday 23 March saw Markham and Noakes up bright and early, heading back to London.

Noakes was in high good humour notwithstanding the early start. It transpired that Natalie was decidedly pleased with her rosary, since "the Madonna look" was coming back into vogue. 'Not Jesus's mother,' he explained to his amused superior. 'The pop singer . . . goes in for crucifixes an' rosaries an' whatnot.' Markham did his best not to boggle at the notion of Natalie Noakes rocking the Catholic vibe at whichever nightclub was currently flavour of the month. He couldn't have been successful, since Noakes added hastily, 'Nat'll keep it tasteful, mind. Don' want to upset her mum.' While Markham struggled to envision a Madonna tribute act that could be classed as tasteful, his wingman moved on to a more pressing preoccupation, namely where they were going to stop off en route . . .

As they sat in Starbucks at Chorley Services sometime later, finishing off their 'elevenses', Markham took a phone call which made the colour drain from his face.

Noakes paused, mug of well-sugared tea halfway to his mouth, studying the guvnor intently.

Bad news.

And so it proved.

They adjourned to the carpark, discreetly out of earshot of neighbouring travellers.

'Whassup?' the DS demanded without preamble.

'The body of David Manners was discovered early this morning.'

Noakes's jaw dropped. Whatever he had been expecting, it wasn't this.

'*Manners?*' he repeated. 'Mister fussbudget . . . the deputy warden?'

Markham nodded gravely, still very pale.

'I don' get it, guv. How come? What happened?'

'Kate's still trying to piece it all together . . . He turned up in the institute crypt wedged behind the little stone staircase next to the lift shaft . . . You remember, there was a disused hydraulic platform used for bringing coffins down from Oratory House?'

'Oh yeah . . . *Spooky*,' Noakes said with feeling. 'How'd he end up down there . . . playing fricking hide an' seek in the middle of the night or what?'

'Presumably he followed someone . . . either by prior arrangement or because he was shadowing them.'

'An' then it got nasty,' the DS concluded grimly.

'Looks like it.'

'How did he die, boss?'

'There were several stab wounds. Dr Dajani says it was a frenzied attack.'

'*Jesus, Mary and Joseph* . . .,' Noakes ducked his head apologetically as Markham shot him a gimlet glance. 'Sorry, boss. But it don' make any sense. Manners weren't the type to go it alone . . . not after three murders. If he knew owt, I reckon he'd have called it in.'

'Not if he believed he was on top of the situation,' the DI said quietly. 'It might be he was on someone's trail without realising they were the killer . . . if he was trying to catch someone out in an illicit encounter, for example.'

'Illicit encounter?' Noakes stared. 'Who'd want to get their end away next to a pile of coffins?'

'Graveyards have long been a favourite trysting place for those who want to add extra spice to a sexual encounter, Sergeant.'

'You mean pervs.'

'No, all kinds of people,' Markham replied. 'I believe they were very keen on al fresco fornication at the time of the Black Death.'

'Dirty buggers.' Noakes was disgusted. 'You'd think they'd wanna be saying their prayers an' stuff instead of behaving like animals.'

'In that particular instance, I think it was a case of keeping death at bay,' Markham said. 'But in more recent times, the sense of the forbidden imparted an extra frisson . . . There's no accounting for tastes, you see,' he added lightly in the face of his subordinate's appalled expression. 'Don't tell me you didn't come across that kind of thing when you were in Vice.'

'Yeah, but not with regular folk. Not like you an' me.' Noakes looked as though he now regretted his Ultimate Breakfast Sandwich with extra fries.

'To get back to Mr Manners,' Markham said, 'he had the reputation of being a snoop. The club staff certainly gave the impression he was always on their case for something or other.'

Noakes considered this.

'An' he weren't happy about gays being at the club . . . said some of 'em were at it, didn't he . . . Donald Trevor—'

'Trevelyan.'

'Yeah an' the accountant bloke . . . plus the Spanish lad Paolo an' Prof Nevin and— *Hey*,' the DS was excited now, 'the shifty theology student . . . Iggy I'm-ever-so-holy wossname.'

'Ignatius Fermor.' Markham thought of the dark-suited would-be priest scuttling away from them at Father Digby's requiem.

The DI unlocked the car and they got in. But he seemed in no hurry to start the engine.

Noakes had found his second wind.

'So Manners might've been doing his morality police number . . . trying to bust this vice ring?'

'Well, no doubt that's how *he* thought of them,' Markham said austerely, 'but of course *we* know better.'

Noakes registered the warning tone. 'Oh yeah, live an' let live,' he said hastily.

His boss started the car and they headed off to rejoin the motorway.

'David Manners wasn't the most congenial individual,' Markham said after a time. 'But no doubt he did his best.'

'He wanted to be the big cheese,' Noakes observed, trying to empathise. The DS scratched his head. 'But for chuff's sake . . . carrying on like a Peeping Tom . . .'

'We can't be sure that's what he was up to,' Markham said carefully, 'but it fits. I remember noticing something strange when we interviewed him after Tom Nevin's death . . . this sort of suppressed excitement.'

'Cos he liked the idea of being a new broom calling time on sleaze an' all that?'

'Well, it would certainly be in character.'

'What if he weren't after nabbing the gay blokes?'

The DS had Markham's full attention. 'How do you mean?'

'Well, it could've been Pauline an' Roisin . . . You could tell he had a hang-up about nuns an' priests . . . Remember the way he talked about Diggers an' them two, like it were all against nature.'

Markham refrained from pointing out it was not so very long ago that Noakes too had demonstrated similar 'hang-ups', but he supposed that in this respect at least the DS had made progress.

And besides, a tingling between the shoulder blades told him Noakes might be on to something. 'Go on,' he encouraged.

'Pauline an' Roisin are round the institute all the time, boss . . . doing stuff on the education side an' messing about in archives an' whatnot.'

The DI suppressed a smile at 'messing about'.

'They've got pass keys for the place,' Noakes continued. ''S like home from home for them, so nowt to say they weren't up to summat.'

'Like what?'

'Dunno.' Noakes struggled with the notion of Roisin and Pauline being involved in illicit sex. 'But if Manners thought he could catch 'em breaking the rules, he'd be like a dog with two tails.'

'It's always possible other people could have laid their hands on a set of keys,' Markham said. 'The club residents or members, for example.'

'Nah.' Noakes was firm. 'Muriel said Miss P made a big song an' dance about that . . . guards the keys with her life. Has to be dead careful who gets 'em cos of the heritage stuff an' important records. Only Father Digby and the nuns had access to all areas. Manners didn't like that cos it meant he had to get permission from her — same as the plebs.'

'So you think David Manners was suspicious of the nuns for some reason and ended up in the crypt because he was tailing them?'

'Mebbe it were jus' Sister Pauline . . . She's the flaky one, right? Mebbe she freaked out down there when she saw Manners an' had some kind of episode, like Dr Dajani said . . . a psychotic break . . . an' then Roisin came looking for her . . . helped her hide the body an' clean up afterwards cos she'd have been in a right state.' Noakes's stomach rumbled loudly, but for once he was too engrossed in his hypothesis to worry about the inner man. 'By the way, boss,' he said, 'who was it suggested where to look for Manners?'

'He didn't turn up for breakfast and when they checked his room, the bed hadn't been slept in. It was Ignatius Fermor who said they should check the crypt.'

Noakes looked very dark, being no fan of the theology student.

'But Noakesy, can you seriously imagine Sister Roisin hiding something like that? There's no way she'd connive at a cover-up.'

‘She might,’ Noakes insisted stubbornly, ‘if it meant there wouldn’t be any scandal. Then later on, the RCs could smuggle Pauline off to a funny farm for religious types.’

Markham shook his head slowly. ‘If Pauline had some kind of psychotic episode which ended in a frenzied knife attack, Sister Roisin would presume she killed our other three victims.’ The DI’s fingers drummed rhythmically on the steering wheel, trying to keep pace with his racing thoughts. ‘Even allowing for her wanting to protect the Church, it would be culpably negligent not to go to the police . . . I don’t see how she could square it with her conscience.’

‘P’raps Pauline ain’t the killer an’ she just lost it when Manners came creeping up on her . . . That way it’d jus’ be a one-off an’ Sister Roisin could make allowances.’

‘Don’t forget, whoever killed Manners was prowling round the crypt with a knife, Noakes. Somehow I don’t think the “one-off” theory holds water.’

The DS sighed gustily, with a well-practised air of injured merit.

‘On the other hand, I think you may have a valid point about our needing to take a closer look at the nuns,’ Markham said thoughtfully.

They drove for a while in silence, revolving the possibilities. It was a grey, dull day but the rain had held off and they were making good time.

‘D’you reckon them letters — the whatchamacallit French stuff — could be hidden in the crypt, guv?’ Noakes asked suddenly.

‘Go on.’

The DS plunged ahead like a desperate man.

‘Mebbe the nuns got wind they were stashed in there an’ went looking . . . not realising ole Deputy Dawg Manners was right behind ’em.’

Markham’s head was beginning to throb, but he tried to follow his wingman’s thread. ‘What, because Father

Digby or someone else put them there and they found out about it?'

'Yeah . . . or mebbe they got hold of the letters somehow an' put them in the crypt for safekeeping, then wanted to take a peek, but Manners clocked they were behaving suspiciously an' went to investigate.'

'Are you saying you think the nuns killed Julia for the letters?' Markham asked.

'Dunno about 'em killing anyone.' The DS sounded at a loss. 'But if they weren't in the crypt diddling each other, what the frick else could they have been doing?' He rumpled his hair wildly. 'You said it yourself, guv — them letters have gotta be the key to it all.'

The DI thought of the chilly stone corridor under the institute with its coffins and the pillars carved with mysterious creatures from St Therese's dreams.

What kind of a creature was it who had murdered four people? Was it possible that the two nuns were somehow behind it?

At the moment, the car speakerphone trilled.

'Go ahead, Kate.'

'How near are you, sir?'

'We'll be with you in half an hour. How's it going?'

'There's been a complication.'

Noakes leaned forward intently.

'What sort of complication?' he demanded.

'We've got a coffin looks like it's been interfered with.'

Even in his wildest imaginings, the DS hadn't envisaged some kind of Black Sabbath.

'How d'you mean?' he enquired hoarsely.

'The SOCOs went over the whole crypt. There noticed a coffin on the bottom tier was clean and not dusty like the rest . . . as though it had been handled recently . . . They checked inside and found skeletal remains.'

'Thass what you'd expect, ain't it, bones?' Tension made Noakes belligerent.

‘Problem is, this corpse had three legs,’ came the shaky reply.

It took a moment for it to sink in.

The crypt had yielded up its secret.

One final victim. Identity unknown.

12. SIGNS AND PORTENTS

The remains had already been removed by Dr Dajani by the time they reached the institute. Meanwhile, two SOCOs were busy processing the spiral staircase beneath which the body of David Manners had been found.

'In terms of family, there's just a sister in Somerset,' Burton told Markham. 'She lives in sheltered housing and there are major health issues. The manager's broken the news but isn't sure it's really sunk in.' She gestured to the iron grates which stood wide open. 'The forensic anthropologist, Dr Grahame Appleby, is checking the coffin that was disturbed.'

'Looks like you've got a stowaway in this one, Inspector,' Appleby said cheerfully, rocking back on his heels on the cold, musty stone flags.

Noakes eyed him with disfavour.

'*A stowaway?*'

'Just my little joke, Sergeant . . . What I mean is that the second set of remains shouldn't be there.'

'*You don' say*.' The DS was looking more mutinous with every minute.

Come back, Doug Davidson, all is forgiven. Markham felt a pang of nostalgia for his pathologist back in Bromgrove.

'Can you say if they're from the Victorian era, Doctor?' Kate Burton asked. 'The interments here date from that period.'

'Yeah, are we talking ancient or modern?' Noakes echoed.

'I would say modern.' Appleby gently extracted something from the coffin and held it up to the light. 'This set of orthodontic braces would tend to support such a conclusion.'

Doyle took the bull by the horns.

'Why aren't there *two* skulls in the coffin? I mean, if two people were put in there, stands to reason there should be two heads.'

'It takes around a year for the corpse to decompose to a skeleton,' the other said brightly. 'Absence of a second skull just suggests that it was removed.'

After the contents of the coffin had been stretchered out of the crypt, the four detectives stood in a huddle, contemplating the tiered biers behind their iron grates.

Noakes was the first to break the silence.

'So now there's a fricking grave robber in the mix.' he burst out. 'That's all we bleeding need! Sidney'll go ballistic.'

'Mind your language, Sergeant,' Markham said levelly. 'This is consecrated ground after all.'

The DS jabbed a pudgy forefinger at the grates. 'Nothing consecrated about what they got up to back there.' He peered balefully through the cast iron squares. 'I mean, are we talking necrophilia or what?'

Burton turned to Markham. 'Do you think the, er, activity with the coffin is connected to the murders, guv?'

'My instincts tell me yes, Kate. But as yet I don't see how.'

Doyle began pacing up and down the narrow space, weaving round the three pairs of pillars.

'So there's someone down here interfering with a coffin, and then Manners catches them at it . . . they lash out and kill him.'

'Keep still, you're making me dizzy doing the cakewalk,' Noakes grumbled.

The younger man duly obliged. 'If that's what happened, then most likely they've killed before and stuck their victim in with another corpse. They figured the crypt was a safe hidey-hole because nobody would ever think of rooting round down here,' he continued his reasoning. 'It's got to be someone who has ready access . . . able to slip in and out with no questions asked.'

'Someone who had a long association with the institute,' Burton mused. 'Someone nobody would ever dream of suspecting.'

Markham became aware that the SOCOs were growing impatient.

'Let's go back upstairs,' he said quietly. 'I'll ask Miss Parkin to find us an empty room where we can thrash things out.'

The little group took one last look around the stark chilling space.

Markham's eye was caught by the engraved eagle on the nearest pillar.

This time it wasn't the wingspan he noticed but the bird's meat-hook beak. Cruelly curved like a scimitar, it made him think of human sacrifice. On an altar of blood.

He recalled Miss Parkin saying that St Therese had dreamed of exotic creatures she had never seen before — nature in all its resplendent glory. But knowing what he now did, there was more a sensation of gargoyles than flowers.

'C'mon, guv,' said Noakes, seeing that the boss looked like he was about to 'go off on one'.

With a barely perceptible shudder, Markham followed his colleagues to the exit which led to the institute's basement.

* * *

The institute's senior receptionist installed them with coffee and biscuits in one of the larger conference rooms, promising to keep the rest of the world at bay. Having ascertained that there was no change in Rosemary Gough's condition, Markham thanked her warmly.

'Inspector, I wonder if I might have a quick word when you've finished.'

'Of course, Miss Parkin.' He noticed there were lines around her mouth that hadn't been there before. 'Would you like to speak to me now?'

'Oh, it can wait,' she assured him.

The DI admired the self-restraint that prevented her from pestering him for information.

Discreet to her fingertips, he thought.

Noakes, whom his detractors were wont to dismiss as without tact or finesse, spotted that behind her self-control the woman was positively vibrating with anxiety.

'Lucky we've got you to keep the clergy off our backs, luv,' the DS told her. 'Mum's the word,' he added tapping the side of his nose conspiratorially.

Some colour returned to her ashy complexion.

'Looks like you could do with a cuppa yourself,' he observed kindly. 'I reckon it were an awful shock finding Mr Manners like that.'

'Oh yes, Sergeant.' Her mouth twisted. 'He must have been so scared.'

'It would have been all over in minutes, luv.'

Minutes that must have seemed like an eternity to the poor sod.

'It feels like the crypt's been . . . *polluted*,' she declared.

The piggy eyes blinked rapidly as Noakes groped for something comforting to say.

'You can get it blessed,' he said. 'Yeah, like an exorcism thingy,' he repeated firmly. 'Once this is all over, the bishop'll do you a nice service with holy water an' all the trimmings.'

Miss Parkin gave him a watery smile. 'That's a very good idea, Sergeant,' she said. 'I'm sure Mr Manners would have been in favour too.'

Remembering the deputy warden's thinly veiled prejudice against priests and nuns, Noakes was by no means sure of this, but he was pleased to have struck the right note.

'Right,' he said. 'Off you hop, luv. Get one of 'em to take over while you have that cup of tea . . . We ain't going nowhere,' he eyed her shrewdly, 'so when you feel up to a chat, jus' give us a shout.'

Gallantly, he escorted her to the door and sent her on her way with a parting smile.

'*Exorcism!*' Doyle scoffed as his colleague padded back into the room. 'Next thing you know, she'll have us all down there with candles and bells and God knows what.'

'*Ackshually*, I think it's a good idea,' Noakes said, affronted. 'It'll help give 'em, whatchamacallit, *closure*.'

Burton boggled somewhat at hearing the touchy-feely terminology, but felt her colleague deserved credit for the suggestion. 'Great idea, sarge,' she said warmly.

Markham nodded gravely. 'Indeed.'

Noakes shot the younger man a look that said, 'I told you so', but the gangling redhead merely grinned. Then suddenly, he sobered up. 'Don't forget, only senior staff have the run of the place . . . That means we can't rule out Miss Parkin.'

Seeing his wingman turn the colour of corned beef, Markham swiftly intervened.

'Noakes and I were discussing the question of access as we travelled down,' he said. 'We also worked through various scenarios that might account for the attack on David Manners.' He gestured to the tray of refreshments. 'Come on, help yourselves and let's brainstorm some theories.'

It was thirty minutes later when Markham wound up his theorising, 'So are you agreed we should narrow our sights on the two nuns?'

'I don't have a problem with the idea of Manners spying and following one or both of them into the crypt,' Burton said cautiously. 'But what happened down there must've had something to do with the bones we found . . . the extra skeleton.'

'The stowaway,' Noakes snorted. '"Not Wanted on Voyage", according to Mister Smarty Pants Crab Apple.'

'Yeah, Doyle concurred. 'But where does that leave the dodgy letters about St Therese? I mean, that gives some cult fanatic or religious weirdo a motive for murdering Julia if it turned out she was shooting her mouth off and showing them to people . . . If it's really all about the bones, are we saying Julia found out about the body in the crypt and that's why she was killed — to cover up a murder from the past? And then Digby and Nevin got suspicious, so they had to be silenced too?'

'Mebbe the murderer bumped 'em off cos of the bones *an'* the letters,' Noakes put in. 'But we don' know how it all fits together. God,' the dishevelled salt and pepper tufts looked more like porcupine quills than ever, 'this case is like summat out of *Poirot* . . .'

'*And Then There Were None*,' Doyle yawned, knuckling his eyes.

'We need to find out the identity of our Jane Doe.' Burton too sounded weary.

'Are we going to tell the club folk about the bones?' Doyle asked.

One of them already knows, thought Markham grimly.

'No,' he said. 'We keep this strictly to ourselves. If anyone wants to know why Appleby was called in, we take the line that it was just a precaution, given the antiquity of the site and the presence of human remains . . . whatever sounds feasible and unexciting.'

'Got it, sir.'

You betcha. Burton was no bore, but she could do unexciting like nobody else, Noakes reflected.

There was a soft tap at the door. Miss Parkin had returned.

'Come an' sit down, luv.' Noakes ushered her to a chair. 'You feeling better now?' he enquired solicitously.

She patted her neat perm nervously then smoothed her skirt, as though working up to something.

'Take your time,' the DS said. 'We're all friends here.'

Markham felt the nape of his neck prickle as she met his gaze.

She's going to give us someone, he thought. *Here it is. At last.*

The others sensed something in the air, too. But no one spoke. A sudden burst of hail rattled against the window making Burton jump. But still the silence continued, as though it would stretch out to infinity.

At last she spoke, so quietly that Markham had to crane to hear her. 'You found something else in the crypt didn't you, Inspector . . . *bones*?'

The DI took a gamble.

'Yes,' he said simply.

'How did you know?' Doyle asked.

'I overheard two of the forensics officers.'

Bleeding blabbermouths. But Noakes didn't say it.

Something in the handsome inspector's lean angular face seemed to give the receptionist confidence.

'There was a girl who went missing,' she said. 'She was doing an MA in Gender Studies and Religion at Queen Mary College . . . Jackie Moor.'

'When was this, Miss Parkin?'

'December 2010, Inspector. Everyone thought she just walked out of her life one day . . . but now . . .' The woman's features were working, and she looked as though she was going to cry.

'There was someone you wondered about back then, wasn't there?' Markham said gently. 'But it seemed unthinkable, so you pushed the thought out of your mind . . . And now it's all coming back.'

She nodded mutely.

'You can talk about it, luv. We'd pretty much got there anyway,' Noakes reassured her. 'Knew Sister Pauline had, what-d'you-call-it, mental issues.'

'Not Sister Pauline,' she whispered, her voice a mere thread. 'The other one.'

Noakes's jaw dropped. '*Sister Roisin*?'

The nice sensible one who managed to talk 'human' and was so approachable . . . The DS just couldn't get his head round it. Doyle too looked dumbfounded.

'What made you suspicious of Sister Roisin?' Markham sounded totally unruffled, but Burton guessed his insides were churning like pistons.

'I'm not sure you could even put it as strongly as that, Inspector . . . It was just that Sister Roisin was the last person to see her . . . Apparently they bumped into each other outside Brompton Oratory and arranged to have a coffee later in the café across the road . . . but Jackie never turned up.'

'And you didn't believe that story, Miss Parkin?' Burton asked.

'Well, they *were* seen talking outside Brompton Oratory. Back then, Sister Roisin worked there as a greeter, a sort of usher — this was before she became a chaplain at the Theresian Club — while Jackie was in and out of the institute as part of her MA research. St Therese was one of the figures she was analysing from the feminist perspective. The thing is . . .' The woman seemed momentarily at a loss.

'There's no rush, Miss Parkin,' Markham said calmly, though he sensed his colleagues wanted to shake the information out of her.

'Well, at the time it just seemed *odd*. The two of them didn't strike me as great friends . . . I knew they'd crossed swords a few times in seminars at the institute when Sister Roisin had got quite worked up about some of the ideas Jackie was pushing.' The receptionist grimaced. 'It would have been distasteful to traditionalists, but Jackie *was* taking Gender Studies . . . Her supervisor was one of those radical feminists, so obviously it was considered a legitimate area of debate even if people found the line she took offensive.'

'You actually witnessed Jackie and Sister Roisin clashing?' Burton pressed.

'I saw the occasional bad-tempered spat when I dropped in on institute events, yes. But there was a fair bit of chatter about other incidents, and I heard on the grapevine that things got quite heated . . . You see, Roisin hadn't long taken her final vows with the Brothers and Sisters of Saint Therese. I believe she was a bit shamefaced about it all later, after she became a chaplain at the club . . . joked to me about it having been her reactionary phase.'

Markham heard the note of doubt. 'What did you think when she said that?' he asked.

'Somehow it didn't ring true. You see, I remembered her being really *angry* with Jackie . . . That's why, when Jackie disappeared, the idea of them going off together for a coffee like they were chums didn't make sense.'

'Maybe they planned to bury the hatchet,' Doyle suggested reasonably. 'You know, draw a line under it.'

Noakes found this idea plausible. 'Yeah, what with Crimbo being the season of goodwill an' all that.'

Miss Parkin raised her hands helplessly palm upwards before letting them drop heavily into her lap.

'That's what I told myself,' she said. 'But I suppose deep down it still niggled away at me.'

'Did you say anything to the police at the time?' Doyle asked brutally.

A painful flush rose up her neck.

'No, I didn't . . . Partly it was cowardice. You see, I didn't want to make waves — hadn't long started my job at the institute. And because somehow it seemed *unbelievable* . . . Sister Roisin was so pious, so dedicated to her vocation and her work. If she came across as a bit, well, fanatical to start with, I figured it was all bound up with her devotion to St Therese . . . When Therese was vilified, even in an academic context, she couldn't help but take it personally.'

Fanatical. Took it personally.

Markham read the question in his colleagues' eyes.

How would the nun have reacted to questionable letters about Therese being put into circulation?

'Would you say Sister Roisin continued to be over-intense in her attitude to St Therese's cult?' he asked carefully.

'People mellow, don't they . . . become less entrenched in their views as they get older. That's why I told myself she couldn't possibly have had anything to do with Jackie's disappearance. To start with, she was just a typical young religious, full of zeal and going through a period of adjustment . . . Quite like St Therese, to be honest.' Miss Parkin was babbling nervously now. 'Therese got carried away in the beginning, you know — went to extremes like deliberately trying to spoil the taste of food or writing out the Creed in her own blood.' Registering Noakes's scandalised expression, she added. 'But as time went on, she learned a different kind of heroism . . . That's why the other sisters wondered what on earth the prioress would find to say about her in the obituary they sent to the other convents, because she was just this "good little nun".'

'Is that how you saw Sister Roisin, then?' Markham asked gently. 'Just a good little nun . . . nothing out of the ordinary.'

'Yes, Inspector.' She bit her lip. 'Though I wasn't *totally* sure about her . . . She was always hanging around the museum, and I sometimes fancied she had this plan to steal one of the relics if ever the senior receptionist accidentally left a cabinet unlocked. It was just a feeling and I told myself not to be ridiculous . . . I mean, the idea of a nun plotting a *heist!*' Bitterly, she added, 'The truth is I didn't *want* to see her as anything other than a good religious person. I was brought up to have respect for priests and nuns, so it went against the grain to imagine they could be capable of murder . . . And besides, the police seemed satisfied . . . there was never any suggestion that they didn't believe Sister Roisin's account. Jackie was from a broken home, highly strung and temperamental, there was an idea that she maybe had some kind of breakdown and didn't want to be found.'

It sounded to Markham as though an overly deferential attitude towards ecclesiastical authority had played its part in the unsolved disappearance of Jackie Moor.

'But despite everything, you still had doubts about Sister Roisin?' he asked.

'I suppose my misgivings never really went away; it was just that I buried them. But when I heard you'd found bones, something told me it *had* to be Jackie.' The receptionist's hands were trembling. 'That she never did a runner . . . never dropped out of her life . . . she was here in the crypt all the time. And suddenly I felt I knew who must have put her there.'

The good little nun.

Burton was thinking hard. 'How easy would it have been for Sister Roisin to gain access to the crypt? You said she was a greeter at Brompton Oratory . . . did that mean she was able to come and go at the institute as well?'

'Yes . . . Strictly speaking, she wasn't senior staff back then. But she had sacristan duties — looking after vestments and altar vessels — and part of her job involved doing the odd conducted tour. So she had her own set of keys to the crypt.' Looking acutely uncomfortable Miss Parkin added, 'She and Sister Pauline, who entered the order at the same time, sometimes used the crypt for private prayer and meditation.'

Noakes's face expressed concentrated distaste.

Prayer and meditation. More like she was lining the place up as her own creepy dumping ground!

Doyle tried to picture it. 'Do the keys to the crypt open the iron grates too?'

'Yes. But they're hardly ever unlocked . . . only for visiting clergy if they request it.'

The young DS was nonplussed. 'Why would they do that?'

'To feel closer to the order's founders I think, or so they can touch objects to the coffins — the squares are too small to allow that.'

Doyle was clearly repulsed and trying hard not to show it.

'It's an RC thing,' Noakes told him, with an all-knowing air. 'Getting up close an' personal helps 'em pray better.'

This elicited a faint smile from Miss Parkin. 'That's right, Sergeant. But there's no doubt it makes some people uneasy,' her lips trembled. 'Father Digby said it's really come down to us as a kind of ancient expression of faith in God.'

Doyle was willing to bet that clerical visitors wouldn't have felt quite so comfortable knowing they were snuggling up to the remains of a murdered student, but he kept this thought to himself.

'So Sister Roisin had access to the crypt and the coffins,' Burton said crisply before they travelled further down the arcane byways of Catholic practice. 'Do you think it's possible that she lured Jackie Moor to the crypt on some pretext?'

'It might not have been premeditated,' the receptionist said with some agitation. 'She might have felt that if they met there, Jackie would be influenced by the holiness of the place . . . might have been *touched* in some way . . . converted to the traditional view of St Therese.'

'And then things got out of hand?' Burton prompted. 'Sister Roisin lost control?'

'That's how I prefer to think of it,' Miss Parkin stammered, 'only now there are these *other* murders . . . Did Julia somehow find out about what happened to Jackie?' The receptionist rubbed her temples. 'And what about Father Digby and Professor Nevin?' She looked at Markham with a pleading expression. 'Was it Sister Roisin who killed all of them and David Manners too?' She restlessly pleated her skirt. 'If I had told someone about Jackie sooner, maybe I could have stopped it.'

'Don't blame yourself, Miss Parkin. It seemed almost as incredible to us when we began to consider Sister Roisin as a potential suspect,' Markham said gently. The DI paused, wondering whether to take her into his confidence. Meeting Noakes's eyes, he made a swift decision.

She's a woman to be trusted.

'There are some letters that we think came into Julia's possession via an acquaintance in France,' he said. 'They originated with the Lemarchand family who were connected to St Therese's Guerin relations.'

Miss Parkin regarded him with rapt fascination, taking off her glasses and polishing them on her sleeve as though to see more clearly.

'What kind of letters, Inspector?' A hesitation. 'Do you mean Jeanne La Néele's letters from her sister, Marie Guerin . . . the ones Marie sent from inside the convent?'

'That's correct, Miss Parkin,' Markham said, recalling that it was the receptionist who had first mentioned the tradition prevalent in Catholic circles regarding the missing letters. 'You said you thought there was a possibility the correspondence had been suppressed because it was controversial in some way and could be manipulated to discredit St Therese and her cult.'

She inhaled sharply. 'Have you found the correspondence, Inspector?'

'No. It appears to have vanished without trace.'

Now she clutched the sides of her chair. 'Was Julia killed for the letters?'

'You used the word "fanatical" earlier to describe Sister Roisin when she was a newly professed nun . . . You wondered if she had *mellowed* as time went on . . . become more balanced in her outlook.' Markham paused. 'But what if she *didn't*? What if it was all an act and underneath she was as hard-line and uncompromising as ever?' He let this sink in. 'What if Julia dangled these letters in front of her or let slip that they were in her possession?'

Burton took up the story. 'Julia's position wasn't all that secure, given the way some members were lobbying the trustees to get rid of "dead wood" and bring the club into the twenty-first century. Maybe she thought of using the letters as a bargaining chip.'

'Or she might just have enjoyed the power they gave her,' Doyle put in. 'An academic like Professor Nevin would have sold his granny to get a look, while the Catholic higher ups would be falling over themselves to keep them hidden from view.'

'She'd have had folk fighting over her,' Noakes concluded. 'But Sister Roisin never let it get that far.'

'On the other hand, Sister Roisin's discovery of the letters could have been accidental,' Burton hypothesised. 'Julia might have talked about the Lemarchands and their connection with the Guerins . . . after that, it would be relatively easy for someone to do their own research, just like we did, and realise that Julia was sitting on dynamite — something that could blow the cult to kingdom come.'

'If Sister Roisin's fanaticism never went away — simply went underground — then it's plausible to imagine that she killed Julia for the sake of her beloved St Therese's reputation,' Markham pointed out.

Miss Parkin looked stunned. 'What about the others?' she stammered. 'Father Digby . . . Professor Nevin . . . ?'

'Something must've put them on to Sister Roisin,' Doyle said.

'Then why didn't they go to the police?' She sounded anguished.

'Maybe like you, they had suspicions but couldn't accept her as a killer,' he told her. 'Maybe they even thought she was covering for someone else—'

'Like Sister Pauline,' Noakes cut in. 'Seeing as *she's* the barm cake.'

Burton looked distinctly pained at this term of art, but held her peace for now.

Suddenly Miss Parkin turned very pale.

'What is it, luv?' Noakes asked in concern.

'I was thinking about Rosemary Gough . . . wondering if that overdose was actually an overdose . . .'

'How d'you mean?'

But Burton had got there before him. 'You think Sister Roisin might have been planning to set Rosemary up for the murders . . . maybe even messed with her head?'

Miss Parkin nodded wretchedly, looking exhausted. 'Rosemary was highly suggestible. If someone pushed the right buttons, I could see her being talked into a false confession.'

Markham decided they should wrap up the interview. The woman looked drained.

Standing up, he extended a hand towards her. 'You've been a great help, Miss Parkin, but I can't stress enough how imperative it is that you don't show any sign of having spoken to us or give any indication that you mistrust Sister Roisin.

I know it's difficult, but we need you to behave exactly the same as normal.'

She got slowly to her feet.

'What did he mean by talking about the "headless wonder"?' she asked.

Noakes wondered if the shock had addled her wits. '*Headless wonder*? Who said that?' he repeated.

'The forensics officer I overheard talking about bones said it had grossed him out.'

Markham's face seemed carved out of granite.

'Gallows humour, Miss Parkin,' he improvised grimly in the face of her confusion. 'A private joke . . . there's something of a repertoire when it comes to scenes of crime.'

'Nice one, guv,' Noakes said after escorting the receptionist from the room. 'Though I don' think Miss P knows *With Her Head Tucked Underneath Her Arm*.' Seeing his colleagues' bemused expressions, he muttered, 'Stanley Holloway. Before your time.'

'Those two clowns will be reviewing their career options when I catch up with them,' Markham said tersely. 'Music hall will be the least of it.'

His wingman didn't doubt it. The boss's carpetings were something to behold. For all his quiet reserve, Markham was lethal when he felt subordinates had fallen below the standards he expected.

For now, though, the DI dismissed the lapse in professionalism.

'I think we finally have our killer,' he told them before turning to Noakes. 'So Sister Roisin Boden murdered Jackie Moor a decade ago in the grip of an obsessive fixation about St Therese . . . There then seems to have been a period of quiescence—'

'Maybe she was so appalled at what she'd done, that it kind of shocked her out of the obsession,' Burton suggested.

'That's one possibility, certainly.'

'Or mebbe she were jus' a crafty so-an'-so who knew how to lie low,' Noakes muttered.

Doyle's bafflement was evident. 'What beats me is how she could've killed Jackie Moor and hidden her body in the crypt without anyone noticing.'

'I think the clue lies in her ordinariness,' Markham said slowly. 'She was just this "good little nun" who never made a ripple.'

'She made a ripple in those seminars, though,' Doyle protested. 'Didn't Miss Parkin say she lost it with Jackie?'

'Yes, but that was in the context of academic debate — perfectly in keeping with her religious calling and traditional views,' Markham pointed out. 'Away from the classroom, she's just this nondescript woman whom you wouldn't notice in a crowd. A colourless shadow. Nothing special.'

''Cept that she's a bleeding serial killer,' Noakes retorted.

'Nobody'd think anything of Sister Roisin wandering round the institute,' Burton said, ignoring this remark. 'She's just another nun . . . Let's face it, the place is crawling with them.'

'Do you think there was something going on between Sister Roisin and Jackie Moor?' Doyle demanded bluntly. 'Something sexual?'

'But they clashed all the time,' Burton objected.

'That wouldn't rule out some sort of attraction in the mix,' Markham replied. 'If there was tension between them, it could have reflected a sexual component.'

'Mebbe Jackie threw it back in her face,' Noakes suggested. '*Taunted* her with it.'

'Or it could have been unacknowledged,' Burton countered, always ready to consider the psychological angle. 'Something that Sister Roisin repressed or denied even to herself.'

'P'raps when they were down there in the crypt, she copped on to how she felt an' couldn't handle it. I mean, nuns aren't *supposed* to have the hots for other women,' Noakes said primly.

Doyle appeared struck by this. 'And then if Jackie mocked her religious views and did the whole feminist number, she would've felt even worse.'

'We can't know what exactly happened between them all those years ago,' Markham said. 'But if the Guerin letters could be construed as hinting at an illicit relationship between St Therese and Sister Marie of the Trinity, or a homoerotic dimension to convent life, then maybe all the buried impulses and tormented memories came surging up—'

'And triggered some kind of mental health crash, just like Dr Dajani suggested,' Burton finished eagerly.

'What about the missing head?' Doyle said suddenly.

'*Eh?*' Noakes shot him a look that suggested the youngster had lost his marbles.

'The skull that wasn't in the coffin,' Doyle explained patiently. 'There was only one in there, remember. So if those are Jackie Moor's bones, what about her head?'

'Mebbe she took it as a relic,' Noakes suggested.

They stared at him.

'The missus tole me,' he continued hastily, 'that when Therese's sister Celine went to have a look at her after she were dug up the first time — like they do when they're thinking about making someone a saint — she took hold of the skull an' gave it a big kiss . . . There weren't anything left in the coffin but bits an' bobs, see, but she didn't care. Jus' wanted to give her a smacker.'

Bits and bobs.

Doyle looked as though he was going to be sick.

'Well, the RCs are big on that sort of thing, right?' Noakes was defiant now. 'They put skulls an' things in glass cases an' whatnot.'

At that moment, Markham recalled a book he had seen as a child, with the photograph of a mummified head in a gilded cabinet wearing a nun's white wimple. Apparently it belonged to St Catherine of Siena and was detached from the vertebrae during some squabble about the dispersal of her remains. The shrivelled face and cadaverous shrunk skin, in conjunction with milky half-open eyes, ruined mouth and part-decomposed nose, had given him nightmares. And yet the faithful thought nothing of decking this severed poll with flowers and parading it through the streets of the saint's home city on a carnival float . . . like some macabre beauty queen coquetting with suitors who competed for her favours.

To a disordered, unwell mind, Noakes's 'bits and bobs' might have possessed a totemic significance that trumped the dismal realities of the grave.

'You could be right, Sergeant,' he said slowly. 'Perhaps it *was* a question of relics.'

Kate Burton was not generally behindhand when it came to psychiatric deviance — as evidenced by the fact that the *Diagnostic and Statistical Manual of Mental Disorders* was her preferred bedside reading — but on this occasion she shared Doyle's discomfort, as though she feared associating a nun *of all people* with some kind of erotic fetishism.

She cleared her throat.

'How do we plan to arrest her?'

'We set a trap,' Markham said.

Burton nodded. 'Who do we use as bait?'

'Miss Parkin. No *look*,' Markham said, eager to forestall Noakes's objection, 'she already suspected Sister Roisin in relation to Jackie Moor, which means we don't have to invent a cover story for her.'

'Plus she thought Sister Roisin might have had something to do with what happened to Rosemary Gough,' Doyle pointed out, 'and there was that business of wondering if she was planning to steal from the museum. She was already *on to her*.'

The idea found favour with Burton too. 'She's intelligent and has the nerve to go through with it . . . knows about the letters too, so no need to drill her about them . . .'

'I think Miss Parkin's also motivated to do it,' Markham added quietly, 'seeing as she blames herself for not having gone to the police when Jackie Moor disappeared.' As a rule, he didn't care to resort to emotional blackmail, but the woman's guilty conscience gave them leverage.

Noakes considered their killer, looking mutinous. 'How d'you know the nun will fall for it?' he demanded.

'We don't,' Markham told him bluntly, 'but it's worth a throw of the dice . . . She's killed four people, and I'm guessing she's haunted by the ghosts of Jackie Moor *and* Therese. So we play on that.'

'You really reckon she'll spill her guts to Miss P?' the DS asked his boss.

'If the right chords are touched, yes.'

Burton sensed Noakes's concern for the receptionist. 'Look sarge, she's the right woman for the job. I know they only call her the "senior receptionist",' it was clear Markham's fellow DI took a dim view of the institute's old-fashioned chauvinism, 'but essentially she runs the place . . . degree educated, fluent and *humane* . . . knows all about St Therese. Even after everything, you can see she pities Sister Roisin . . . empathises with her, if you like. She's the best one to do it.'

'The only other two who could really take on a *nun* are Sister Pauline and Ignatius Fermor,' Doyle mused. 'And I don't see either of them being up for it.'

'They'd be more likely to tip her off,' Burton murmured.

Noakes saw that he was outnumbered. 'So what happens next?'

'Council of war with the bishop and Sidney,' Markham said decisively, 'and then Miss Parkin makes her move.'

'Where're they gonna have this girlie chat then?' Noakes rumbled.

'*Think*, Noakes . . . Where better than the place where it all started.'

'You mean . . .'

'Yes. We take Sister Roisin back to the crypt.'

13. IN HEAVEN

As it turned out, DCI Sidney stood by his team in the conference with DCI Moriarty and Bishop Buckley.

The bishop was visibly shell-shocked at the idea of a *nun* being a four-times killer. Five if you counted Jackie Moor.

'We always knew the murders could have been committed by a woman, since they didn't require extraordinary strength given the element of surprise.' Markham said. 'The likelihood of its being an "inside job" was also extremely high . . . Julia Porter, Father Digby and Professor Nevin met their deaths in circumstances which strongly suggested that they were taken unawares and by someone who knew their routines . . . The encounter with Mr Manners led us to focus on those with unrestricted access to the crypt. What we learned about the unsolved murder of Jackie Moor pointed to Sister Roisin Boden as our prime suspect.'

'Are you *sure* about this, Inspector?' the bishop asked, his face ashen. 'Sister Roisin's reputation stands very high . . . She's regarded as an asset to her order and the diocese.'

Noakes experienced a spasm of compassion for the clergyman who appeared to have aged ten years in the space of a single afternoon.

'We think she kind of fell in love with St Therese,' the DS said kindly. 'It sent her round the twist, see.'

Unsurprisingly, neither Buckley nor Sidney appeared greatly reassured by this explanation. But the DCI took it better than his team might have anticipated.

'I gather this particular individual has had a phenomenal impact,' he said carefully. 'I don't pretend to understand the, er, cult of saints, but from what you've said it seems plausible that a devoutly religious person might succumb to some form of religious mania.'

'Yeah. Prince Philip's mum had summat like that,' Noakes chipped in. 'She ended up living in Buck House, but it were all dead embarrassing cos she insisted on dressing like a nun an' telling everyone she were in love with Jesus.'

For all his interest in royalty, Sidney looked as though he could happily have dispensed with this contribution.

'Quite so,' he said shooting a wary glance at the bishop who was examining the DS with an expression of mingled fascination and outrage before continuing hurriedly, 'In which case, Sister Roisin cannot be held fully responsible for her actions.'

'It seems likely Sister Roisin buried the memory of what she did to Jackie Moor, so that she was able to function successfully in relation to her religious calling,' Markham continued. 'But then she learned about the existence of correspondence which posed a potential threat to the cult of the Little Flower and became obsessed with the idea of suppressing it.'

'You haven't found any trace of these letters though, Inspector?' the bishop asked with marked anxiety in his tone. It was clear that Buckley hoped fervently Marie Guerin's correspondence would never see the light of day.

'No, but it seems likely Sister Roisin discovered that they had come into Julia Porter's possession and reacted violently to their contents—'

'*Particular friendships*,' Noakes said meaningfully, with the air of someone pronouncing 'open sesame'.

The bishop continued to regard Markham's wingman with the expression of an explorer encountering a previously unknown entity. Hearing the specialised vocabulary of religious life on the lips of this strangest of policemen rendered him temporarily mute.

Markham took advantage of the bishop being struck dumb to continue with his analysis.

'Sister Roisin may have wanted the letters, but Julia refused to hand them over,' he said. 'Or she may have feared that Julia was going to disclose their contents to others . . . We can't be sure exactly what happened between them, but we believe it led to Julia being strangled.'

The DCI nodded.

So far so good.

'It looks as though Father Digby Peake arranged to meet with Sister Roisin in the library stacks at the institute.' Markham steepled his long musician's fingers as he tried to envisage what had taken place in that basement. 'Possibly Julia had let something slip to him, and whatever it was spelled danger. Julia might even have told him about the letters and mentioned that Sister Roisin was keen to get her hands on them.'

'Or Dig— er, Father Digby might've guessed it were Roisin who killed Julia an' wanted to give her a chance to come clean . . . go to confession, like,' Noakes added helpfully.

The bishop found his voice.

'Without a firm purpose of amendment, there would have been no question of absolution,' he said faintly.

The DS nodded solemnly 'So then she went tonto.'

Doyle joined in. 'Maybe Sister Roisin gave herself away by saying something incriminating in front of Father Digby — something about the Guerin letters — and it got him wondering.'

'He might not have realised *she* was the killer,' Burton pointed out. 'Just suspected she knew something.'

'One thing is certain,' Markham said. 'Father Digby wasn't expecting to be attacked.'

'God rest him,' the bishop said. 'It could be he thought to cure a tormented soul—'

'Like that woman in the gospel,' Noakes said. 'The one who had seven devils an' Jesus got rid of 'em all.'

Seeing that Buckley was unlikely to relish his wingman's brand of biblical exegesis, Markham smoothly interposed, 'Again, we may never know what passed between them, but it sealed Father Digby's death warrant.'

There were no 'RIPs' from the bishop when it came to Tom Nevin whom he clearly regarded as a dangerous freethinker.

'I think Professor Nevin may have wanted to pull off the religious publishing coup of the decade,' Markham said. 'It would have secured his place in the annals of religious scholarship and turbo-charged his academic career.'

'You think Sister Roisin somehow betrayed herself and then he *blackmailed* her?' Buckley asked, as though such a scenario was only to be expected.

'Actually, I'm not sure that Professor Nevin ever connected Sister Roisin with Julia's murder,' Markham said. 'But like Father Digby, he'd somehow got wind of the existence of the Guerin letters and was on the trail of the mystery.'

The DI felt he somehow owed it to Tom Nevin's memory to counter Bishop Buckley's insinuation that the man was an unscrupulous opportunist. He didn't think it was in character for the affable academic with his courtesy and lazy Southern drawl to have sought personal advantage courtesy of a murderer.

'If Professor Nevin imagined for one minute that Sister Roisin was a murderer, I believe he'd have turned her in,' Markham said firmly. 'It's more likely he simply picked up on something — maybe something Julia or Father Digby let drop — and in Sister Roisin's overwrought state, she decided it was too big a risk to let him live.'

'You're saying the Guerin correspondence was the key to everything, Inspector?' It was obvious the bishop would dearly love it to have been otherwise. In the clergyman's carefully calibrated scale of scandals injurious to the Church, it was obvious the mental derangement *tout court* suited him far better than the spectre of compromising correspondence with sapphic overtones.

Markham stood his ground. 'Yes, My Lord, I am.'

'Then we must go where the evidence leads us, and it would appear the existence of these, er, *billets-doux* or whatever they were, triggered Sister Roisin's break with reality.'

At that moment, Markham felt almost affectionate towards Sidney. However potent the lure of ecclesiastical honorifics, the DCI wasn't going to allow the Church to bury this mess six feet deep and then play cricket on top. Out of the corner of his eye, he saw DCI Moriarty wink at Noakes.

'The best outcome would surely be for Sister Roisin to enter a medical facility,' the bishop said.

'*Best for who?*' Noakes demanded indignantly. 'She killed five people an' one of 'em a young lass.'

'We need to secure a confession, My Lord, and then it will be for the courts to decide if she is competent to stand trial,' Markham said firmly.

Buckley's head swivelled towards Sidney. The DCI's rictus smile suggested he was swallowing a dose of bitter medicine, but his response was unequivocal.

'Inspector Markham is correct, My Lord. It would only harm the Church's reputation should any suggestion of undue influence arise.'

Before Markham could stop him, Noakes stepped forward and wrung the DCI's hand.

'You never said a truer word, boss. An' what's more, the Little Flower'll see you right.'

Doyle looked as though he anticipated dining out on this story for the foreseeable future, while Burton squirmed in an ecstasy of embarrassment and DCI Moriarty smiled a Cheshire Cat smile.

Sidney executed an adroit discarding manoeuvre.

'Excellent, excellent,' he mumbled as he extricated himself from the sweaty handclasp, looking both pleased and abashed.

Markham only wished Olivia could have been there to see DCI Sidney in his newly acquired character as an adherent of the Little Flower. Truly St Therese's fabled 'shower of roses' fell in the strangest of places.

But he was gratified at the way Sidney had come through for the team and wondered if this perhaps heralded a détente in their relationship. For all the DCI's brown-nosing and undoubted obstructionist tendencies, there were still signs of the essentially upright officer who, so Markham had heard on the grapevine, had put his neck on the line more than once at the start of his career. When it came to Sidney, Olivia invariably quoted the old saying, 'Power corrupts and absolute power corrupts absolutely,' but on the strength of this case Markham saw hopeful glimmerings of a new era.

In the meantime, there was a bishop to bring onside.

Carefully, Markham explained the choice of Miss Parkin as bait.

'And where do you propose that this encounter should take place?' Buckley demanded.

'In the crypt.'

'I've just thought — it's a crime scene now because of David Manners, sir,' Doyle pointed out. 'Won't Sister Roisin smell a rat?'

'We'll make an announcement that the SOCOs are finished down there — processed the area extra fast due to its being consecrated ground. We can say something about wanting the institute's routines to get back to normal asap . . . whatever it takes to lull her into a false sense of security.' Markham resisted the urge to cross his fingers. 'Sister Roisin's antennae won't be on full alert,' he added. 'Don't forget, she's bound to be traumatised over what happened with Mr Manners.'

The bishop's lips thinned almost to invisibility. 'I'm glad you appreciate the crypt's status as consecrated ground, Inspector. I was afraid you had overlooked that point.'

'I'm very conscious of it, My Lord. But we need to ratchet up the emotional tension to secure a confession. The crypt will have a unique significance for Sister Roisin as the burial site of her first victim. Even though she somehow absolved herself of guilt for the murder of Jackie Moor and went on with her life, it seems likely she returned there on a regular basis.'

An unwelcome image flashed into his mind . . . Sister Roisin behind the iron grates bending over the rotten wooden coffin, crooning to the remains of the woman she had murdered. The very notion of the corpse of Jackie Moor slowly rotting atop the remains of some venerable Victorian clergyman, her flesh dissolving into the ancient skeleton by some obscene alchemy, made him shudder. Awful even to imagine the killer *gloating* at the incursions of decay and corruption on firm, youthful flesh . . .

He wondered what had happened to Jackie Moor's skull. Something told him they would never find it.

The DCI and bishop were looking at him.

'Has the corpse in the crypt actually been identified as Jackie Moor?' Buckley asked.

Burton had been busy since the discovery. 'The family emigrated to Australia the year after the murder,' she said, 'but I did a Zoom call with her brother who told me she had customised straighteners on her teeth . . . it fits with what Dr Appleby showed us.'

Noakes and Doyle exchanged glances. Dental records weren't going to be much use in the absence of the victim's skull. Aware that Markham had withheld that gruesome piece of information from the bishop, Burton added, 'We can't conclusively identify the remains as Jackie Moor, sir, but we'll obviously expedite the process as much as possible.' So unlike Noakes in every other respect, she resembled the DS in her reluctance to address anyone as 'My Lord'.

'How do you intend that Miss Parkin should proceed, Inspector?' The bishop sounded resigned. 'Is she going to challenge Sister Roisin about these Guerin letters . . . or will she come right out and accuse her of the murders?'

'Miss Parkin's suspicions about what really happened to Jackie Moor in 2010 were reawakened when she overheard a SOCO mention the discovery of bones in the crypt . . . So *that's* our way in. It has the merit of being true, so we don't have to coach her in some elaborate pretence . . . Plus we need to bring Sister Roisin to the tipping point of confessing—'

'And you think it's the Jackie Moor murder that will provoke a reaction?' Sidney asked urgently.

'Yes I do, sir.' Markham's voice rang with conviction. 'Sister Roisin's anxiety must be very near the surface after what happened with David Manners. It's a question of touching the right chord.'

'How will you guarantee Miss Parkin's safety?'

'Yeah, boss.' Noakes leaned in anxiously. 'It's a tight squeeze down there . . . nowhere to hide.'

'There's the derelict lift shaft,' Markham said, 'with the disused hydraulic machinery . . . adequate cover for a stake-out. We can hide in there.'

Noakes still looked dubious.

Markham offered reassurance. 'Miss Parkin and Sister Roisin will have their backs to the shaft . . . it's at the bottom of the passageway, remember.'

Doyle looked as though he was coming round to the idea. 'We'll tell Miss P to stay as far away from that end as possible . . . keep Roisin's attention focused on the coffins. If the guvnor's right about her being close to the edge, it's a question of pressing the right buttons so she lets her guard down.'

'Are we wiring Miss P for sound?' Noakes demanded.

'Yes,' Markham confirmed.

'An' giving her a stab proof vest?'

'That too.'

'It might work,' the DS conceded.

'It *has to*,' Markham said earnestly. 'If we are right, this is a very guilty human being who has killed five innocent people.' As he made this comment, he was struck by the bishop's withered look; somehow the man appeared even dimmer and more faded than at the start of their interview. 'It seems likely that monomania centring on St Therese played a large part,' he said gently. 'With the right help, her life need not be totally thrown away.'

'That's right,' Noakes said solemnly. 'Jesus said in heaven they get more excited over one bad person who says sorry than ninety-nine who behave thesselves.'

'In heaven,' the bishop repeated dully.

The DS peered at the clergyman in concern, thinking the bish looked properly out of it. He racked his brains for some titbit to cheer him up.

'My missus tole me that were the last thing St Therese's dad ever said to her. Pointed to the sky — well the ceiling really — an' said, "Au ciel". *In heaven*, see,' he translated helpfully, 'cos he were going to die an' he wanted his girl to know he'd be up there waiting for her.' A beatific smile. '*Beautiful*.'

It couldn't be said that Bishop Buckley looked especially comforted by this edifying anecdote, but he forced a pale smile. 'I never expected to find such enthusiasm for St Therese's cult amongst the police.'

Noakes beamed. 'Full of surprises, that's us.'

* * *

When the end came, it came quickly. Afterwards it seemed to Markham that time had mysteriously speeded up as though unseen furies were whipping the case to its denouement.

Calmest of all was Miss Parkin who, as instructed, sought out Sister Roisin and suggested a meeting somewhere private. By a code agreed with the team beforehand, she moved a vase of roses from in front of St Therese's statue in the chapel to the reception desk, so they knew it was Game On. In the meantime, the team ostensibly busied themselves about the building, with Markham duly making a short announcement in the library about the 'suspicious death' of David Manners and imminent re-opening of the crypt. Sister Roisin stayed close to Sister Pauline and appeared the same as usual, though Markham noticed an almost imperceptible facial tic that would not be suppressed. Her fellow residents appeared subdued and shocked, dispersing after Markham's announcement to their temporary accommodation or one of the institute's two common rooms.

At six o'clock when reception closed, Burton made a great show of descending on Miss Parkin with a clipboard, ostensibly with a view to arranging interview rooms for the following day. The two women disappeared into the back office from which Burton emerged a quarter of an hour later with a cheery 'Goodnight'.

The team then headed off together in Markham's car, but instead of returning to Southampton Row, they installed themselves round the corner in the Brompton Café.

It was dreary and sleety outside, but their spirits were high as they sat over hot drinks. For a wonder, Noakes was too wound up to worry about food, ruminating instead on the strange coincidence of their waiting in the very spot where Jackie Moor was supposed to have rendezvoused with Sister Roisin Boden all those years previously.

'Poor lass,' he said, thinking of the pathetic braces found in the crypt. 'Everyone thinking the world were her thingummy—'

'Oyster?' said Doyle.

'Thass right. But that fruit loop had shoved her in a box on top of some ole priest.' Noakes shuddered. 'Fricking horrible.'

'Sister Roisin must've been pretty strong to lug her into the coffin,' Doyle mused.

'She's stocky,' Burton observed. 'And besides, an adrenalin surge gives people extra strength. Like those stories you read about with people trapped under vehicles . . . Y'know, rescuers get this superhuman energy from somewhere and manage to lift the car off.'

'I wonder if we'll ever find out what it was in those letters that got Roisin in such a lather,' Doyle went on, with a wary eye on Noakes. 'Do you reckon there *was* anything going on in the convent that wasn't, er, strictly kosher.'

Burton felt they were on dangerous ground.

'No,' she said firmly, surprised at the force of her own revulsion. 'I think Miss Parkin's right about how you could get completely the wrong end of the stick because they used such over-the-top language back then.'

'Yeah, *nasty*,' Noakes said emphatically. 'Like we're all, whatchamacallit, *voyeurs*.'

'Miss Parkin thinks Sister Roisin might have been extra-sensitive because of impulses in *herself* that she'd tried to bury.' Burton sipped her coffee thoughtfully. 'She also mentioned St Therese having some sort of ecstasy in the convent, when she experienced a burning sensation all over her body — a fiery wound, she called it . . . Apparently it was the one and only time anything out of the ordinary happened. But if Marie Guerin wrote in detail about stuff like that, you'd have all kinds of Freudian "experts" crawling out of the woodwork sensationalising it.'

Noakes had no time for Freud. 'Mebbe it were jus' family things she talked about,' he said. 'They were cousins after all, so Marie could've told stories about when they were kids.'

'According to Miss Parkin, Therese's childhood has had a lot of attention . . . There were all sorts of psychosomatic illnesses. Plus, she almost competed with Marie for attention by complaining of headaches and sore throats.'

'Well, she *did* die of TB,' Noakes glowered. 'So I reckon the sore throats must've been genuine.'

'I'm not saying they weren't, sarge,' Burton replied pacifically, 'but it's possible Marie said unflattering things about Therese's childhood . . . Her father Isidore didn't always see eye to eye with Louis Martin, remember, so she might've been spiteful about how her cousin went on in the convent.'

'Yeah, the prioress usually checked what the nuns wrote,' Noakes said, casting his mind back to convent lore, 'but she were a jealous bitch, so mebbe she didn't mind someone else slagging Therese off.'

'Or, for some reason, the letters somehow evaded censorship,' Markham pointed out. The aquiline features wore an absorbed expression. 'Either way, I suspect we'll never know if there was anything inflammatory in the correspondence.'

'Cos Roisin's squirreled 'em away you mean, boss? Like *trophies?*' Noakes asked.

'Something like that, yes. She was definitely determined they would never get into the public arena.'

'Her an' the bish agree on *that*, at any rate,' the DS muttered.

'Would people *really* pay all that much attention?' Doyle asked. 'Okay, so this nun who died in her twenties wasn't as holy as everyone thought . . . *Big deal, hold the front page!*'

'But it *is* a big deal to hordes of worshipers,' Burton told him, seeing that Noakes was working up to an explosion. 'And there are all kinds of people who look to her for inspiration . . . Forget those stories about the smell of roses drifting down corridors and the rest of that crap.' Registering Markham's sardonic expression, she blushed. 'Sorry, sir, but you know what I mean.'

Having heard something similar from Olivia, he did.

'She's someone folk can relate to,' Noakes said. 'Gives 'em a map to heaven.' His colleagues recognised the familiar stubborn note. 'She were a young lass stuck in a kind of prison,' for such was Noakes's view of the convent. 'Her life were bobbins . . . But she stuck at it an' never stopped working even after she died. 'Sides, how d'you explain all the miracles an' cures an' things? God must've felt he *owed* her, like.'

If he was startled by this bizarrely mercantile evaluation of Therese's merit, Markham showed no sign.

'Special without a doubt,' he said. 'And an important figure in Christendom.'

'So the letters would be a bit of a time bomb if they got out,' Doyle suggested.

'I think the Church could weather any "revelations",' Markham replied. 'But to someone as disturbed as Sister Roisin, any discordant notes — any hint of demonic impulses or erotic temptations — might have been unbearable . . . And once Julia Porter had decided to light the fuse, it was all up with her.'

'An' the others too,' Noakes gloomed. Then, 'What time's Curtain Up?'

'Half past seven,' Burton told him. She turned to Markham. 'Probably time to get set up in the crypt . . . We can go through the church, so there's no risk of anyone from the institute clocking us.'

'Where's Sister Roisin now?' Markham asked.

'She and Sister Pauline are leading evening prayers in the chapel till quarter past seven—'

Doyle was appalled. '*Jesus*.' He caught Markham's eye. 'Sorry, sir, but I can't get my head round it . . . killed all those people and she's in there rattling her rosary beads!'

'She'll be dissociating,' Burton pointed out. 'Thinks she's on a holy crusade . . . defending St Therese's honour in heaven.'

Noakes got to his feet. 'Jus' so long as she don' send Miss P there any time soon,' he growled.

* * *

The chill mustiness of the crypt as Noakes and Markham manoeuvred themselves into position behind the hydraulic rig felt even more oppressive than on their previous visit. From where they were standing, they could not see the pillars with their strange engravings nor the coffins behind the iron grates. But it felt to the DI as though a legion of unseen presences was there waiting in the darkness alongside them.

When the electric light snapped on, it was a shock. But they both managed to remain very still, listening to the first set of footsteps.

A cough.

The agreed signal.

Miss Parkin was there.

Another set of footsteps and then the pleasant Irish brogue. Knowing what he knew, it made the hair on Markham's neck stand on end.

'Now, Miss Parkin, what's all this about? Sure, I wouldn't have thought you'd be wanting to come in here after what happened to poor Mr Manners.'

'You *know* why I wanted to meet you here, Sister.'

'Are you feeling quite yourself, Miss Parkin? I've no idea what you're talking about.'

'*Jackie Moor.*'

And then something in the darkness felt different, as though evil had come slithering out of one of the coffins like a noisome gas to fill the air with its stench.

Steadily, inexorably, Miss Parkin accused the nun of murdering the young student all those years before.

'You see, they've found her down here, Sister. Even after so long, they *found* her. You weren't quite careful enough the last time you came to visit her . . . when David Manners caught you.'

In that instant, Markham wondered . . . had the nun subconsciously *wanted* them to find Jackie Moor's remains? Had that careless slip not been so careless after all?

Miss Parkin followed her script, aware of the need to secure a confession for her concealed auditors. 'You murdered the others too, didn't you? Julia . . . Father Digby . . . Professor Nevin . . . David . . . ?'

The nun replied in the same sing song bouncy accent, but this time Markham heard something else — a shrill intensity like a high-frequency sonic alarm that only the most attentive listener would detect.

'They would have brought the Little Flower into the mud with their disgusting insinuations,' she said. 'That's why I had to kill them. For the sake of the Faith.'

'Is *that* what they planned to do?'

Still the same eerie lilt, a grotesque contrast to the confession and the words themselves.

'Julia was looking to make herself important . . . hints and come-ons . . . blabbing to Father Digby . . . And that poor simple man imagining I could ever regret stopping the woman's stupid mouth!'

Miss Parkin asked hoarsely, 'Was Professor Nevin on to you as well?'

A gurgling laugh, as though they were chatting across the tea table.

'I think the big booby wondered about Sister Pauline to start with . . . and her such a *good* soul, but of course she's had her *trials*. It was the Guerin letters . . . I could have kicked myself afterwards, but it was too late.'

'What was too late?'

'We were talking about St Therese, when I mentioned a conversation between the Lisieux convent chaplain Father Youf and Sister Margeurite-Marie who eventually left the convent. He pricked up his ears at that . . . never left off about it afterwards because it isn't in any of the bibliographies . . . knew I had to have seen something that no one else knew about. He was becoming suspicious of me . . . Julia had dropped something about having friends in France, you see. I couldn't take the risk.'

'And David Manners?'

A tiny hiss.

'Always too busy minding other people's business, I'm afraid.' A deadly pause. 'Much like yourself.'

Miss Parkin's voice was hoarse. 'Put the knife away, Sister.'

At that, the two detectives emerged from their place of concealment.

The diminutive Irishwoman's broad, open face was the colour of whey. But the hand that held the knife to her own throat — profession ring glinting on her third finger — was perfectly steady.

'*My wedding dress is ready*,' she said.

One sure slicing movement and it was all over.

* * *

A week after the conclusion of the institute murders found Markham, Olivia and Noakes sitting companionably in their favourite Bromgrove hostelry the Grapes.

The quaint little pub with its brasses, nautical knick-knacks, old-fashioned prints, and carpet with Prince of Wales feathers had steadfastly resisted passing trends and was all the better for it. Ensconced in their favourite booth in the back parlour, watching the flames of a good fire cast leaping shadows on the uneven oak floorboards, the trio enjoyed their pre-dinner drinks while mulling over the recent investigation.

'Sister Roisin was the coolest killer of them all,' Noakes said thoughtfully, gazing into the amber depths of his Ruddles. 'An' as for that exit line . . . she didn't turn a hair.'

'It shows how far gone she was,' Olivia commented. 'Quoting St Therese like that.'

'I thought it were summat to do with her being married to Jesus,' Noakes ventured shyly. 'Though obviously she turned out to be more like the Bride of Dracula in the end.'

'Well yes, I think that *was* part of it, George. But I read somewhere in Professor Nevin's papers that those were the words Therese said just before she made her profession.'

'Maybe she was imagining some mystical union with St Therese,' Markham said, suppressing a smile at his wingman's aghast expression.

'Or the Church,' Olivia put in hastily.

Noakes didn't appear enamoured of either theory.

'In a strange way, I reckon she saw herself as some sort of martyr for the Truth,' Olivia said thoughtfully. 'Custodian of the Little Flower's purity or something.'

Noakes's devotion to Olivia prevented him from saying '*Pshaw!*' out loud. Even so, the screwed-up expression that he made, giving him the look of a man with a bad case of piles, said it all. It was clear he found this dubious in the extreme.

'She were a barm cake,' he said darkly. 'With a thing for young girls.'

'Yes, that poor student,' Olivia said softly. 'And now she's dead, Jackie's family will never know the whole truth.'

Not least what happened to the missing skull. But Markham had withheld that particular detail from Liv and, with a warning glance at Noakes, he steered the conversation into safer waters.

'There's the mystery of the Guerin papers as well,' he said lightly.

Instantly diverted, Olivia said, 'Not a trace of them then?'

'As if they'd never been,' he confirmed.

'I wonder what was so terrible that people had to die?' she pondered. Pensively, she sipped her G&T. 'If the letters are still out there somewhere, then the threat to the cult hasn't gone away.'

'I doubt Sister Roisin could bear to part with them,' Markham said. 'But wherever her hidey-hole is, it's resisted all our efforts to find it.'

'Betcha the bish has his gofers on it.' Noakes chuckled. 'Ten years off Purgatory for whoever gets there first!'

Olivia pretended to be scandalised, but her eyes were dancing. 'Have some respect, George,' she said, thumping him on the arm.

'Miss P will fill us in when we go down for Professor Nevin's memorial service,' he said.

As yet, there was no news about the other funerals, but Olivia knew Markham would be there for those as well. The Theresian murders had added new entries to the roster of victims he carried close to his heart.

'This Miss P appears to have taken quite a shine to you, George,' she said roguishly. 'It appears I have a rival.'

Blushing furiously, Noakes buried his nose in his pint glass as Markham and Olivia exchanged a glance of amused complicity.

* * *

Afterwards, when they were walking home hand in hand, Olivia said to him.

'It's odd, Gil. She's not with us anymore.'

'Who?'

'St Therese. It's like she's been there behind us all this time but now she's gone.'

Markham recalled that moment in the Theresian Club.

The black-veiled figure he had seen in profile . . . The rounded chin, convex forehead and penetrating gaze.

'She doesn't need us now,' he said with absolute conviction. 'Her legacy is safe.'

They continued on, oblivious of the March showers, and Markham's heart was strangely light as he walked.

THE END

ALSO BY CATHERINE MOLONEY

THE DI GILBERT MARKHAM SERIES

Book 1: CRIME IN THE CHOIR
Book 2: CRIME IN THE SCHOOL
Book 3: CRIME IN THE CONVENT
Book 4: CRIME IN THE HOSPITAL
Book 5: CRIME IN THE BALLET
Book 6: CRIME IN THE GALLERY
Book 7: CRIME IN THE HEAT
Book 8: CRIME AT HOME
Book 9: CRIME IN THE BALLROOM
Book 10: CRIME IN THE BOOK CLUB
Book 11: CRIME IN THE COLLEGE
Book 12: CRIME IN THE KITCHEN
Book 13: CRIME IN THE SPA
Book 14: CRIME IN THE CRYPT

Thank you for reading this book.

If you enjoyed it please leave feedback on Amazon or Goodreads, and if there is anything we missed or you have a question about, then please get in touch. We appreciate you choosing our book.

Founded in 2014 in Shoreditch, London, we at Joffe Books pride ourselves on our history of innovative publishing. We were thrilled to be shortlisted for Independent Publisher of the Year at the British Book Awards.

www.joffebooks.com

We're very grateful to eagle-eyed readers who take the time to contact us. Please send any errors you find to corrections@joffebooks.com. We'll get them fixed ASAP.

Printed in Great Britain
by Amazon

82585974R00133